MAREHO KIKUISHI

Illustration by
Tsubata Nozaki

I

YOUR FORMA

Electronic Investigator Echika
and Her Amicus Ex Machina

Harold W. Lucraft

An electronic investigator aide (Belayer) working for Interpol's Electrocrime Investigations Bureau from the Saint Petersburg branch.

A blond, blue-eyed, highly intelligent humanoid robot (Amicus). Despite being a machine, he's bold and cheeky in ways that annoy Echika to no end. He is, however, extremely devoted to his job. His specs are much higher than a normal Amicus model, and he has extraordinary observation skills. His past is shrouded in mystery.

The suture of the brain—Your Forma.
It records all that your mind experiences.
Everything you see, everything you hear...
and everything you feel...

Echika Hieda

An electronic investigator (Diver) working for
Interpol's Electrocrime Investigations Bureau.

A prodigy with extraordinary data-processing
abilities who was made the youngest electronic
investigator in the world. Since none of her
investigator aides can match her overwhelming
faculties, she often fries their brains, sending them
to the hospital. As a result, her peers shun her. Hates
robots of all kinds due to childhood trauma.

Bigga

A Sami girl living in a technologically restricted zone in Norway. Becomes a material witness after crossing paths with Echika and Harold as they investigate an important electrocrime. She's actually a skilled bio-hacker.

Steve H. Wheatstone

An Amicus who is the spitting image of Harold save for the mole on his face, which appears on the opposite cheek as his counterpart's. Serves as a secretary for the adviser of Rig City, a major IT corporation. Seems to have worked together with Harold somewhere in the past, but he refuses to elaborate. Unlike Harold, he's straitlaced and curt, though his specs are just as high as those of his doppelganger.

PROFILE

YOUR FORMA

D A T A B A S E

Your Forma

A smart thread device also know as the "suture of the brain." Inserted into the brain via laser surgery. Was originally developed for treating encephalitis but is mostly used as an information terminal in the present day. Saw widespread adoption after Rig City, a major IT corporation, equipped it with advertisement features that made it cheaply accessible for the average citizen.

Brain Diving

The act of viewing a subject's Mnemosynes by connecting a unique cord into their Your Forma. Brain Diving has revolutionized the criminal investigation field, but due to both a shortage in electronic investigators and the violation of privacy this act entails, it is managed exclusively by Interpol and only used in the most important cases.

Amicus

Colloquial term for humanoid robots. Unlike industrial robots, which are optimized for efficient labor, Amicus are built to appear as convincingly human as possible. The matter of whether they should be treated as "friends" of mankind or as "mere machines" has become the subject of much debate, though "Amicus sympathizers" seem to be on the rise. Some developed countries are even considering granting Amicus basic human rights.

Mnemosynes

A function of the Your Forma that records the user's experiences, from what they see and hear to even their emotions. The only means of browsing these records is to have a specially trained electronic investigator physically connect to a person's Your Forma and Dive into them.

Electronic Investigator (Diver)/ Electronic Investigator Aide (Belayer)

A profession reserved solely to those with high affinity with the Your Forma and extreme stress tolerance. They work under Interpol. Since electronic investigators can't willingly end a Brain Dive, they require the assistance of an electronic investigator aide. The Belayer experiences mental strain proportional to the Diver's data-processing abilities.

Rig City

A leading international IT corporation based in Silicon Valley. Repurposed a medical thread device to develop the Your Forma, which they made accessible to everyday people by granting it advertisement features. Their corporate advisor, Elias Taylor, is both an IT innovator and a known recluse who refuses to appear before the media.

Maybe she'd have actually been better off quitting a long time ago.

That way of life had seeped into her heart and body, had made her like a machine.

She hadn't wanted to turn out like this.

YOUR FORMA

Electronic Investigator Echika and Her Amicus Ex Machina

CONTENTS

MAREHO KIKUISHI

Illustration by

Tsubata Nozaki

I

Electronic Investigator Echika and Her Amicus Ex Machina

YEN
ON

New York

YOUR FORMA

I

Electronic Investigator
Echika and Her Amicus
Ex Machina

MAREHO KIKUISHI

Illustration by
Tsubata Nozaki

Translation by Roman Lempert
Cover art by Tsubata Nozaki

YOUR FORMA Vol.1 DENSAKUKAN
ECHIKA TO KIKAIJIKAKE NO AIBO
©Mareho Kikuishi 2021
Edited by Dengeki Bunko
First published in Japan in 2021 by
KADOKAWA CORPORATION, Tokyo.
English translation rights arranged with
KADOKAWA CORPORATION, Tokyo, through
TUTTLE-MORI AGENCY, INC., Tokyo.

English translation © 2022 by Yen Press, LLC

Yen On
150 West 30th Street, 19th Floor
New York, NY 10001

Visit us at yenpress.com
facebook.com/yenpress
twitter.com/yenpress
yenpress.tumblr.com
instagram.com/yenpress

First Yen On Edition: May 2022

Yen On is an imprint of Yen Press, LLC.
The Yen On name and logo are
trademarks of Yen Press, LLC.

Library of Congress Cataloging-in-Publication Data
Names: Kikuishi, Mareho, author. | Nozaki, Tsubata, illustrator.
Title: Your forma : Electronic Investigator Echika and Her Amicus Ex Machina /
    Mareho Kikuishi ; illustration by Tsubata Nozaki.
Other titles: Your forma. English
Description: First Yen On edition. | New York : Yen On, 2022.
Identifiers: LCCN 2022010527 | ISBN 9781975339654 (v. 1 ; trade paperback)
Subjects: LCGFT: Science fiction. | Light novels.
Classification: LCC PL872.5.I38 Y6813 2022 | DDC 895.63/6—dc23/eng/20220311
LC record available at https://lccn.loc.gov/2022010527

ISBNs: 978-1-9753-3965-4 (paperback)
        978-1-9753-3966-1 (ebook)

10 9 8 7 6 5 4 3 2 1

LSC-C

Printed in the United States of America

YOUR FORMA

Electronic Investigator Echika and Her Amicus Ex Machina

Ceremony celebrating the sixtieth anniversary of the Queen's ascension to be held next June

New cutting-edge Amicus models to be presented as a gift

On the fourth of this month, the British royal family's PR department announced that a ceremony celebrating the sixty-year anniversary of Her Majesty Queen Madeleine, fourth queen of the Windsor dynasty, will be held in June of next year.

On the fifth of this month, Novae Robotics Inc. (London) was officially notified of the event and revealed there is a project underway to develop and present new Amicus units to Her Majesty for the occasion. The three robots are currently under development and are known as the Royal Family (RF) Models. They will differ in appearance from existing Amicus and are to be equipped with unique, next-generation multipurpose AI. In response to the media, Her Majesty replied that she will gratefully accept the Amicus. "I'm currently thinking of the right names for them," she said. (23 related articles)

Article from *The Times*, May 5, 2014

Obituary:

Chikasato Hieda (programmer for the Your Forma development team) was a former employee of the tech corporation Rig City (based in Santa Clara, California) and a major contributor to the development and adoption of the invasive augmented-reality device Your Forma.

On the twelfth of this month, Chikasato Hieda passed away with the help of Fenster, a Swiss assisted-euthanasia company. He was forty-four. In response to queries from the media, Fenster admitted to being involved in his death but refused to give any further details since it would "encroach on their client's privacy."

In response to a request for comment on this news, Rig City replied, "we deeply apologize, but we are not in any position to speak on a former employee's activities and choices."

The funeral was conducted privately by his relatives. He is survived by his daughter, Echika Hieda.

From *The Los Angeles Times*, August 18, 2022, Obituaries

Prologue
Blizzard

Prologue
Blizzard

Every now and then, a thought blew through her mind like a violent gust of wind: *I never wanted to turn out like this.*

"So based on the victim's testimony, how many centimeters of *snowfall* are in his room now?"

"About forty-eight centimeters before we applied the suppressant. The blizzard is pretty terrible, so he'll probably start exhibiting hypothermia symptoms once the suppressant wears off."

Much to her surprise, the Brebis Égarée Hospital didn't reek of disinfectant.

Echika walked down the hospital wing's corridor with her eyes fixed on the two men ahead of her. One of them was a doctor clad in a white coat, and the other was her partner, Benno Kleiman.

Benno was a twenty-five-year-old German man with squarish facial features and short, tidy beige hair. His overall appearance gave a somewhat neurotic impression. Two weeks had passed since he'd started working with her, but the only thing Echika knew about him was that he had a girlfriend two years his junior.

He continued. "...So we will connect to the patient's Your Forma and attempt to trace back the virus's infection source."

"I am aware of the procedure, yes. Brain Diving, correct? You trace back the personal history and Mnemosynes recorded in his Your Forma to find where he was infected… I have to admit, though. It's my first time seeing a self-propagating virus that induces illusions of a blizzard."

"That's what the doctor in Washington, DC, said, too," Benno replied. "'There's no doubt that this is a new strain."

"DC was where it showed up initially, right? I'm glad we weren't the first case. We've learned how to handle it effectively through precedent."

The Seine River flowed serenely outside the window. Rays of cold winter sunlight sparkled against the water's surface in an almost irritatingly calm fashion.

"That said," the doctor started, before pausing to stifle a yawn, "I'm sure you two have it worse, but I've hardly gotten any sleep. I really hope you can resolve this as quickly as possible."

"Why don't you leave the Amicus to handle the workload at night?"

"We're letting them take the reins wherever possible, of course, but we don't want to overwork the poor things."

"Poor things?" Benno asked, raising an eyebrow. "They're just machines. You lose out by not using them when you can."

"Oh, I see, you're a luddite. Well, personally, I'm an Amicus sympathizer, so I can't help but feel for them."

Benno shrugged awkwardly and moved away from the doctor, approaching Echika. Based on his expression, she could tell he was about to give her his usual warning.

"Listen, Hieda. Only broach as far as their surface Mnemosynes. Find how they were infected and look for clues on who did it."

Yep, same old, same old…

"With all due respect," Echika said, "I'm a Diver. It's your job as my aide and Belayer to decide when to pull me up. What I mean is, how deep I go is up to you, not me."

"I'm only saying this because whenever I try to reel you back up, you drag me down there instead. You've almost fried my brain three times from the strain already. Are you trying to kill me or something?"

"I've gotten people sent to the hospital before, but I've never killed anyone."

"Makes sense no one works with you for long." Benno spat the words out bitterly. "Now listen to me, Little Miss Genius. While we were out investigating something else, our colleagues were working their butts off, Brain Diving to trace the source of the infection. You better produce results."

"I always do."

"Fine, let me rephrase that. Produce results without *breaking your partner*. You follow?"

Having said his piece in a clearly one-sided manner, Benno walked back to the doctor. Echika exhaled hard. He loathed her, to an almost refreshing extent. Not that she made any effort to make herself likable. This meant her relationship with him could only keep getting worse, but she didn't mind.

After all, as unpleasant as it was to admit, he was right. Their partnership wouldn't last long anyway.

The doctor led them to a luxurious hospital room, where a young French man was sleeping in a dull, undecorated bed. He was the source of the viral infection in Paris. In addition to Echika and the other two, a nurse Amicus robot stood in the room. Its appearance was modeled on a woman in her thirties, with a well-featured, tidy face. It was a mass-produced model she'd seen quite often.

"Thank you for coming," the Amicus said with a sociable smile. "We applied the suppressant twelve minutes ago, and the patient's condition has been stable since. He's already consented to Brain Diving."

"A pleasure to meet you, Monsieur Ogier," Benno said, flashing his ID badge. "I'm Investigator Aide Benno Kleiman from Interpol's Electro-crime Investigations Bureau, and this is Electronic Investigator Echika Hieda. In accordance with International Criminal Procedure Code Article 15, we will exercise our authority to connect into your personal Your Forma."

"He's comatose," the doctor said, snickering. "Was there a point to that?"

"It's standard procedure. We get complaints sometimes if we don't say it."

"Let's begin, Benno. Jack in."

Echika reached into her coat pocket to produce her Lifeline—the

Umbilical Cord, a threadlike cable with connectors on both ends. Echika and Benno each took an end and plugged it into the connector ports embedded in the skin on the nape of their neck.

"Next, the Brain Diving cord."

At Echika's instructions, Benno plugged the Brain Diving cord into the boy's neck and tossed the other connector over to her. This one was a good deal thicker than the Umbilical Cord. She plugged it into a second port on her body. This manner of connection was colloquially known as a triangle connection, the most basic form of attachment that the Brain Diver needed to investigate someone's mind.

"Hieda, what about the antivirus infection cocoon?"

"All green. It's operating normally."

"Then get going."

Echika jerked her chin back; the next moment, she was plummeting into the infected boy's mind. The wintry trees of Luxembourg Gardens filled her field of view, and the fluffy pleasure of stuffing her cheeks with a *pain au chocolat* from a bakery flooded her taste buds.

The name of Paris's index case—the first person to be diagnosed and the source of the infection—was Thomas Ogier, a student at Grande École, an elite French institution specializing in technology and the sciences. According to his surface Mnemosynes—which detailed records of his activities over the last month—having breakfast in this park was part of his everyday routine.

After eating, he would get in a carpool, which would make his heart race a little with excitement. This began a day's worth of fascinating research.

As the car sailed past the cityscape, advertisements of the latest Bluetooth-equipped sneakers, improved sleep earphones, and carbon-fiber sportswear flew into his field of vision. They all sparkled and shone. These were all products Ogier would likely be interested in.

Echika continued her free fall, letting his emotions flow past her without allowing them to settle in. As she viewed his Mnemosynes, she traced his footprints through the network, from his purchase history through e-commerce sites to his browsing history in video-streaming services. She checked his social media accounts by forcing open his registration info. As an aspiring engineer, he had strong interest in technology. Because of this, he'd taken a prolonged leave from work on All Saints' Day to go to America, where he'd toured Rig City and Clear Solution Inc.

But she discovered no clues pertaining to the virus. His mailing apps were mostly full of exchanges from his family and friends, and even the few advertisements she found there seemed innocuous.

I see, thought Echika. *It's just like the electronic investigator from Washington said...*

Even when they'd Dived into patient zero there, the investigators had found no traces of either the culprit who'd infected them or even the virus's method of infection.

By this point, she'd finished browsing through the surface Mnemosynes, but Benno wasn't pulling her up yet. Their processing speeds were so disparate that his monitoring couldn't keep up with the rate at which she Dived. Echika continued to plummet, accelerating with every second.

No good.

She sailed past the patient's surface level, into the depths of the medium layers of his Mnemosynes—when suddenly, she felt something jolt in the nape of her neck.

"Aide Kleiman!"

She jerked her head upon hearing his name shouted. Her field of vision dissipated, and she found herself in the hospital room again. Benno had crumpled to his knees, the cord yanked out of his neck. The doctor hurried over to him, but he was already unconscious and completely limp. The Amicus nurse bolted out of the room, its expression alarmed.

Aaah. It happened again.

Echika stood rooted in place, not terribly surprised by what had transpired. She had thought Benno would probably reach his limit any day now, and sure enough, today was the day... Echika pretended not to notice the stinging in her heart.

These kinds of malfunctions occurred when a Diver's and a Belayer's processing speed didn't match. Their abilities hadn't been equal to begin with, so Benno forcing himself to work with her was bound to wear him out eventually.

Echika was used to seeing her partners break down.

Before long, several nurse Amicus hurried into the room. They brought in a stretcher and carried Benno away. He would probably get out of this with a week of hospital stay. *That's what always happens,* Echika told herself as she silently stifled the guilt bubbling up from the pit of her stomach.

"I've seen investigator aides exhibit these symptoms before," the doctor standing next to her said.

Echika took a silent deep breath as she felt his condemning gaze.

"Which one of them was it?" she asked. "Clidat? Algren? Cerbère, maybe? Who else was there...?"

"Enough." The doctor's eyes had long since filled with disdain. "They told me that there was a genius out there who fries all her partners' heads and sends them to the infirmary. That's you, isn't it? Electronic Investigator Hieda."

She already knew how to give him the answer he wanted. What he wanted to hear was something along the lines of, *I'm not doing this on purpose* or *No one enjoys seeing their colleagues suffer.* Those kinds of lines, full of transparent goodwill.

But no number of pretty words could sweep away the facts. That was something she'd learned all too well a long time ago.

"Benno will recover. The Your Forma will mend his cranial nerves, and he'll be fine," Echika said, her face expressionless to an almost cruel degree. "I'll be taking my leave, then. Thank you for your coop-eration with the investigation."

She walked out of the hospital room, not regarding the doctor, who stared at her as if he couldn't believe what she'd just said.

Tracing the information Your Forma records to find clues that would solve criminal cases.

That was an electronic investigator's—Echika Hieda's—job.

Chapter 1
Amicus
Ex Machina

Chapter 1
Amicus Ex Machina

1

\<Today's temperature stands at −7°C. Attire index A, warm clothing, is recommended>

Despite it being eight in the morning, the stars continued to faintly twinkle in the sky. With the psychological-horror movie she'd watched during her flight still burned into her eyelids, Echika stood at the roundabout by Pulkovo Airport, located in northwestern Russia.

Her jet-black hair, typical of her Japanese descent, was styled in a bob cut that reached down to her jawline. Her thin frame was covered by a sweater, short pants, tights, and boots—all of them black. People had ribbed her countless times about being a raven in the body of a human.

Cars flowed into the roundabout, their headlights activated. Buses with Cyrillic letters written on them pulled over to spew out their passengers before sucking in more people. As Echika's eyes met with a few of the riders', their personal data—like their names and professions—danced through her field of vision in a pop-up display.

Ever since the popularization of Your Forma, this kind of personal information had become visible just by looking someone in the face. Not for the average citizen, mind you, but for people whose professions granted them the necessary permits to access it. Names, dates of birth, addresses, lines of work… These were all visible to Echika without even a command.

At any rate…

Despite it being fifteen minutes past the agreed time, Benno hadn't shown up.

Fine, Echika thought, licking her dry lips as she decided to call him. *Audio call to Benno Kleiman.*

Converting her thoughts to a textual command, she issued that order to the Your Forma inside her head. The boring ringback tone buzzed through the earphone she'd left on her ear.

She knew Benno hated phone calls, so she didn't expect him to pick up. And despite that, she'd made the call anyway. Sometimes, he'd answer if he was in a decent mood. Besides, she had half a mind to complain to him about his perpetual tardiness.

But today wasn't a good day, it seemed. The call timed out and automatically closed. A moment later, she received a text from him. She opened up the message window floating at the corner of her field of vision.

"I'm still at the hospital. When Chief Totoki said yesterday I'd be arriving on the scene, that was a lie."

She lied? Echika knit her brow.

"The chief ordered me to keep quiet about it, but our partnership ends today."

Figures.

She'd seen this coming. Her partnerships got canceled pretty often, so she wasn't disappointed or dejected by the news. The problem was that Chief Totoki had kept it a secret from her until today. That gave Echika a vague, ill premonition.

"Someone from the local branch should be in the airport to pick you up. Stay at the roundabout."

"Understood. Did you hear anything about my new aide, by the way?"

Echika replied with a question, but Benno didn't answer it. That pissed her off a little, but she was the one who'd gotten him hospitalized, and he hadn't liked her to begin with. Him turning a cold shoulder to her didn't come as a surprise.

A new partner, huh?

She wasn't enthusiastic at the prospect, to say the least. After all, no matter who showed up, they wouldn't last long. Most electronic investigators worked with the same aide for a year or so, but in Echika's case, her partnerships lasted only a month at best. Her data-processing abilities were so outstandingly high that no one could match her, so her aides kept failing and getting hurt.

Feeling a wave of melancholy creep in on her, Echika took out her electronic cigarette and sucked on it. As she was about to blow out a wisp of water vapor that contained neither nicotine nor tar, an alert popped up from her Your Forma.

<Smoking is prohibited on airport grounds>

Restraining the urge to click her tongue, she turned off her cigarette and instead resorted to fiddling with the nitro-case necklace hanging from her neck in an attempt to distract herself.

The person picking her up arrived only thirty minutes later. As Echika stood there, almost freezing over, an SUV pulled up in front of her. It had a squarish body with a stylish maroon coating, and its roundish headlights seemed like an expression of how this car was meant for driving off the road.

Her Your Forma swiftly analyzed the car's make. A Lada Niva. An ancient, *respectable model* that hadn't seen a full makeover in some forty-odd years. An artistic city like this had a unique taste in automobiles, indeed.

"Good morning. Are you Electronic Investigator Hieda?"

The driver's-seat window rolled down, revealing the face of a young Caucasian man. But despite looking him straight in the face, no personal information popped up in her field of vision. That alone instantly made Echika that much more depressed.

The person at the wheel was an Amicus. Though they were once called androids or humanoid machines, they were now considered an indispensable part of human life.

"Did I keep you waiting long?" he asked, holding up an ID badge identifying him as an Amicus working with the local police. "I was told to meet you at nine AM..."

"We were supposed to get here at eight." Benno had relayed that to her, so this was another one of his petty attempts at harassment. Typical. "Never mind, let me get in."

No sooner did the Amicus unlock the door than Echika slid into the passenger seat. Finally, she could warm herself up a little...or so she thought, but her expectations were dashed when she found the interior of the car was terribly cold.

"Oh, excuse me. The cold helps my processing speed," the Amicus said, flipping the switch for the heating with a friendly gesture.

As far as Echika knew, it couldn't tell the difference between hot and cold. Being a machine fashioned in human form, it was compelled, by its system, to act "human."

"But if I was to catch a cold because of this, it would be a breach of your Laws of Respect."

"Right you are. Of course, I take care to watch over my behavior accordingly."

To respect humans, obey the orders of humans, and never attack a human being—all Amicus were programmed in accordance with these Laws of Respect.

Honestly speaking, Echika didn't like these machines much. Or rather, she flat-out hated them.

The semiautomatic vehicle slowly started moving and drove out of the roundabout. The streets of Saint Petersburg sailed past in all the glory of their anachronistic architecture. It was an elegant, beautiful sight, but it was blotted out as advertisement holograms unfurled over the walls.

One of the Your Forma's features was an augmented-reality advertisement system. By reading the user's tastes, it displayed business advertisements tailored to their preferences. These days, buildings around the globe were covered in commercials, and no matter where one went, one couldn't appreciate the view. You could opt to turn them off, but it came with a steep fee.

After all, the developer of the Your Forma, Rig City, was mostly funded by ad revenue. What's more, the Your Forma installation procedures were performed free of charge for all users, which was also thanks to this revenue source.

"According to today's schedule, you should be heading for the Union Care Center next. You're to Brain Dive and identify the source of the virus today, yes?"

"Correct."

"After Washington, DC, and Paris, there's a third incident here in Saint Petersburg."

"Forget the schedule—what about my new aide?"

"He's ready and waiting for you. Would you like to hear more about him?"

"No, I'll find out when I meet him."

Cutting off the conversation there, Echika used her Your Forma to browse the news. Lines of headlines tailored to her interests danced before her eyes.

<AI author to be final nominee for literary prize>

<Massive cold wave hits Japan's Kanto region>

<Notre-Dame Cathedral restricts end-of-year countdown event>

<Switzerland announced as the leading country in number of assisted suicides>

<Bookstore networks to increase year-end sales of paper volumes>...

The identity of her new aide didn't interest her per se. She'd just do the work laid out before her regardless. Echika had stopped thinking about her partners a long time ago; that way, she could shield her heart from all kinds of guilt.

<The age of the pandemic is behind us. Won't you grasp the thread of your new life?>

That was the slogan for the first advertisements.

The invasive augmented-reality device, Your Forma, was an information terminal fashioned after a sewing thread that sat within one's head. After being shaped into a three-micrometer smart thread, the device was inserted directly into the brain using laser surgery.

With the Your Forma, one could do almost anything, from monitoring one's health to online shopping and updating social networks, via thought alone.

It all started thirty-one years ago, the winter of 1992, when a virus that came to be known as The Spore caused a worldwide pandemic. The development of vaccines and antibodies couldn't keep up with the virus's rapid mutations, which swiftly paralyzed society. The death toll climbed to thirty million, with the most frequent cause of death being viral encephalitis. As such, preventing brain inflammation became a matter of urgent concern.

Under a World Health Organization initiative, different corporations and groups cooperated to create a prototype of a brain-machine interface, which they eventually rolled out for general use.

Over the next several years, they developed the invasive medical-thread device Neural Safety. With its help, treating the encephalitis symptoms became easier, and the mortality rate was greatly curbed. Future iterations could outright prevent the disease.

And the population, exhausted from years of fighting the virus, had no reason not to be drawn to this new thread.

And now, long after the pandemic's conclusion in the year of 2023, Neural Safety had since been reborn under a new name, evolving into the Your Forma, the cutting-edge, multipurpose, multifunction information terminal.

One of its most noteworthy features was Mnemosynes—records of real events, plus the emotions and impressions of the user at the time. They were formed through converting the memories in the hippocampus into binary data and producing a visualization of the heart.

Mnemosynes went on to revolutionize the face of criminal investigation. Interpol's Electrocrime Investigations Bureau became the sole organization with the authority to investigate Mnemosynes, which they exercised to solve major offenses. There were, of course, rare instances of criminals tweaking or erasing Mnemosynes to escape judgment. Still, since it was impossible to falsify Mnemosynes with current technology, they nevertheless contributed greatly to the solving of criminal cases.

The people who plunged into Mnemosynes were electronic investigators—also known as Divers—like Echika.

Divers connected to a victim's or perpetrator's Your Forma to quite literally plunge into their minds in search of key clues for solving crimes. Mnemosynes were stored in a stand-alone environment that was disconnected from the network, which meant you had to interface physically with them through a wire. On top of that, Mnemosynes were housed in a multilayered structure resembling a mille-feuille. This ensured people with average processing speed couldn't so much as view the surface level of this data.

As such, the job had very specific compatibility requirements. These basically boiled down to a genetic resistance to stress and an affinity with Your Forma.

When brains grew accustomed to using Your Forma from the early stages of development, some would, in rare instances, adjust themselves to the device to an extreme degree, spurring a formation of myelin. In simple terms, the brain grows too used to the Your Forma and exponentially increases its information-processing speed as a result.

Those kinds of slightly distorted people were selected to become electronic investigators. And Echika stood head and shoulders above her peers, to the point where even now, no aide had ever been able to match her processing speed.

In other words, people calling her a genius wasn't a compliment but sarcasm of the highest degree.

2

Her destination, the Union Care Center, was a building designed in the style of Gothic Revival architecture. Echika couldn't help but stare at it, but that soon prompted ads to flash into life on the outer walls. Her Your Forma automatically read their data matrices, instantly opening the products' purchase pages in her browser.

Ugh, stop that.

Needlessly exhausted, she arrived at the center's lobby with the driver

Amicus in tow. The lobby was full of haggard outpatients, and none of them looked like the kind of person who might work as an electronic investigator aide. Echika exhaled hard. Her partners being late wasn't anything new.

"Maybe I should tell you about him anyway," the Amicus started again. "Your aide's name is Harold Lucraft, and he recently transferred to your department from the city police. He has blond hair and is about 175 meters tall."

"I said it's fine. I'll just check his personal data when I see him—"

But as Echika turned to the Amicus to complain, she got her first good look at him, then froze up in amazement. She didn't care much for him because he was a machine, but his features were incredibly handsome.

His age had been set to his mid to late twenties. He had blond hair held in place with wax, and he had uniform brows and gentle eyelashes. The bridge of his nose was perfectly straight, and his lips were thick in just the right way. The back of his hair stood up a little, and he had a faint mole on his right cheek, granting him a very human appearance.

From top to bottom, he looked like a work of art that a craftsperson had put their heart and soul into. He clearly wasn't a mass-produced model but a customized one that cost a great deal of money.

"As for Lucraft's attire, today, he's wearing a tartan scarf and a melton coat."

Echika couldn't even blink anymore because the Amicus in front of her was wearing exactly that. Even his coat, with its mundane design, somehow accentuated his slender, well-proportioned physique.

"No way…," she uttered, her mouth feeling awfully dry all of a sudden. "You're joking, right?"

He smiled serenely—a smile so sophisticated, it almost gave her heartburn.

"My apologies for not introducing myself sooner. I'm Harold Lucraft," the Amicus—Harold—said, extending his hand for a shake.

Hold on. No. Stop messing with me.

"That can't be. I've never heard of Amicus working as electronic investigator aides. You just do the chores—"

"True, Amicus in investigative organizations usually manage evidence-storage rooms and security. Humans and analysis automatons handle the investigations themselves. My title isn't official, either."

Since their productivity didn't match that of industrial robots, Amicus were usually charged with routine tasks. As AGI—Artificial General Intelligence—they stressed human appearance over efficiency. Back when AGI was still a theoretical concept, scholars dreaded the possibility of them becoming a hyper intelligence that could overshadow humankind. But once they actually came to be, they didn't amount to anything more than "clever but obedient robots" that served as reliable partners to humankind.

The Amicus traced their origins to the height of the pandemic. They were developed by the England-based Novae Robotics Inc. as a humanoid machine. Much like the Your Forma, the fields of robotics and AI research had made great strides during that time. With risk of infection discouraging physical contact between people, investments were made into robots that could work in their place.

And so the English government sunk vast funds into Novae Robotics Inc.'s research, allowing them to make their humanoid machines a reality. The first androids were supplied only to medical institutes. Though they were the spitting image of humans, they were also incredibly expensive.

Not only did the robots perform their assignment well, but they also behaved the way people sought; they comforted, encouraged, and sympathized with them, caring and relieving the stress of both the patients suffering from the virus and their healthcare providers.

The machines were later rebranded and put on sale as Amicus, and they soon spread throughout society, both in home and business environments. It only made sense that at present, clashes between the Amicus sympathizers and the luddites were creating frequent problems in society.

Yet as "human" as the Amicus were, and despite how flexible and capable of adapting to different situations they could be, they were jacks-of-all-trades, masters of none. Their depth of understanding of any specific field was shallower than industrial robots.

That was why analysis ants were preferred over Amicus when it came to specialized tasks like criminal investigations. And yet the Amicus gazing at her had nevertheless introduced himself as her new assistant.

"If you really are my aide, then why didn't you tell me you were when we met?"

"Oh." Harold retracted his hand in a carefree manner. "My apologies. It's just that I wanted to observe what kind of person you are... Did you happen to watch a movie on your flight?"

"Huh?" She had. "So what if I did?"

"It was *The Third Cellar*, correct?"

Echika blinked a few times. He was dead-on, but how did he know that?

"No way. Who told you?"

"Oh, no one told me. I assumed you were taking an Étoile France flight. And if you check their home page, *The Third Cellar* is highlighted as one of their recommended in-flight pictures."

"...And?"

"If you're someone who isn't particular about their tastes, you'd likely pick the recommended title. And given your profession, only a very thrilling story would draw you in. Your eyes are congested on account of you blinking less, and your lips are dry because you lick them more when you're frightened. Meaning the movie was likely a psychological-horror thriller, and the only recommended movie of that genre in their catalog was *The Third Cellar*."

"What the hell are you...?" Echika muttered, taken aback.

"Which makes me think that you're something of an indifferent person, aren't you, Investigator? I'm picking up the scent of an electronic cigarette's flavor on you, too. And if I may be so bold, a very cheap flavor, at that. That makes me think you don't have any preferences when it comes to smoking, either—you only do it to distract yourself. People like you don't usually have any interest in their daily lives. You care little for fashion or romance, and you're married to your job."

She was speechless. And as Echika stared at him, stunned, Harold regarded her with a satisfied smirk.

"It's basic human observation. I think that demonstrates my aptitude as an investigator, don't you?"

This isn't funny—what is this thing?

Amicus knew how to read people's emotions so they could communicate effectively, but this level of accuracy was abnormal. Just what was going on?

"Investigator Hieda," Harold whispered, his lips curled into a soft smile that left no room for argument, "I will do my utmost to be a suitable partner until we solve this case."

Give me a break.

An Amicus investigator aide? With skills so honed, they could violate her privacy?

"I, hmm… I need a minute," Echika managed somehow. "Let me call my superior."

<Holo-call to Vi Totoki>

Stepping outside the Care Center, Echika immediately called Chief Totoki. The temperature was as low as it had been earlier that morning, but for some reason, she couldn't feel the cold; that was how shaken she was.

Holo-calls, or Holographic Telepresence, were one of the Your Forma's features. It used holographic models to make it feel as though you were standing directly across from your conversation partner.

"Oh, good morning, Hieda."

The call connected, and Chief Totoki's image appeared before her eyes. She had sharp facial features, so she gave a rather stern impression despite being a woman. Her black hair was bound and reached down to her waist, and her gray suit didn't have a single wrinkle on it.

This woman in her midthirties led the team that managed all the electronic investigators. Totoki's official title was senior police investigator, and she'd worked her way up the ladder through a different route than electronic investigators and their aides.

"Do you have any idea what time it is right now here in Lyon? Eight AM. People are only getting out of bed this time of day."

"My apologies." Echika held back the urge to snap at her. *Keep your cool.* "Did you stay quiet about my partnership with Benno being annulled because my new partner is an Amicus?"

"Not at all. I was just busy, so I forgot to get around to breaking it to you." Lies. Totoki wasn't above tricking people like that. "I get that you hate Amicus. It's just that we only have a limited number of investigators. And with you causing your aides to go kaput and sending them to the hospital every so often, we're starting to have holes in our investigations."

"But that's because—"

"Yes, I know. No aide can match you, and I'm also to blame for turning a blind eye to the disparity in your abilities. But we finally found you a better partner."

"And they're an Amicus?" *How is that better?* she almost asked. "Besides, the Your Forma and the Amicus's AI operate on completely different standards. He probably can't connect to the Lifeline anyway."

"We've prepared a special Lifeline with an HSB to USB converter for him. He can definitely connect to it."

"And if his processing speed doesn't match mine, I'll just end up frying his circuits regardless."

"He's a special model, so you don't need to worry about that."

"What, because he's bespoke? Don't tell me you had that thing made to order."

"Originally, he was working for the Saint Petersburg police's detective division. He was put in charge of this incident and assigned to our office instead, that's all." Totoki said it so matter-of-factly that the more Echika listened, the more she doubted this was true. "He's a special model, but we didn't order his production. As you well know, we don't have that kind of budget."

"But you just said you had a special Lifeline prepared for him."

"Because that's a necessary investment. We're not just doing this for you; this could end up benefiting many electronic investigators in the future."

Was she saying she wanted Amicus handling the aide duties in the future? Absurd.

"Hieda, his computation rate is a match for your data-processing speed. The numbers don't lie," Totoki insisted, trying to persuade her. "There was talk of sacking you in the general meeting, you know. But I fought tooth and nail to reject that suggestion. You're a rare talent, and the fact that you're the world's youngest electronic investigator is proof of that."

The world's youngest electronic investigator, a prodigy. Thinking back to the time when the media had made a big deal out of her and kept calling her that made Echika quite bitter. She'd entered this job three years ago. She was sixteen at the time, having skipped grades to graduate high school early. People calling her a genius had put quite a bit of pressure on her, but at least when they called her that back then, it didn't reek of sarcasm like it did today.

But all that changed when she unintentionally fried her first aide's brain.

"Besides, this method won't end up hurting any human aides."

She couldn't deny this was good news. That one point alone seemed to drown out any other counterarguments.

"And if you have any other complaints, figure out how to Dive in and escape by yourself."

"That's impossible. No one can do that, which is why we have the partner system in the first place."

Divers like Echika specialized in data processing alone, so when they'd begun Brain Diving, they couldn't control it. It was like skydiving in the sense that once she plunged in, she could only continue plummeting straight down. This was why she needed the Belayer to hold on to her Lifeline, carefully monitor her condition, and pull her up in time.

"Are you satisfied now?"

Totoki clearly wasn't going to budge on this. Echika didn't think she could really refuse, either. More than anything, the fact that the chief had covered for her in the general meeting was big. Any normal person would feel grateful and indebted after that.

But the price for that was partnering with a machine.

Echika apologized to Totoki for the sudden disturbance and hung up, then ruffled her bangs. She understood now that she had no choice but to give in. That Amicus would break before long anyway. Totoki seemed convinced that his abilities would match hers, but it wasn't like his compatibility with her had ever been tested.

And it couldn't possibly be as simple as letting an Amicus robot take over that role.

"That was a pretty long call, Investigator Hieda."

The Care Center's hospitalization ward was dark and quite old-fashioned in style. As a human doctor led Echika and Harold down the hall, they passed by hospital visitors and nurse Amicus.

"So what?" Echika retorted bluntly.

"I can tell even if you won't say anything. You asked for a change in partner, right?"

"No," she replied on the spur of the moment. Dammit. "I didn't go that far."

"That's good." Harold smiled. "If I may ask, do you hate Amicus?"

So he noticed. That question felt like he'd just lunged at her throat. Given her attitude earlier, it was an obvious thing to inquire about, but having it pointed out so plainly did make her a little embarrassed.

"No offense to you, but…yes, that's right."

"I don't mind; things like that don't bother me. What makes you despise us, though?"

"I'm not interested in sharing my personal history. Don't ask me about it again."

"I see. Well, I'm fine with the stoic sort. Those kind of people are respectable."

"No…" *What's with him? Is he not gonna get it unless I say it to his face?* "What I'm saying is, I'm not going to pretend like we're friends."

"Hmm, excuse me… Can I start giving you the details about the infected patients?"

Echika stopped with a start. The slender doctor walking in front of them turned a reproachful glare at their pointless chatter.

"My apologies." *Aah, time to switch gears.* "You said the first patient was hospitalized two days ago, right?"

"Correct, and this morning, we've gotten to the point where we have twelve others hospitalized. More than half of them are students of the ballet academy, and they were brought in for hypothermia symptoms. They all say that they see an intense blizzard."

The doctor gestured with his chin toward the window, where they could see a dimly lit, almost sleepy sort of sky. There wasn't a speck of snow to be seen, and the only things dancing busily through the air were delivery drones.

"The patients' minds really are seeing a blizzard," Echika noted. "That shared delusion is one of this sensory crime's distinctive features."

Sensory crimes were caused by cyber viruses that infected the Your Forma. The first of these serial offenses showed up in Washington, DC, followed by Paris, and now Saint Petersburg. Common symptoms included seeing an illusory blizzard, followed by signs of hypothermia.

"I've only seen the patient records and past cases on the news, but this seems to be a new strain of a self-propagating virus."

"Yes, and even a Your Forma's full scan can't detect it. The developers in Rig City have organized an analysis team to look into it."

As of now, only two things had been made clear about the new infectious agent.

First, it started with a single infected source and spread to others via Your Forma messages and phone calls.

Second, the virus had a very short incubation period, roughly fifteen minutes, which was the only time it was contagious.

Thus, the disease's problem wasn't so much its infectious capacity but rather the fact that after its outbreak, the Your Forma became inoperable, which hampered its capacity to spread.

At present, no one had discovered a means to remove the virus yet. There were only limited ways of dealing with it: either applying a suppressant drug that made the Your Forma's functions shut down or undergoing a surgical procedure to remove the Your Forma altogether.

"Delusions of a blizzard are one thing, but why would imaginary snow actually affect the body...?"

"The Electrocrime Investigations Bureau is grappling with that question, too," Echika remarked. "At the moment, we suspect it's a nocebo effect. Like the old water droplet experiment."

"What's that?"

"Briefly speaking, it's an experiment that proved a person can convince themselves to die. The subject is blindfolded and strapped to a bed. The doctor tells them they'll die once they lose two-thirds of their blood, then makes a small nick on their big toe with a scalpel, causing a bit of blood to trickle out."

"But in truth, they never actually made an incision, and what the patient thought was the sound of their blood was droplets of water." Harold continued the explanation from where Echika left off, despite not having been asked to do so. "The experiment goes on to give the patient hourly updates on how much blood they've lost. And a few hours later, when they're told they've bled out two-thirds of their blood, the patient passes away, despite being physically unharmed."

"You're well informed," Echika snipped peevishly.

"I read it online once. *Once we've seen something, we never forget it.*"

"Oh yes, our nurse Amicus are like that, too," the doctor added. "Whenever crucial clinical records end up getting lost along with their backups, they can output them from their memories and reproduce them."

"That's simple work for us." Harold smiled. "But, Investigator, isn't that experiment a little too forceful of an explanation, rationally speaking?"

"The brain is surprisingly easy to fool," Echika said, lowering her voice. "And since the Your Forma is integrated with it, the experiment is considered a viable explanation."

The three of them arrived at a large hospital room housing fifteen beds. On them lay the infected patients, sleeping soundly under the effect of the suppressant. Every one of them seemed to be in stable condition.

"Per your request, we've attached Brain Diving cords to each person," the doctor said.

The Brain Diving cords and Lifelines they used were all HSB cables. *HSB* stood for *Human Serial Bus*, the unique standard the Your Forma used. Possession of HSB cables was legally forbidden for individuals due to privacy-abuse issues, but certain medical institutions and investigative organizations were allowed to use them.

"Oh, so you're going to discover the source of the infection from here," Harold mused. "Do you think you'll discover the culprit, too?"

"I'm not sure about that. I'll only know once I Dive in."

In Washington and Paris, they'd traced the sources of the infection— Ogier, in Echika's case—but that didn't reveal any clues about how the patients had been exposed to the virus to begin with or the identity of the culprit. And since there were no vestiges of the infection in the Your Forma and Mnemosynes of the source patients, it proved that the people suffering from it had no idea where they'd contracted it.

So this time, she had to pray this Dive wouldn't turn out to be in vain, too.

"That being said," the doctor started, looking around the room anxiously, "processing twelve people in parallel. I've never seen electronic investigators handle more than two at once… Won't it impact your mental faculties and scramble your ego?"

"Don't worry. They requested me because I can handle it."

Since electronic investigators experienced the memories and emotions stored in the Mnemosynes as if they were their own, their Dives resulted in many cases of ego scrambling that required mental care. In Echika's case, however, she could handle processing multiple people in tandem. Not once in her career had those emotions engulfed and overtaken her.

If there was anything to be worried about in this situation, it was Harold's processing abilities.

"So." Echika glanced at the Amicus. "Aide Lucraft, where's our Lifeline?"

"I was told to use this one."

Harold took out an Umbilical Cord meant to connect electronic investigators to their aide. Its design was a bit different from a typical Lifeline, though. It looked like it was made of golden and silver threads woven around each other, and it gave off a faint glint.

"It's…custom-made." Echika knit her brow.

"Yes. It converts the data sent to me when monitoring you into a protocol I can understand."

Chief Totoki had deemed this a necessary investment, but Echika still had her doubts about things working out. She'd had one negative experience too many until now, and they'd left a lasting impression on her.

Despite her lack of enthusiasm, Echika plugged the Lifeline into the port in the nape of her neck. Harold approached her to connect the cord himself and stood right in front of her, prompting her to look away and suppress the urge to pull back from him.

It's been a long time since an Amicus has gotten so close to me. If this wasn't for work, I'd never be doing this.

"I'm connected, Investigator."

"Aaah, yeah." Echika glanced at Harold before freezing up.

He slid his entire left ear out of place and plugged the cord into a USB port behind it. "Is...is there anything wrong?" Echika asked.

Moments like these were stark reminders that Amicus were nothing more than machines in human form. And honestly, it was a little... No, it was *very* unsettling.

"Nothing in particular, though I'm a bit nervous," he said with a relaxed smile that belied his words. "You look like you're doing all right, too."

"...I'm used to this."

That was a lie. Her heart was rumbling with anxiety. And of course it was—she'd never been wired to an Amicus's head before. There was no going back now, though.

It'll be fine. You're good at shutting off your thoughts, aren't you?

With the triangle connection complete, Echika took a deep breath.

Just do it like you always do.

"Let's begin."

As soon as she whispered that word, it felt as if her senses tilted for a second—and the next moment, she was plummeting into a cybernetic ocean.

She started with the surface Mnemosynes. The feel of a pet dog's fur against her cheeks—a desire to protect it. The sight of a friend raising their voice—heart-wrenching sorrow. The feel of a new pair of toe shoes in her hands—excitement, a longing to dance. Browsing through a friend's social media timeline out of boredom. A photo of coffee with cheese scrolled by. The Mariinsky Theatre, shining beautifully, even when covered in ads—admiration...

The daily lives and emotions of a dozen people as recorded by their Your Forma swirled around like fragments of glass. This hail of human emotions haphazardly pelted Echika. But none of them was hers. She cloistered herself, wrote them off as the emotions of another, and let them flow through her.

"If they died, I would have hated you for the rest of my days."

A sudden whisper reached her—who was this?

"I almost keeled over because of you."

"I'll never partner with you again."

No. These were Echika's memories. Why was she Diving into her own Mnemosynes? She was falling in the wrong direction... Right, this was a *countercurrent*.

This is bad.

She could see it. A dark hallway. She shuddered. It was a hospital, and outside the window was a town bathed in starlight. The moans of all the partners whose lives she'd ruined emanated from somewhere. She heard sobbing. It was from their families, friends, lovers.

"You're terrible."

"She's like a machine."

"I shouldn't have paired with her."

"Apologize."

"And they call her a genius?"

I'm fine. This is fine. Nothing they say hurts. Because they're the ones who are really in pain, and I'm the one who hurt them.

She told herself this time and again.

Shut it down. Get away. This is unnecessary.

The world stiffly shifted around her as she somehow managed to change course. Using the network, she traced the infected patients' action history, from their mailboxes to their social media accounts. Good, she was back on track. Countless exchanges passed her by like a storm.

See you at school tomorrow. I had a fight with Dad. My friend bought a new Amicus. I got brand-new toe shoes. About the countdown party...

They rushed past her like a current. Points of scattered information, Mnemosynes, gathered, clashed, and connected. And little by little, they formed a path to the source of the infection.

Suddenly, sparks obscured her field of vision. Her sister's nostalgic face came into view, her cherubic features forming a mature smile. White teeth peeked between her peach-colored lips. This was another one of Echika's Mnemosynes.

"Hold my hand, Echika. I'll cast a spell to take the cold away."

I want to see her. To hold her hands again. And this time, I won't ever let go. I won't let anyone separate us—

No. Calm down. Don't let your own feelings get the better of you. Shut them off.

Echika flailed about. She'd picked up too much speed, and now she wanted to stop. But she couldn't. No, she had to turn rudder, to make her way toward the source of the virus. A convulsing sensation filled her mind. It was hot. She turned back to the twelve Mnemosynes. The dozen sets intersected. There, she searched for the origin of the infection.

And finally, *she saw it.*

And then Echika's field of vision shook. An old scent filled her nostrils as she found herself back in the hospital room. She panted, her forehead dripping with sweat. She steeled herself, preparing to hear the doctor scream, just like the other doctor had done when Benno collapsed.

Go on. Scream.

But she waited and waited, and the scream never came.

"You found it, didn't you?"

Breath catching in her throat, she turned her gaze to the beautiful voice. Next to her stood Harold, calm and composed, his expression as serene as it had been before she Brain Dived. He held the Umbilical Cord, which he'd pulled out of Echika's neck, in his hand. He didn't collapse like Benno did, nor did he seem any worse for it. In fact, he looked totally fine.

She couldn't believe it.

"What's the matter, Investigator?"

Aaah. Chief Totoki was right.

This was the first time this had ever happened in her career as a electronic investigator. Any other aide would perhaps not collapse after Brain Diving, but they'd definitely look exhausted. And after experiencing several instances of that fatigue, they'd eventually break down. Without exception.

But not only was Harold fine, he also didn't even look mildly tuckered out. Echika was flabbergasted. How was she able to successfully Dive while connected to a machine? That made no sense. It shouldn't be possible. She couldn't accept it. But reality, it seemed, was not without an ironic streak.

She'd finally found a partner to match her, and of all things, they were a bloody Amicus.

"Investigator? Did I pull you up at the wrong time?" Harold peered at her dubiously, his eyes as cold as a lake at dawn.

The depth of his artificial irises, the clear blood vessels tracing behind the whites of his eyes. Beautiful, cold, perfect eyes.

"No...," she managed in reply, her voice somewhat raspy. "Your timing was...perfect."

"Thank you."

"I'm shocked," the doctor uttered in an overwhelmed fashion. "You really processed twelve people in tandem... How's your head doing? Are you in any kind of pain?"

Echika replied she was fine and licked her dry lips, forcing her train of thought back to the investigation at hand. She looked up at Harold to put the information she'd obtained in order.

"The source of the infection is called Clara Lee, a student from the ballet academy. But...*she's not in this room.*"

3

Saint Petersburg's index case, Clara Lee, had been absent from the ballet academy on the day she was infected. Based on the Your Forma's records, Lee was an eighteen-year-old Norwegian girl, hailing from Kirkenes in Finnmark county. She had joined Saint Petersburg's ballet academy as an exchange student and lived in the student dorms. Lee had no criminal record and, much like Washington's and Paris's index cases, was an upstanding but otherwise ordinary civilian.

But for some reason, she had disappeared somewhere.

"As far as I can see, she's nothing but a victim. So why would she need to run?" Echika mused.

"Guilt at infecting her friends, perhaps," Harold replied. "I'm looking through Lee's social media accounts right now."

Echika and Harold were currently sitting in the Niva. It had been two hours since they left Saint Petersburg, and the border checkpoint for entering Finland from Russia was coming into view.

After inquiring about her at the academy, they learned that Lee took time off from her studies due to her grandfather's funeral. But according to the database, her grandfather had passed away several years ago. In other words, Lee lied.

By cross-referencing Saint Petersburg's security drones, they found out Lee rented a car from the closest parking lot to the dorms. After following its route, they confirmed Lee had taken it to the city of Kautokeino, which was some four hundred kilometers away from her hometown.

They didn't know why she went there, but they were at least able to confirm her current location, which made things quick.

However, her infected Your Forma's signal seemed to have shut down, leaving Echika with no choice but to track her by foot, the old-fashioned way, which was why they were driving to Kautokeino now. Being crammed into a car with an Amicus for hours on end did leave her rather dejected, though.

"Look at this, Investigator. A perfect dance," Harold told her, holding up a holo-browser window. Inside was a video of Lee, clad in a tutu and engaged in a flexible, graceful performance. Harold probably found it somewhere on her social media. "It's a variation on *Flames of Paris*, but she doesn't so much as tremble on tiptoe. Her technique puts some pros to shame."

"She might be talented, but I don't see how that has any bearing on the case."

Echika placed her hands on the steering wheel to distract herself from the cold. The car was currently in automatic-driving mode. Harold was in the passenger seat, fiddling with his wristwatch-model wearable information terminal 'to browse through Lee's social media. Amicus were always online, but that connection was limited to IoT (Internet of Things) purposes. They still needed information terminals to browse the web.

"How about this, then? Don't you think it's a weird way of drinking coffee?"

He showed her a picture of a mug of coffee with a generous amount of cheese in it. It was accompanied by a caption reading, "**my favorite.**" Echika had seen a glimpse of it earlier in the Mnemosynes. She had the Your Forma analyze the image, and it only took a moment for it to look up the answer.

"Coffee with goat cheese… That's part of the indigenous Sami people's culinary traditions," she remarked, as additional information flowed into her field of vision. "And apparently, Kautokeino, the city Lee is in right now, has many Sami residents."

"That area is a technologically restricted zone populated by luddites, who object to the use of machinery. And the Sami also make a living off reindeer husbandry, but some of them work as back-alley doctors behind the scenes."

"Yes, that's a pretty famous anecdote back in the office. But to be exact, they're not back-alley doctors; they're bio-hackers."

Bio-hackers were those paid to use cyborg technology to modify, or bio-hack, their clients' bodies. To accomplish this, they utilized illicit drugs and muscle-control chips, which was why they were sometimes referred to as back-alley physicians.

Many bio-hackers were minority people hired by underworld organizations. Their struggles to maintain their culture drove them to poverty, and so there were many observed cases of such bio-hackers working for large sums of money.

Needless to say, this was all highly illegal.

"So Lee went to a bio-hacker to have her infected Your Forma removed…?" Echika asked, puzzled. "But wait, why not just go to a normal hospital for that? Why take that risk?"

"Yes," Harold said, nodding. "I believe Lee is under the impression the hallucinations she's seeing are the result of some other machine malfunctioning inside her body. Don't you think that's plausible?"

"What do you mean? The database says she's healthy and has no chronic diseases. She shouldn't need any machines inside her body except for the Your Forma."

"Incidentally, Investigator, have you ever watched ballet?"

Echika blinked. *What's this all of a sudden?*

"Do I look like a dance fan? You're the one who called me indifferent."

"Allow me to apologize for that, even if it is belated. That wasn't appropriate to say to a lady," he said, bowing his head.

"That's not the issue." She didn't want him to treat her as anything but a coworker anyway. "But what about ballet?"

"It's just..." Harold hesitated for a moment. "Never mind. I'll explain later."

Following that, silence settled over the Niva. It was awkward. Feeling uncomfortable, Echika lowered the window. The freezing wind cut into her cheek, but she ignored it and placed the electronic cigarette between her lips.

Harold knew she hated Amicus. Things would be so much easier if he was like Benno and openly expressed his feelings, but Harold wasn't like that. He was always calm and collected, which made it hard to tell what was on his mind.

Echika blew out a wisp of smoke outside the car's window.

"How long have you been smoking, Investigator?" Harold suddenly asked, making her jolt.

Leave me alone.

"I told you not to ask about my private life. If the cigarette's bothering you, I'll turn it off."

"I don't mind. I like the scent of mint."

"...Some people say it doesn't taste much like a cigarette, though."

"Well, you should tell those people that it's much healthier than nicotine."

As part of their Laws of Respect, Amicus always have to behave

amicably toward humans. He won't act any different, no matter how much I try to close my heart off to him. That's how they slither their way into people's hearts.
Like I'll fall for that.

"Let me ask you about work," Echika brought up curtly. "Did functioning as my Belayer really not cause you any damage?"

"None at all. My abilities are verified as equivalent to yours. Can't you believe the numbers?"

It wasn't so much that she couldn't believe them as she *didn't want to.* Much as she hated to admit it, his data-processing speed was a startlingly close match for hers, and to prove it, she'd experienced a countercurrent during the Brain Diving earlier.

When their affinity with their Belayer was high, a Diver could sometimes accidentally draw on their own Mnemosynes. Since she'd never worked with an aide who matched her before, she'd experienced it for the first time in the hospital just then.

"I had a countercurrent earlier... Did you see anything?"

"No. The Belayer only sees the Mnemosynes of the targets the Diver is exploring. Even then, I only see it like a movie on fast-forward."

"That much I know." *And when they can't catch up to that quick current of information, their brain fries over, like with Benno.*

"When you slipped into your own Mnemosynes, the footage cut off, and all I saw was static noise. In other words, I could tell you were going through a countercurrent, but I couldn't make out your Mnemosynes."

"I see... Well, I'll try to keep the countercurrents to a minimum."

The fact that Harold couldn't glimpse into her Mnemosynes was honestly a relief. By contrast, the fact that she was so highly compatible with an Amicus of all things was far less encouraging. Scratch that, it was terrible.

"You don't have to act so fed up."

"I'm not acting fed up."

"It'll take us thirteen hours to get to Kautokeino," Harold said with a graceful smile. "That's enough time for you to overcome your aversion to Amicus and get to know me."

Echika grimaced. *What is he thinking?*

"I told you, we aren't friends."

"Because I'm an Amicus, right?"

"No, that would be true for anyone. I'm not going to go out of my way to play nice."

"Well, I, for one, would love to get to know you."

"Well, good for you, but I refuse."

What's his damage?

If a human said no, an Amicus was supposed to respect that and keep their distance. She'd felt this way since she met him, but there was something oddly cheeky about Harold. It was like he had his own unique personality.

"What's the point of us getting chummy? Letting our personal feelings get involved in this will just make it harder to do our jobs."

"I'm shocked," he said, widening his eyes in deliberate surprise. "You were thinking of getting that close to me?"

"Huh?" *What is this bucket of bolts saying?*

"I mean, personal feelings that would get in the way of doing our jobs refers to a *very particular* kind, right?"

She mentally gave herself a weary pat on the back for not knocking the Amicus down on the ground for that one.

"Aide Lucraft... Can you see what's strapped to my leg?"

"Yes, it's a Flamma 15, the Electrocrime Investigations Bureau's standard-issue automatic pistol."

"Correct. And being an Amicus, you're forbidden from possessing weapons. In other words, you're defenseless."

"It was just a joke; you don't need to get worked up," Harold said, placing his hand on the window frame with a composed smile. "You're a pretty interesting person. I'm sure we'll get along swimmingly."

As she contemplated the pros and cons of pumping a round into him, Echika angrily switched off her electronic cigarette, closed the window, and grumpily turned on the heating.

"It's been five minutes, so it's my turn to warm up."

"Yes, I'll put up with it for five minutes, then."

Harold preferred the cold, while Echika had a normal human body temperature, so they'd decided to alternate between switching the heating on and off every five minutes as a compromise. Folding to a damn machine's demand was humiliating, though.

"Listen to me, okay? Stop teasing humans."

"I wasn't teasing. I really do want to get to know you."

"Say one more weird thing, and I'll be claiming the right to keep the heating on for three hours."

"I've been meaning to ask, but if you're so cold, why wear tights instead of something thicker?

"These fibers produce heat and are easy to move in. They're warm, but they're far from perfect."

"So you're just sensitive to the cold."

"No, you're the weird one here. You'd have to not be human to be fine when it's below freezing."

"How well-informed of you."

"...That's not what I meant."

What a pest!

Their destination, Kautokeino, turned out to be a rather deserted rural settlement. Its buildings weren't even built densely enough to really be called a town. The main road was paved in the middle of the snowy field, the residential houses looked like nostalgic mountain shacks, and a church, a post office, and a school dotted the area.

Technologically restricted areas like this one were populated by luddite minorities, who'd rejected all manner of technological devices during the era of the pandemic, including thread devices. These segregated communities spanned the globe.

The pair had arrived during polar night, so the sun wouldn't be rising even at nine AM. The sky just barely lit overhead, the Niva pulled into a parking lot adjacent to the only supermarket in town.

"We can't do anything," Echika bemoaned, seated at the driver's seat as she sucked on a jelly pouch. "Without any surveillance drones in the area, we don't have any way of tracking Lee down."

The most dependable method of locating targets who Your Forma couldn't detect was to rely on surveillance cameras or drones set up around a city. That hadn't changed in years. But much to her displeasure, Echika realized that Kautokeino had neither cameras nor drones. Even deliveries had to be made by hand. Some restricted zones still had surveillance cameras set up, strictly to maintain the public order, but this section wasn't one of them.

"This town is simply sticking to the principles of a restricted zone," Harold said, tearing a jelly pouch open. "Why don't we enjoy this serene scenery a while longer?"

"What's so interesting about looking at a town from the Stone Age?"

"Oh, no, this is Bronze Age at worst."

"You really meant that, didn't you?"

"Let's stay on the lookout here," Harold said, glancing at the super-market. "This place is the only food source in the city. And without any drones flying around, I doubt e-commerce sites deliver to the area, so if anyone needs to shop for food, they'd have to come here. There's a high probability Lee will show up."

Something that convenient couldn't possibly happen. To begin with, Lee had only gotten out of the rental car in Kautokeino, so they didn't know for sure if she was even staying in its limits.

That being said, the fifteen-hour drive had been exhausting. Echika's body felt like mud as she leaned against the car seat. She glanced at Harold, who was sucking on his jelly pouch. Much like humans, Amicus could ingest food, but their energy source was a power-generation system based on liquid circulation, so it wasn't like they converted what they ate into energy.

Eating was simply an option for them, included for the sake of making them look and feel more human, and their artificial stomachs simply broke down and disposed of anything they consumed.

"When we get back, I'd like to have some hot borscht," he remarked. "This jelly is just nasty."

"Nasty?" Echika asked indifferently. "It's got all five major nutrients included, and you can finish it in no time. It's convenient."

Harold knit his brow in a clear gesture of disappointment.

"Are you sure you're not hiding a charging port somewhere under those clothes, Investigator? Like some of the early Amicus models."

"Huh? If anything, why are you going on about whether food tastes good or not? Act more like a machine."

In all the time she'd spent with him on the way here, Echika had come to a single conclusion—she'd never get along with this robot. That would be true for any Amicus, but in his case, he was her polar opposite.

Either way, Echika pulled herself together. She'd need to come up with her next move. Using her Your Forma to deploy her data on this case, she scavenged for any clues she might have overlooked. Meanwhile, Harold continued observing the customers entering and leaving the market. Did he have some basis to believe Lee might pass through? Echika hoped so but couldn't bring herself to expect much.

Time ticked by, and the cold air seeping in through the window sapped the warmth from her fingertips little by little. The sky brightened slowly before gradually fading away. Then the lights of the settlement flicked on.

Echika had already thrown in the towel and started to doze off when it happened.

"Investigator, wake up."

"Nn, no... Nothing's getting me out of bed today... Nng..."

"You're half asleep, aren't you? I found Lee."

What?!

Echika awoke at once. Peering through the Niva's windshield, she saw a blue jeep parked near the entrance of the market. The door of the driver's seat had just slammed shut, and she couldn't make out who had settled into the car.

"It's that jeep. To be exact, it's not Lee herself but a Sami who's sheltering her."

"What are you talking about?" That didn't make any sense. "We didn't get any information on someone sheltering her ..."

"No, there's no mistaking it. You know about my eyesight, right? Trust me."

How could she trust him? Was she really supposed to believe he could discern, just by glancing at someone, not only their ethnicity but also if they were sheltering Lee in their house?

That couldn't be, but she was too groggy to piece together a logical argument. As they spoke, the jeep's taillights flickered red, and the vehicle began driving away.

"Tail her, please. And you should probably wipe your chin off as soon as you can. You're drooling."

"I'm not. I wasn't sleeping that deeply! Besides, even if I was, I wouldn't drool!"

"Investigator, the jeep is getting away."

"Ugh, fine!"

If this is just a wild-goose chase, you'll never hear the end of it!

Switching the Niva to manual, Echika stomped down on the accelerator. She pulled out of the parking lot, sliding onto the main road in pursuit of the jeep. But there were no other cars around, and visibility was too good.

"We're in plain sight. How is this tailing them…?"

"Well, there aren't many streets the residents can take, so it's not that suspicious."

"Like you can say that with such an obviously Russian vehicle," Echika noted, exasperated.

After driving roughly five kilometers, the jeep suddenly decelerated, cutting a left turn without turning on its blinkers before entering the premises of a residential dwelling, where it parked.

Echika passed the residence and stopped the Niva at the shoulder of the road a few meters ahead.

"She got out of the car," Harold whispered, using his superior Amicus eyesight to observe the house. "See, she didn't notice us."

Echika reached for a pair of binoculars sitting on the dashboard and stared at the jeep. Thanks to the night-vision scope outfitted to the binoculars, she could see clearly even amid the darkness.

The jeep's driver was a relatively young girl, about the same age as Echika. She was petite, and her chestnut-colored hair was tied into adorable braids. She was just barely carrying a hefty paper bag. All things considered, she resembled a perfectly ordinary girl, and nothing seemed to imply she was sheltering Lee, of course.

"So why do you think she's the one? Did you find a picture of her on Lee's socials?"

"No, let me explain. Look at her closely," Harold instructed, and Echika reluctantly obeyed. "See that jewelry on her wrist? That's a

Duodji bracelet, made of reindeer horns, tendon, and skin weaved together with pewter. It's a traditional Sami handicraft."

"So she's Sami. But you can't assume they're all bio-hackers. It's jumping to conclusions to presume she's sheltering Lee just because of the bracelet."

"But she bought a lot of instant food, and she was the only customer I saw who was doing that. Maybe she avoided buying perishables to minimize the number of times she has to go grocery shopping? What if, for instance, she had a reason to avoid going outside and being seen?"

"Wait... How can you tell all she bought is instant food?"

"Based on the way her bag is swollen, I'm sure of it."

Just as she was about to tell him this was absurd, she saw the girl trip and spill the contents of her bag—packages of instant food—onto the snow. Echika clicked her tongue quietly. She'd felt this way since she'd met him, but this Amicus definitely had some kind of X-ray vision feature.

"But what stood out to me most was the way she acted in the parking lot. She kept looking around and had her hand on her neck. Touching one's neck is a nonverbal gesture for trying to calm nerves, but why would she be so stressed by visiting the local supermarket?"

"I don't know... Did something else catch your eye?"

"Yes, she was acting suspicious. It was especially striking when she loaded the bag into her car after she finished shopping. She stood at an oddly open stance, and one of her legs was always turned to the entrance of the parking lot. It was like she was mentally priming her-self to bolt at any moment. Why would she want to run, then?"

Beats me.

"If nothing else, she didn't shoplift. It's a small town, so the clerks probably know her personally," Echika stated.

"Exactly. So she was wary of someone realizing that she was shelter-ing Lee."

"You're jumping to conclusions. We don't even know if Lee came to a bio-hacker for help—"

"You said you've never watched ballet before, right, Investigator?" Harold cut her off. "Lee's dancing was perfect. Too perfect, actually.

The way she danced didn't fit her musculature... Need I say anything else?"

Echika put down her binoculars. Finally, she arrived at the answer to the question that had been weighing on her mind for a while now.

"So you're saying Lee *was using bio-hacking to cheat from the start*?"

"Indeed. And that girl right there operated on her. That's why she's sheltering Lee."

That did make for a coherent explanation. From the very beginning, Lee had modified her body to become a ballet student. Bio-hacking was judged as harshly as doping, and it was heavily restricted in the sporting world. So if Harold was correct, Lee had mistaken the viral infection for a malfunction in her bio-hacking, hence why she went back to her Sami bio-hacker instead of going to a hospital.

But they didn't have any decisive proof yet. Absurdly arrogant as she was, Echika refused to acknowledge that an Amicus was this capable.

"But what about this?" Echika countered, forcibly coming up with another hypothesis. "Something bad happened to the Sami girl recently. Like, she was bullied or something, and that made her dread contact with people. It makes her so anxious that she can't even go to her local supermarket. She's too depressed to bring herself to cook, so she bought instant foods that last and take little effort to prepare... Hey, are you listening to me?"

"I am. That's a possibility, yes," Harold acknowledged, peering into the rearview mirror and fixing his hair. *Why this all of a sudden?* "I thought I should make sure I look right before we go confirm the truth."

"Uh, sure." *Like a machine needs to worry about appearances.* "Well, the hair on the back of your head is standing up, though," Echika pointed out venomously.

After blinking a couple of times, Harold smiled.

"That's intentional. Leaving a few flaws in my appearance makes me come across as likable."

God help me, I want to sock him in the face.

4

As they got out of the Niva, fleeting snow began to sprinkle down from above. The girl's house was very much an old-fashioned lodge. Icicles dangled down from its triangular roof, and its vividly colored outer walls were frozen from the snow blowing against them. Echika stepped onto the sundeck and knocked on the front door a couple of times. A few seconds later, the girl opened it.

"Who are you? What do you want?"

The girl was visibly wary, but upon closer inspection, she was surprisingly pretty. She wasn't wearing any makeup, and her unwavering eyes were a clear shade of green. Her beauty wasn't the artificial, fabricated sort belonging to a city girl but rather the dignified presence of a fruit tree hidden deep within the forest, away from the prying eyes of humans.

"We're from Interpol's Electrocrime Investigations Bureau." Echika flashed her ID. "We're questioning people around the area with regard to an ongoing investigation. Can we have a few minutes of your time?"

"...What kind of investigation?" the girl asked, still wary.

"We're not at liberty to elaborate, but it's an electrocrime," Echika answered, picking her words carefully. "It seems someone involved with the incident is hiding in the area."

After a moment's hesitation, the girl let them inside. If Harold's story was right, Echika would have expected her to resist a little more. Or maybe she thought rejecting them would just come across as suspicious? Echika couldn't tell.

She led them into a living room with a country-like interior. *Duodji* bracelets woven with silver threads hung over the hearth, and the sofa she had them sit on was furnished with reindeer fur.

"Can I ask your name?" Echika asked as she took a seat on the sofa.

"It's Bigga," the girl said, placing a tray on the table. "Hmm, I'm sorry, but I'm the only one at home right now... My father went out to the mountains, and he won't be back for a while. There's a lot of ice fog this time of year, so the reindeer herds tend to separate."

This girl was definitely Sami, like Harold predicted. Echika snuck a glance at the Amicus sitting beside her, and upon noticing her gaze, he curled his lips a little. He almost looked smug.

"Is reindeer husbandry your father's only source of livelihood? Does he have a side business in the primary sector?"

"He couldn't have one if he wanted to. Even in the restricted zone, outside contractors take up all the jobs with their robots, so it's hard to find work... That's the state's policy, so we can't do much about it," she said, pushing a mug toward Echika. "Drink this, if you'd like?"

The mug was full of normal coffee. It was a sleek black color and gave off a fragrant smell. It didn't have cheese in it, like she'd seen on Lee's social media. Apparently, that was their private way of drinking coffee, and they didn't offer it to guests.

Did this mean she regarded Lee as more than just a guest, then? Were they close?

"Ah!" Bigga blurted out suddenly.

It seemed that she'd bumped her hand into Harold's as she passed him the cup and spilled a bit of coffee over his fingers.

"Oh, I'm sorry; I can't believe how clumsy I am...!" Bigga hurriedly wiped his hands with a towel she had nearby. "Did any spill on your terminal? It might break if it gets wet."

"Don't worry—it's waterproof," he said, glancing at his wristwatch-shaped wearable terminal. "Besides, it's provided by the bureau, so even if it breaks, I can just use my Your Forma."

Harold indirectly implied he was human by claiming he had a Your Forma. Since the restricted zone's citizens were predominantly luddites, he'd deemed it wiser to pass himself off as one.

But even without him actively pretending, Bigga didn't seem to have realized he was an Amicus. Having been born and raised in a city without any drones, to say nothing of robots, she probably couldn't tell them apart from humans.

"Did you get burned? Are you sure you're all right?"

"It's fine. Thank you—you're sweet." He smiled, holding on to her hand gently.

Hello? Echika cocked an eyebrow at his oddly saccharine compliment.

Bigga's eyes widened like she'd just snapped out of a stupor, and her cheeks turned visibly rosy.

"*Ahem.*" Echika cleared her throat. "Don't worry about him, Bigga; just take a seat."

"Ah, yes. Excuse me…"

She gingerly sat down on the opposite sofa as Echika shot a sidelong glare at Harold. The Amicus simply sipped on his coffee with an innocuous look on his face. What was he thinking?

"So," Echika said, massaging her brow gently to pull herself back together, "I'd like to ask you a few questions. Do you go to school?"

"I graduated high school. I decided not to go to college."

"To focus on work?"

"Yes. I'm on my day off today, but I spend a few days a week sorting out the mail at the post office…"

"I see. Does anyone but you and your family visit this house?"

"The neighbors and my father's friends come to visit sometimes."

"Do you have any siblings or friends who stop by?"

"I don't have any siblings, and my friends don't come over. They're all busy with college, jobs, or housework."

"Have you been bullied or harassed recently, then?"

Bigga suddenly knit her brow, then started fiddling with the *Duodji* bracelet on her wrist in annoyance.

Drat.

Echika realized, a moment too late, that she'd asked the wrong question. The atmosphere tensed up for a moment.

"That's a pretty pattern," Harold said abruptly, his gaze fixed on a tapestry hanging on the wall.

It was a woven image of a herd of reindeer in vivid reds and blues. Echika couldn't say if *pretty* was the right descriptor for it, but his comment did come in a timely fashion.

"My deceased mother made it," Bigga said, narrowing her eyes wistfully.

"It's very well-made. Does it employ the same colors as your traditional *gáktis*?"

"Huh? How can you tell…?"

"I majored in northern European ethnology in college," he said with an especially soft expression. "I'm honored to finally meet a Sami, even if it is for an investigation. I'm very glad to have met you."

"Hmm, uh…" Bigga blushed again and suddenly got to her feet. "I'll, um, go pour you some more coffee."

She bolted out of the living room, like she was trying to run from him. And she did this despite their mugs still being just as full as they were when she brought them. It was quite the sweet sight, but Echika couldn't feel particularly moved at it.

A sizable piece of kindling crackled within the hearth.

"I've got more than just a thing or two to say," Echika started, glaring pointedly at Harold. "But which college did you graduate from, exactly?"

"Lies are a means to an end," he said, reverting to a serious expression. "I needed to have her open her heart to us."

"Forget getting her to open her heart; you just about won her over. What was that back there?"

"Whatever do you mean?" Harold furrowed his brow as if baffled.

Stop playing dumb.

"More importantly," he continued, "what was that 'have you been bullied or harassed' question? I almost shuddered when you said that. If you were bad at questioning people, you should have said so."

Echika was at a loss for words. Up until now, she'd gotten by with just her outstanding abilities at Brain Diving; interpersonal communications were a weak spot for her. She always let her aides handle that part of the investigation.

"It might be for the best if you take care of things like that in the future," she finally admitted.

"I think that's a wise decision," Harold replied.

"But that said, it doesn't look like Bigga's sheltering her, and she doesn't strike me as a bio-hacker."

"Why not? Because she didn't realize I'm an Amicus?"

"Not that. A bio-hacker's area of expertise tends to be focused on gadgets and cyborg technology. They wouldn't know much about robotics."

"Yes, you're right about that," Harold said, looking down at his wrist. "But earlier, Bigga could tell with a glance that this was an information terminal. A luddite's knowledge of gadgets would usually stop at ordinary cell phones, so this shouldn't have looked like anything but a wristwatch to her."

She hadn't paid it any attention at the time, but when he put it like that, it did make sense. Bigga had been so shaken by spilling the coffee that she let slip that she knew it was a portable information terminal. His point did seem to be credible.

"But what about Lee, then?"

"Oh, she's here, of course. The fact that Bigga stepped out proves it."

"Maybe your creepy smile just scared her off."

"How is it creepy?" Harold asked shamelessly. "She'd have left the living room either way, because she needs to smuggle Lee out of here so we won't catch her. I'd imagine they're preparing as we speak."

"How can you tell?"

"Go outside and wait at the back door. You should find your proof there."

She'd considered laughing it off as a joke but knew better than to underestimate Harold's observation skills. She still didn't want to admit it, of course, but Echika sullenly got up from the sofa.

"And while I'm at the back door, what are you going to do?"

"I'll stay here and draw the truth out of Bigga."

"Just don't do anything funny," Echika emphasized and left the residence.

An almost painful wave of cold air whipped against her body. She stepped off the sundeck, shivering, and headed for the back of the house. If Lee showed up there, she'd have no choice but to accept Harold's "discerning eye."

Behind the house, she found a single snowmobile sitting alone in the backyard. There was no one in sight, and a deep silence hung over the place. But something felt off, and Echika soon noticed what it was. There wasn't a speck of snow on the vehicle. It looked like it had only just been carried out of a garage.

Just as she approached the snowmobile to examine it, it happened. The back door swung open, as if someone had been waiting for her to make a move. At first, Echika thought it was Bigga who'd bolted out of the door, since the silhouette was very similar to hers. But this new girl was wearing a poncho-like overcoat, and she sprinted toward the snowmobile without so much as looking around.

Echika couldn't make out the girl's face beneath the hood of her coat. But if a girl who wasn't Bigga had just sprinted out of the house, it could mean only one thing. Echika took off after her, spurred by urgency.

"Stop!"

The girl straddled the snowmobile and glanced up in shock. It seemed she'd just noticed Echika's presence for the first time. And Echika finally saw her face under the streetlights' fading illumination.

Their eyes met, and the database immediately read her facial features and brought up her personal data. Echika felt her blood starting to surge in her veins.

"Clara Lee!"

She didn't have time to stop her. Lee vigorously hit the throttle, and the snowmobile took off, kicking up a spray of snow that turned everything white before Echika's eyes.

Dammit!

Echika quickly wiped the snow from her eyes, but when she looked again, the snowmobile was already speeding away in the distance, moving so fast that it would be impossible to catch up to it on foot.

"Shit…!"

She'd finally found Lee. She couldn't let her get away here.

"Investigator!"

Turning at the call, Echika found Harold leaning out from the back door. "Where's Lee?!"

"She got away!" They wouldn't have time to go back to the shoulder of the road and get in the Niva. "Bigga lent her a snowmobile!"

As she shouted, Echika activated the Your Forma's marker feature. A distinct track surfaced in the snow—Lee's tracks. She placed a holo-marker on it, her last ray of hope. With this, she wouldn't lose her.

Returning to the front of the house, Echika froze at a jeep's horn blaring at her. It was Harold, who'd swiftly gotten into the driver's seat of Bigga's car. The owner wasn't in sight, so she was probably still inside. Bigga now had nowhere to run, so Echika elected to disregard her for the time being.

Echika plopped into the passenger seat quickly and closed the door. "I placed a marker on her. Get going—we need to be fast."

"Driving safely is my personal policy, though." Harold stomped down on the accelerator.

Much to her surprise, this rickety jeep had its automatic-driving feature removed. She felt like she ought to be grateful just for the fact that the heating was still working, but she was shocked Bigga could drive around in this lump of metal.

"Did Bigga talk?"

"Of course," he said, nodding composedly. "Lee is her cousin, as it turns out. Apparently, they got along like sisters when they were little, and Bigga let her stay, since she came to her for help with the malfunctions. She didn't imagine a virus could be behind it, though. She thought the delusions were side effects of the bio-hacking."

Echika had assumed as much since the moment Lee appeared, but this meant Harold had predicted everything perfectly. By this point, she'd grown tired of being surprised by him, and after witnessing everything today, she felt stupid for pridefully refusing to admit this Amicus's capabilities. Yes, he was undoubtedly a police investigator.

In the end, Echika could only say, "I'm surprised you figured everything out in just that one moment."

"Bigga seemed like the pure, emotional type, so I figured drawing attention to myself as a member of the opposite sex might do the trick. It went well, thankfully," Harold said with a very innocuous smile.

Echika couldn't mask her weary expression. That meant this had been his plan from the get-go. It finally dawned on her.

"So you had her spill the coffee when she handed you the mug on purpose."

"Yes. I wanted to check if she was a bio-hacker and draw her attention to me."

"And she fell for it, hook, line and sinker."

"Physical contact has all sorts of meaning, but the most prominent of all is narrowing down emotional distance."

Listening to his spiel gave her a headache.

"Did they load a module for toying with women's hearts into your memory?" Echika asked dryly.

"Perish the thought. I only did it in the name of furthering the investigation."

"I'm sure you breached one rule or another with what you did. Pull another stunt like that, and I'll have to report you to Chief Totoki."

Echika was confident about one thing: People said Amicus were supposed to be humankind's best friend, but this android was definitely an exception.

Lee's trail winded along the snowy field, heading south down a trackless path. After pursuing her for a while, the Altaelva River came into view, and they saw a snowmobile speed across its frozen surface. It was Lee. Harold skillfully turned the steering wheel, driving the jeep along the riverside. But their target noticed them and picked up speed, drawing away from them in a feat of reckless driving.

"Isn't she infected? Where is she getting all that energy?!"

"Bigga told me she applied a self-made suppressant to Lee, which paused every machine inside her body. Since it's used for bio-hacking, it's much more powerful than the legal machine suppressants used by hospitals."

"Guess they don't call them back-alley doctors for nothing," Echika whispered sarcastically.

Give me a break!

"That said, it was almost time for her to inject another dose, and she ended up not getting it because we stopped by."

"So you're saying we should stay patient and keep chasing her until the suppressant wears off?"

Just then, however, a gust of wind whipped by, and a spray of snow overran the windshield. Echika drew back, but Harold continued speeding up unflinchingly. The snow clung to the window, and when Echika's field of vision cleared, the jeep was still clutching the riverside and driving directly parallel to the snowmobile. Now was her chance.

"Hold!" Echika shouted, rolling down the window. "This is the Electrocrime Investigations Bureau!"

But Lee didn't so much as turn to look at her. The moment Echika made to reach for the gun holstered on her leg, Lee's small body started shaking like a toy with its batteries running out. Her hands, which had been gripping the snowmobile's handles, slackened, and she soon slid off the vehicle.

Wait.

Lee's body tumbled violently over the snow, her limbs banging against the ground. Even with its rider missing, the snowmobile continued speeding ahead before finally toppling sideways with a concerning *crunch*.

"Oh my…" She heard Harold's breath catch. "This is horrible."

They shouldn't have gone after her like they did. But that realization came far too late.

Echika and Harold got off the jeep and ran over to Lee, who lay faceup. She was already unconscious, though, and bleeding profusely from a cut on her forehead.

"She's already developed hypothermia symptoms," Harold said. "The suppressant probably wore off a while ago."

"I'll call an ambulance." Echika used her Your Forma to make the call, a bitter taste in her mouth all the while.

They had, without a doubt, approached this the wrong way. She hadn't assumed Lee would be so desperate to get away. Having finished her call, she turned around to find Harold kneeling on the frozen river. He'd taken off his coat and wrapped it around Lee's body, then removed his scarf next, which he used to wipe the blood off her forehead.

"Hold on," she said, bewildered. "You might be a machine, but if your circulatory fluid freezes, you'll malfunction."

"I don't mind. They can fix me as many times as it takes, but you can't recover a lost life."

Harold's deadly seriousness made Echika's stomach churn with anxiety. *Right, that's what all Amicus are like. They're made to conform to their Laws of Respect and sympathize with humankind.*

She stifled down her annoyance. Their job wasn't done yet.

"Aide Lucraft."

Echika removed her gloves. Despite her hand going numb from being exposed to the freezing air, she took out a pair of cords.

"We need to inspect Lee's Mnemosynes before the rescue team gets here."

"What are you talking about?" Harold looked up at her in disbelief. "She's in a dangerous condition right now."

"We still have to do it. The Brain Diving won't make her any worse."

"But we should keep her body as still as possible. There's the risk it could cause a ventricular fibrillation—"

"Yes, and the possibility her situation becomes critical is exactly why we need to do this now."

The Your Forma was integrated with the brain, so if its user's vital signs stopped, it would shut down as well. The problem was that the Mnemosynes were programmed to prioritize the user's privacy and self-erase themselves upon death. And once that happened, restoring the lost data was a huge headache that required extracting the Your Forma. But not only was a request to do so not legally binding, the bereaved family could also object to it, which could make things very problematic. Many times in the past, families had dragged out talks by arguing the bureau down, then "accidentally" had the deceased's remains buried.

That's why any electronic investigator would realize that now could be their last opportunity to plug into Lee. Echika knew this to be fact, and any other electronic investigator would do the same.

"Put her facedown."

The howling wind passed by, coiling around her legs. Harold looked up at her in blank amazement, as if to say he couldn't believe her. But he wasn't really thinking that; he was just a machine, compelled by its emotional engine's programming to make this Echikal reaction.

Give me a break.

"Aide Lucraft, do I need to remind you what our job here is?" Her voice spilled from her lips as she failed to keep her emotions restrained. "It's to track down the culprit of the sensory crime, not looking after Lee. I'm not saying we have to kill her or leave her to die; I called the ambulance myself. We took the necessary measures to save her."

Harold remained silent.

"Hurry up and jack her in," Echika ordered, extending the Lifeline toward him, but he didn't accept it.

Not just that—he placed his hand over Lee's body, like he was trying to shield her from Echika. Then he stared at Echika almost as though trying to arouse her pity.

Stop that. Why do I need a stupid machine looking at me like that?

"Investigator, please consider this calmly."

"I'm calm, as you can clearly see," Echika said firmly. "Are you trying to interfere with the investigation?"

"No, I just believe there are priorities to everything."

"Well said. Jack her in, then."

"I meant that her life and survival take precedence over all."

"If we don't Brain Dive into Lee now, there's no telling how it could stall the investigation. Are you going to convince her family to cooperate if anything happens to her?"

"That's not what I'm talking about."

"But this is what it's about. We can't save her right now."

They glared at each other for one long moment, neither of them blinking. The snow kicked up at some point, pouring down on them like tears. Amicus were just machines—they were good at pretending to do the right thing, but in reality, they were empty on the inside. All they did was display their Laws of Respect and put up an illusion of humanity and emotion.

I hate Amicus.

Eventually, Harold bit his lip, and after a piercing silence, he spoke in a conflicted manner.

"Fine. Then…let's jack her in while she's lying faceup, so as to not disturb her."

Finally.

Echika gave him the Brain Diving cord, and he gently raised Lee's head to avoid jostling her too much, then plugged it into the nape of her neck. Next, they connected the Lifeline to each other. Harold looked displeased with this, but Echika didn't mind. She didn't care what he thought; this was for the best.

"Begin," she uttered as always, and the next moment, she was plummeting down.

She entrusted her body to the velocity of her free fall, letting it wash away her annoyance. No matter what happened, none of it mattered once she started Diving. That's how it always was.

Lee's surface Mnemosynes washed over her. The ballet academy's lesson room came into view. The feel of the bar against her hands. Her classmates, clad in leotards. She liked dancing. Someday, she would become a prima ballerina. But somewhere in that firm resolve, a black shadow clung to her like ichor, like it was something she had to look away from. Guilt over bio-hacking.

This made Echika's heart oddly restless. The darkness never released its grip on Lee. Not during lessons, or on her days off with friends, nor from the cold grays of Saint Petersburg's cityscape, where commercials for ballet gadgets jumped at her from every direction. They promoted old-fashioned toe shoes and the newest sneakers, sneering at her for her muscle-control chip. And whenever she saw them, the shadow, the anxiety, grew larger.

Don't sympathize with her. Let it pass through, like always.

Echika moved through the surface level and entered the middle layer of her Mnemosynes. Harold hadn't pulled her up yet. Whenever it felt like a countercurrent might be beginning, she managed to keep control of the rudder one way or another.

Suddenly, a familiar building skirted through the corner of her eye. Its streamlined roof was adorned with a gigantic spherical monument. She'd seen it countless times in news footage: the headquarters of technology company Rig City.

Lee had visited there on a prolonged vacation when she went on a trip to America with her parents. Apparently, she'd been part of a field-trip tour of Rig City. Her involvement with bio-hacking led her to develop an interest in modern gadgets, which brought her there.

Echika felt something was off and immediately realized what it was. Thomas Ogier, who was Paris's index case, had also gone on a tour of Rig City.

5

The revolving lights of the ambulance disappeared into the night as it carried Lee away. Gazing at the bright glow spilling over the snowy field, Echika blew out a wisp from her electronic cigarette. The temperature had dropped even further, and by now, the air wasn't so much cold as it was painful.

Based on the diagnosis AI the rescue team brought, Lee had gone unconscious when her hypothermia symptoms worsened, and she couldn't keep driving. She apparently hit her head hard when she fell, and there was chance of a contusion. Thankfully, her condition wasn't life-threatening, but since she was infected, they couldn't use her Your Forma to treat it.

Echika could only hope she'd recover somehow. But more importantly, she'd found a lead.

"There might be a common denominator between the index cases. They were both in a tour of Rig City," Echika said, white vapor streaming out of her lips. "Ogier in Paris was a science student, but he was interested in technology, so it didn't come as a surprise. But Lee's a ballerina-in-training, so I doubt this is a coincidence."

"Yes," Harold replied dispassionately. "I contacted the Washington branch to check if the index case there went to a tour of Rig City, too."

He'd been down since earlier and was leaning against the jeep in a depressed manner. The coat and scarf in his arms were wet with Lee's blood. Apparently, this Amicus saw human injury as more important than the investigation. The very image of Echikal behavior. It pissed her off.

Anyway…

"How did you know all that just by looking at her?" Echika asked him.

Harold turned a dejected gaze toward her and answered:

"Once, I was guided by a skilled detective. That's it."

If a bit of guidance really would be enough to make one develop such keen observation skills, all the Amicus in the world would be geniuses by now. Totoki had called Harold "special," though, likely because of this.

"You were like a modern Sherlock Holmes."

"'You see, but you do not observe. The distinction is clear,'" Harold quoted without so much as a smile and moved away from the jeep. "Do you like reading, Investigator Hieda?"

"I've read enough to mistake you for R. Daneel when we first met."

"Asimov, eh? Well, unlike R. Daneel, I don't hail from Spacetown."

"I see you still want to chat with me." She couldn't stop herself from saying that. "I thought what happened might have muddied the waters and made you realize we can't get along. But being estranged would be better for both of us. You'll understand that eventually."

She'd thought this would convince Harold, but he simply sighed at her. She didn't get it. Noticing that she'd turned off her electronic cigarette, he opened the door of the jeep for her. His attempts at gentlemanly politeness ticked her off. Hadn't he learned his lesson yet?

"Aide Lucraft, I told you that acting like this is unnecessary—"

"Why do you try to present yourself as cold and unfeeling?"

His gaze practically stabbed into her.

"What are you talking about?" Echika glared back at him.

"You know what I'm talking about," Harold insisted, his face expressionless. "You were desperate to jack into Lee for some reason, but though you may not have noticed, you looked like you were holding back tears of remorse. Why are you trying so hard to bury your emotions?"

"Did the cold screw up your visual system?" Echika spat over her shoulder as she turned to the jeep. "Let's go back to Bigga's place. I'll drive."

"No. I can't let you be behind the wheel right now."

What's his problem?!

This feeling that he could read right into her heart annoyed her to no end. What did he know?

"Listen to me. I don't feel anything about this. You're reading this all wrong, understood?"

Ignoring Harold's attempts at kindness, she forced her body into the driver's seat. He seemed intent on saying something but, in the end, relented and took the passenger seat. Now that they were both in the car, the inside felt even more frigid than the outside.

I'm not trying to pass myself off as cold. I'm just doing my job.

And I don't want this stupid machine creeping into my heart.

Chapter 2
Scattered Candies

Chapter 2
Scattered Candies

1

She could remember it even now. That despite the refreshing scent of spring filling her lungs, she couldn't shake off her nervousness.

"It's nice to meet you, Dad."

Cherry blossoms blew in from somewhere, flying into the mansion's common hallway. Echika, then five years old, was carrying a rucksack roughly her size as she looked up at the large front door. And the person peering down from the gap in the entrance was none other than her father.

Today was the first time she'd ever met him.

"No, it's not the first. I saw you in the hospital nursery," her father remarked, not a smile on his face. "Who did your mother remarry?"

Echika hung her head and fell silent. Her mother would often fly into hysterics, but she was kind sometimes. A young man had delivered her to her father's place. She didn't know his name.

"A different question, then. How did you get injured?"

Her father's gaze raked over the Band-Aids on Echika's cheek and knees. She tried to hide them with her hands, feeling as though she was being scolded, but she couldn't cover every one of them.

"This is, I…um, I tripped, that's all."

"Listen to me, Echika. I probably won't ever love you."

And this was why her father had emphasized that they would have to make a promise if they were going to live together.

"Remain a machine for my sake. Never speak to me unless spoken to. Want for nothing, don't show your emotions, and never make a fuss."

Echika nodded. She had no choice but to. She got the ominous impression that miserable days were ahead of her, but that was what things had been like until now anyway. In the end, no matter where she went, it was all the same. She only came to realize a single thing—for whatever reason, no one cherished her.

Her father let her into the house. The entrance hall was beyond clean and organized—it was sterile. As Echika took off her shoes, her heart heavy with melancholy, a woman approached them.

"This is Sumika. She will be looking after you starting today."

Sumika was about the same age as Echika's mother. Her features were flawlessly fair, and she had braided black hair. She wore a one-piece dress blue enough to burn itself into one's memory, and her limbs were slender. Echika's first impression was that she was a very pretty lady.

"Hello, Echika," Sumika said with a smile, extending a hand toward her.

Echika accepted it and shook. Her smooth, well-proportioned fingers felt slightly colder than they should have been. And that's when she realized—Sumika was an Amicus.

"And you also have an older sister, Echika. You'll get to see her soon."

"Huh?" Her eyes widened in surprise.

Her father's words glowed with enough magic to blow away any anxiety toward her new life or her doubts about Sumika. Her heart, which had felt as heavy as lead just moments ago, jumped for joy.

She'd been alone for so long, but now she would finally get a sister.

∗

During winters, California's moist air took on a certain chilliness.

The taxi carrying Echika and Harold ran down a freeway along the

San Francisco Bay. The cityscape was lined with skyscrapers, and drones buzzed through the air like flies. Standing right beneath them would no doubt make the sky look pure gray and blot its stars out of sight.

"Once we get to Rig City, we'll Brain Dive straightaway," Echika said. "Thankfully, we have some company employees willing to cooperate with us. Once that's done, we— Aide Lucraft? Are you listening?"

Harold sat next to her, his arms crossed gently and his head hung. He was wearing a thick sweater today, but it clearly wasn't part of the Amicus clothes the bureau had provided. She had to wonder where he got it…before shaking the thought off. That didn't matter right now.

Their flight to California was decided after they left Bigga's residence, on their way back to Saint Petersburg. The electronic investigator from Washington called back and answered their question.

"The index case here was part of a study tour of Rig City, too. They took a few days off for the Fourth of July and went on a trip to California."

It did seem that the common denominator among the index cases was that they'd all taken a study tour of Rig City. Echika quickly contacted Chief Totoki and arranged for an investigation there. She'd just spent a total of thirty hours being rocked around inside a car, and then she had to put up with a daylong flight. If this was a business issue, they could settle it with a holo-call, but Brain Diving required her presence on the scene.

"Given the virus's traits, we can probably assume the culprit behind it has some advanced technology," Totoki said through the holo-browser, as stone-faced as ever. "It wouldn't surprise me if the culprit happens to be one of Rig City's programmers. The company does gather capable manpower from around the globe, after all. For all we know, we could be dealing with multiple culprits."

"Yes, we have to account for every possibility."

"The situation's getting worse, but the fact that we found that Rig City is the common point to all the cases is our one ray of hope."

Apparently, while Echika and Harold were going after Lee, virus outbreaks were confirmed in four other major cities: Hong Kong, Munich, Melbourne, and Toronto. Each branch's electronic investigators were in a hurry to identify the sources of the infection, but their progress was terribly slow. Few investigators could handle parallel Brain Diving like Echika could, which inevitably made their investigations lag.

"That's why we're counting on you, Investigator Hieda."

"Rest assured that I'll dig up some kind of clue."

But even as she said this, Echika couldn't contain the bitter emotion filling her heart. Honestly, just hearing Rig City's name filled her with dread.

"By the way, Chief, will Aide Lucraft be accompanying me there?"

"Of course. I have him registered as one of your belongings."

Harold, who had remained silent so far, furrowed his brow.

"Are you telling me to sit in the cargo hold?"

"The cargo hold? Why? There are Amicus compartments in the plane."

"I am aware, yes. They stuff us into a dark, cramped, closed space. It's *effectively* a cargo hold."

"Just give it up. Even with more and more Amicus sympathizers cropping up, the world nations still consider Amicus to be objects."

"But… Please, could you reconsider and let me travel first-class, like a human?"

"Excuse me?" Echika raised her voice in disbelief. "I don't get to travel first-class, so why should you?"

"I want the results of the viral analysis and the personal data for Rig City's employees, understood?"

At this, Totoki closed the call with little fanfare, leaving Echika alone with a clearly distraught and despondent Harold.

After that, the two arrived in California and took a taxi to Rig City, bringing them to the here and now.

"Aide Lucraft, wake up already."

Harold was depressed and hadn't said a word ever since he got off the flight.

"Hello?" Echika peered into his face.

She then recoiled a little. He was sitting there, with his eyes wide open.

At least blink. It's creepy.

"What's gotten into you? Don't tell me you malfunctioned or something—"

"Good morning, Investigator Hieda."

"Yikes!"

Harold suddenly sat up, as if someone had flipped a switch inside him, prompting Echika to pull away from him so quickly that she bumped the back of her head against the taxi window.

"Oh?" he asked, his expression nonchalant. "What's the matter?"

"I should be asking you that!" Echika shouted, feeling as if her heart had nearly just jumped out of her chest. "Don't startle me like that!"

"My apologies. Being in the cargo hold was so terrible that I had to switch my thoughts off."

"Ugh." *The hell?* "So you were...sleepwalking the whole time?"

"That would be a suitable analogy, yes."

"You got off the plane and got into the taxi with your own two feet. It really looked like sleepwalking."

Echika was clearly being sarcastic, but Harold simply smiled. If nothing else, it was a relief that he hadn't broken down or whatever. The last thing she needed was for the investigation to get held back because of something like that.

The taxi eventually turned off the freeway and entered the gate leading into Rig City. Echika had learned of the sheer size of the premises from looking the place up on the internet, but seeing it with her own two eyes was overwhelming nonetheless. It had an integrated sports facility, a golf course, and even a private beach. It was like a small resort.

Rig City was a multinational technology enterprise whose main office was located in Silicon Valley. During the early stages of the pandemic, they bought out the developers of Neural Safety, contributing to its production and distribution using their vast funds and production plants. The corporation went on to create the Your Forma.

In addition to that, they also became the providers of all manner of internet services. It was no exaggeration to say that Rig City was the largest technological driving force on the globe.

They got off the taxi at the roundabout in front of Rig City's headquarters, where they were greeted by a woman Amicus clad in a suit.

"We've been expecting you, Investigator Hieda and Investigator Aide Lucraft," she said, flashing a smile that showed off her perfectly aligned teeth. "My name is Anne, and I'm in charge of showing visitors around."

Echika nodded at her vaguely and looked up at the building. She saw the streamlined roof she'd witnessed in Ogier's and Lee's Mnemosynes, with the distinctive circular monument shining atop it.

Aah. I really ended up coming here, didn't I?

Although it was her first time visiting Rig City, she didn't have many good memories of the company.

"Is something wrong?" Harold suddenly asked, prompting her to jolt.

But he didn't pose that question to Echika. It was directed at Anne instead, who was staring fixedly at him for some reason.

"Not at all," Anne replied, flashing a perfect, mechanical smile. "Allow me to show you the way. Follow me."

The two of them went with her into Rig City's main building. The entrance hall was unusually wide, and it was adorned with a chiseled statue of the company's logo. The employees passing by were clad in casual outfits, and Echika could see Amicus walking among them. Everyone they passed by called out to Anne to say hello.

"I see everyone here knows you, Anne," Harold noted.

"Oh, not particularly. Everyone is very friendly toward Amicus here, is all. And not just within the company, mind you. Most of the citizens around here act the same way. Many people even want to give us time off."

"Huh?" Echika made this surprised utterance. "Time off?"

"Yes. Many of California's representatives are Amicus sympathizers, and Congress is considering granting Amicus basic human rights. The request to give us time off will undoubtedly become reality in the near future."

What the hell?

That was the first Echika had heard of that. The times were progressing at an almost terrifying clip. Harold, however, seemed to have known about this already and didn't look very surprised.

"Silicon Valley really is our home turf, isn't it? Maybe I should consider moving here."

Anne regarded him with apprehension.

"I don't feel much of a need to take breaks. Do you feel differently about it?" she asked Harold.

"Well, yes, I think taking time off is important. Anne, could you give me your number for when I move in here?"

Wait, what is he doing?

Echika poked Harold in the ribs, but he pretended not to notice it. She could overlook it when he did this to Bigga—though not for lack of misgivings—but why would he try to curry favor with Anne? Weren't conversations between Amicus just shams they kept up for the sake of seeming human?

"I don't have a personal terminal, so simply call the office and ask for me. I'm sure I'll be able to help you." She smiled at Harold, though Echika couldn't tell if she understood his intent here.

"Thank you kindly, Anne. I think I'll do that."

"Aide Lucraft," Echika chided him. "Watch your behavior. Investigators need to set a standard."

"Of course," he said.

Liar. You're not listening at all.

Meanwhile, Anne led them to a nap room, where four employees who had agreed to cooperate with the investigation were waiting for them. They were all young programmers working on the same team.

Of course, they weren't the sole people Lee and the other index cases had come into contact with. But all the other employees had refused to assist with the investigation and only agreed to go through questioning.

After all, Brain Diving was, first and foremost, a violation of one's privacy, and many people disliked the idea of it. So long as you weren't a direct suspect and the electronic investigator didn't have a warrant, you had no legal obligation to allow it.

Thankfully, these four weren't terribly opposed to the idea.

"If anything, I really want to know more about Brain Diving."

"How does it feel to have someone look into your Mnemosynes?"

"I heard you're just asleep and don't feel anything. Is that true?"

"Don't you get pulled in by other people's emotions?"

This flurry of questions gave Echika a look into the intellectual curiosity driving the people who worked on the Your Forma. But she didn't come here to explain what Brain Diving was like.

"We're grateful for your cooperation. Please sign the letter of consent and lie down on the bed."

At Echika's curt statement, the four of them exchanged disappointed looks but did as they were told. A nurse Amicus—who was dispatched from the local hospital to remain on constant standby in the office infirmary—showed up a few moments later to inject the four of them with sedatives. Brain Diving was clearer when the recipient had a lower level of consciousness, so using sedatives was indispensable for the process.

Echika only hoped she'd find some kind of clue to the source of the virus and how it originally infected people. After confirming everyone had gone to sleep, she set up the triangle connection like always.

"I'm ready, Aide Lucraft—"

She suddenly cut off. Harold had just moved aside his ear to reveal the connection port and plug the Lifeline into it. This wasn't a sight Echika could ever get used to, and as she stared in surprise, their eyes suddenly met.

"What's wrong, Investigator?"

"Nothing," she replied, unable to mask her displeasure. "I have to ask, couldn't they have put your port somewhere better?"

"Oh, is seeing my ear slide away that uncanny?"

"Of course it is."

"I see," he said with an amused smile for some reason. "Would you like a closer look at it, then?"

"Stop that—get away from me! I'm starting the process!"

Sooner than Harold could bring his face closer to hers, Echika Dived into the cybernetic ocean as if trying to flee from him.

Did they really program the Laws of Respect into him? He teases humans a little too frequently. Forget that, though. I have to switch gears...

The four employees' Mnemosynes unfurled before her eyes. She traced them back to the study tours, passing through their daily routines in Rig City. Lines of code fluttered by. Then there was a Christmas tree covered in shining ornaments. It was an enchanting sight, but a sudden feeling of annoyance filled her consciousness.

Periodic mental examinations. They plugged an HSB cable into their necks, but the emotions recorded in their Mnemosynes were all stable. There were hardly any records of anger or sadness. There was mostly just enthusiasm toward work and composure.

Most employees of this leading firm were people with balanced mental states. Thanks to the sizable budget of the company's mental health care program, the office environment had been crafted so people could work without getting overstressed, which meant there weren't many disputes among the employees.

Echika didn't find the Mnemosynes she was looking for, so she Dived faster down. But then suddenly, she passed by something—a negative emotion that throbbed like a festering wound.

What's this?

She turned her eyes to it. It was a scene in a bar. A bunch of employees were gathered in one place, drinking and chattering. It looked like a farewell party.

"See you, Salk."

"Take care."

"The office will feel empty without you."

She saw someone—a man who looked to be Russian—sitting at the center of these exchanges.

This must be Salk... Wait, what?

This was the only Mnemosyne she saw where all four of them were overcome with hatred that bubbled up from the pits of their stomachs. This made Echika stare. On the surface, the four of them didn't seem to regard Salk with disdain at all. If anything, they acted like they were sad to part with a friend.

Their feelings and behavior were mismatched. And while everyone had times when what they said didn't line up with what they felt, these were all emotionally stable human beings, all four of who seemed to dislike this specific individual. Despite feeling off, these Mnemosynes appeared to be unrelated to the index cases. Connecting them to the incident would be difficult.

Salk took another sip of his beer and discussed programming with his colleagues. The noise of the scene washed over her like a wave, and somewhere behind the breezy jazz music, she could hear someone utter a word—*Matoi*.

"We were working on the Matoi at the time—"

But the rest was drowned out. Echika felt a shiver run down her spine.

"It's nice to meet you, Dad."

She felt a countercurrent settle in.

Calm down. Keep it suppressed. Don't touch on the wrong place, Echika reminded herself, straining her thoughts.

Matoi. She wished she could flush that word out of her ears and mind, but it clung to her persistently. She found her way to the study tours and began going through the Mnemosynes one by one.

First, she looked at Ogier, then Lee, and after that, Washington's index case—and saw, much to her surprise, that Salk was among the employees guiding them. He proudly told them about cutting-edge programming technology. And these Mnemosynes didn't include the deep-seated hatred that had been present before. It felt wrong. But apart from that, there was nothing suspicious about the Mnemosynes of the people who'd attended the study tour. No clues that might link the index cases to a culprit who'd infected them.

"Matoi."

The name nudged at her again.

Aah, just stop it. Shake it off.

"—Investigator Hieda?"

Her head felt awfully heavy when she was pulled back up to reality, and her breathing was a little shallow. Echika forced herself to suck in a lungful of the nap room's dry air and then realized Harold was looking at her with concern. She pulled out the Lifeline as calmly as she could, attempting to hide her disconcerted state of mind.

"I didn't find anything," she told him, her voice raspy. "Nothing seemed suspicious."

"Yes, the Mnemosynes seemed perfectly peaceful. Did you possibly overlook something?"

"No, that can't be," Echika said, ruffling up her hair. "Anyway, let's stick to schedule. You go around and question the other people who came in contact with the index cases. I'll go obtain the employees' personal data and the results of the virus analysis."

"Understood." Harold nodded, but his expression remained concerned. "You look pale. Do you want to take a rest before we continue?"

"I'm fine. Oh, and while you're out questioning people, could you ask for details about an employee named Salk?"

"You mean the Russian man who was with them? He didn't look related to the case."

"I agree, but something's bugging me about him… Anyway, see you later."

Harold seemed like he had something else to say, but Echika left the nap room without looking him in the eye. She wanted to be alone before he noticed anything.

Matoi. Matoi. Matoi—the word echoed time and again inside her head.

Aaah. This is why I didn't want to come to Rig City.

2

The lounge in the first floor's southern area was full of employees who'd brought their work over. Echika sat alone on one of the sofas, puffing out smoke from her electronic cigarette. Since the room had an ozone generator, the minty smell of the smoke soon faded away entirely.

She'd finally calmed down a little. It had been a long while since the last time Brain Diving left her this shaken up. That might have been back when she'd still been a rookie and needed to Dive into the Mnemosynes of a murderer. That had made her lose her lunch. What she saw just now was nowhere near as gruesome.

This is pathetic.

Heaving a sigh, Echika switched off her cigarette and glanced around the lounge. After she left the nap room, Anne had instructed her to wait here, but no one seemed to be showing up. But after five more minutes of idling…

"Investigator Hieda, yes? Thank you for waiting."

Echika gazed up at the voice that called out to her...only to find Harold standing there with his back straightened out, his expression uncharacteristically hard and stiff.

"What, are you done questioning them already? That was awfully qui—"

But then she paused. Upon closer inspection, he wasn't wearing a sweater but a neat business shirt and vest. He had an Amicus's employee's badge dangling down at his chest that read *Steve H. Wheatstone*.

This wasn't Harold but another Amicus produced using the same appearance preset as him.

What is this?

Echika couldn't mask her bewilderment. She knew, of course, that Amicus could share the same appearance, but she didn't imagine she'd run into one with the same model as Harold. Wasn't he custom-made?

"Ummm...," she finally managed to utter. "I'm sorry. I mistook you for someone else."

"I don't mind," Steve said without a smile. "Our company's adviser wishes to speak to you directly about the virus-analysis results. Please follow me."

"Adviser?"

The company's busy CEO had sent her a video message prior to this, so she didn't expect an adviser. But before Echika could say anything, Steve walked off. She was quite unhappy with this, but she had no choice but to follow him given the circumstances.

The two of them went to the elevator hall and entered one elevator that was more gaudily decorated than the rest. The doors closed, and a thick silence filled the elevator. Steve was almost frighteningly sullen, and seeing someone with Harold's face make that sort of expression was kind of suffocating.

Generally speaking, Amicus were supposed to act as friendly and presentable as possible to humans, but Steve was different. He was extremely polite, but his lack of expression was the very image of a soulless machine.

"Investigator Hieda." He suddenly spoke up just as that thought crossed her mind. "Your partner is the same model as me, correct?"

He was an Amicus, so normally, she'd ignore him, but Echika wasn't indifferent enough to remain silent at this point.

"Have you met Aide Lucraft, by any chance?"

"I saw him in the corridor, but it seems he didn't notice me," Steve said matter-of-factly. "I was surprised. I didn't know Harold was still functional."

"You knew him beforehand?" Echika asked, perplexed.

"Yes. We used to work together."

"Together? Here in Rig City?"

"No," he replied, but he didn't seem to intend on elaborating. "I hope he hasn't been causing you any unnecessary trouble?"

"He's a talented aide," she said.

And his observation skills were phenomenal, in fact. However...

"...Are you going to figure out my private details just by looking at me? Do you wrap women around your little finger?"

"My only impression of you is *clad in black and inapproachable*, but I haven't the foggiest as to any of your private details. Also, my little finger is nowhere near large enough to wrap a human around."

He's the polar opposite of Harold. Are they really the same model?

"I can see that Harold's given you some grief, though. Allow me to apologize."

As they spoke, the elevator reached the top floor. Echika found herself staring at a polished marble floor and a pair of double doors that reminded her of a medieval church. It felt as though she'd just stepped onto the set of some fantasy film.

The whole place made Echika sick. This was why she hated companies with this much money to spare.

"Excuse me, sir. I've escorted Investigator Hieda from the Electrocrime Investigations Bureau over," Steve announced.

The doors opened on their own from the inside. The view behind them made Echika furrow her brow yet again. It was more greenhouse than room. The atrium's ceiling was open to the air and overrun with subtropical plants in their original forms. Those were all replicas, covered with blooming, vivid flowers. A drone fashioned after a bald eagle was perched on one of the treetops.

"Where are we?" Echika asked.

"This is a guest room," Steve replied. "Please take a seat on the sofa over there. I'll get you something to drink."

"Thank you," Echika said, still bewildered. Could you really call this a guest room? "So, um, maybe it's a little too late to ask this, but you're basically...?"

"The adviser's secretary."

Leaving it at that, Steve disappeared behind the plants. Echika wouldn't be surprised if someone told her the Amazon River was flowing through here. The atmosphere of the place was so unique, it was almost intoxicating.

For the time being, she took a seat on the nearby leather sofa.

"Hello. It's been some time, Echika," a voice suddenly called out to her, making her gasp in shock.

She looked up to find a Japanese man seated on a sofa opposite her. He was short and middle-aged, with well-chiseled facial features that didn't look much like hers. His hair was thoroughly slicked down, a clear indicator of the sheer amount of wax he applied every morning. The shirt he wore was a refreshing shade of blue that suited him greatly.

This was Echika's father.

She couldn't even blink as she stared at him in bewilderment. This couldn't be; it was impossible. Because her father was already...

He beamed at her.

"I have a hobby of startling people when they meet me for the first time. People often tell me it's in poor taste."

The figure of her father suddenly melted away, out from which appeared an elderly man. He had a white head of hair that suited his age, but his round, almondlike eyes still had a youthful glint to them. His features looked quite friendly, and nothing about him seemed mean-spirited.

"Welcome, Investigator Hieda. I'm Taylor, the corporate adviser."

Elias Taylor. The promising technological revolutionary who led the Your Forma's development, and also a known recluse who refused to show himself before the press. When Steve said he would take her to the adviser, the whimsical thought that she would be seeing him had crossed her mind, but she didn't actually expect she'd get to meet Taylor himself.

"Excuse me," Echika said, just barely managing to hang on to her composure. "But what was that just now...?"

"That was the projector system's newest holo-model. It hasn't been disclosed to the public quite yet, but it's currently under development here. In fact, the image of me you're speaking to right now is a holo-gram, too," Taylor explained, looking up at the bald eagle.

Apparently, that was the laser drone for the projector system.

"I am currently ill, so I've been avoiding direct contact with other people...," Taylor continued. "Of course, I've been doing this since before the illness became an issue, too. I'm not one for face-to-face interaction."

Echika had seen on the news that he was afflicted with terminal pancreatic cancer. He only had a month left to live, so he'd refused treatment and entered palliative care. Not at the hospital, though, but at the top floor of the company headquarters, which was his place of residence—the room they were standing in.

"I'm Hieda, from the Electrocrime Investigations Bureau. We appreciate your cooperation with our investigation." She glanced at the eagle and managed to calm herself somehow. "Hmm... How did you obtain a holographic model of my father?"

"I based it on our surveillance cameras' scan data. Very realistic, don't you think?"

"...Yes."

If anything was clear, it was that she shouldn't expect any kind of sensible consideration out of Taylor.

"I was friends with your father. As you may know, I'm something of a recluse, so I never met Chikasato Hieda face-to-face, but we spoke so much over the phone. He was a very skilled and avaricious program-mer, and thanks to his involvement, the Your Forma was completed years ahead of its time."

This was what he really wanted to talk to her about. Echika felt her stomach churn with anxiety. Her father, Chikasato Hieda, used to work for Rig City, at least for a time. But honestly, she preferred to think about her father as little as possible.

"Mr. Taylor, I'm sure you've heard, but today, I came for…"

"The personal data and the viral-analysis results? I sent Steve to get them."

As if on cue, the Amicus returned, carrying a cup of black tea. He set the saucer and cup down with practiced motions and placed an HSB memory stick next to them.

"This includes the personal data of all our employees, including retirees, and the results of the viral analysis. I'm afraid I have to ask you to copy the data here and leave without the stick, though. These are company secrets, so it has security placed on it to prevent it from being copied more than once."

"Understood," Echika replied, plugging the HSB stick to the port in her neck. After confirming the data was being copied, she turned her eyes to Taylor. "So about the virus, did you manage to discover any connection between the delusions and the bodily symptoms?"

"We did." Steve was the one to answer the question. "The virus uses the signals transmitted from the Your Forma directly into the brain to stimulate the thermoregulation center in the hypothalamus. In other words, it's not that the illusion of the blizzard causes them to develop hypothermia. It's showing the illusion of the blizzard, while simultaneously interfering with the brain's thermoregulation center to cause hypothermia."

That was a much more plausible explanation than the water-droplet experiment. But now Echika had another question to pose.

"Weren't you his secretary, Steve? Or are you part of the analysis team?"

"Steve likes to call himself my secretary, but I have no one filling that role for me," Taylor revealed with a smile. "He's my caretaker and is also employed as an engineer and programmer for Rig City. And a modeler, too, on the side. He wears many hats around here, if you will."

Apparently, Steve was as much of a Renaissance man as Harold was.

"Based on our analysis," Steve continued, "this virus was created with an almost telltale level of precision, so only someone in the field could have produced it. We're working on correcting the Your Forma's vulnerability, but the creator will probably find a way around it as soon as we patch it out. We need you to catch the culprit as soon as possible."

"That's our intent, of course," Echika said.

"We're counting on you. I'll be off, then. Mr. Taylor, if you need anything, don't hesitate to call."

With that, Steve once again disappeared among the plants.

"He's a good boy, isn't he?" Taylor said, narrowing his eyes affectionately. "He came to me on his own."

"...What do you mean?"

"Apparently, he ran away from somewhere. He was repeatedly resold because of his rare model. Citizens are forbidden from trading Amicus themselves, but many people still put them up for sale on the black market."

"Yes, I'm aware of the phenomenon." Expensive Amicus with customized models sold for good money on the black market, with some of them even being illegally smuggled on an international scale. Except... "Hmm, I've heard Steve worked somewhere else before coming to Rig City?"

"Let's drop the issue," Taylor said, still smiling. "I'm sure he doesn't appreciate us talking about him and doesn't want people snooping into his past."

Echika furrowed her brow. *Is Taylor an Amicus sympathizer? Even if an Amicus shows displeasure at something, it's just a part of their human act. And besides, even if Steve and Harold used to work together, what does it matter? It's got nothing to do with the task at hand.*

Being in Rig City is really throwing me off.

The files finished copying, so Echika extracted the HSB stick and placed it on the table.

"Thank you for sparing me your time, especially when you're not feeling well," she said, trying to force the conversation to an end. She'd gotten what she came for and wanted to leave as soon as she could. "Then, if you'll excuse me..."

"Wait. There's no need to rush."

Echika already sat up, but she had to sink back down into the sofa. She knew Taylor was curious about her, since she was Chikasato's daughter. And that was exactly why she wanted to leave as soon as possible.

"There are a few questions I always ask people when I first meet them. Most people get to know others through boring small talk, but I opt for more efficient methods." Taylor got to his feet slowly. "Would you be so kind as to answer? I'll start out with just one."

His tone was soft, but something about it didn't allow her to decline. Echika had to keep her irritation from showing on her face. She wanted nothing more than to walk out of here despite his pleas, but Taylor had cooperated with the investigation, so she couldn't offend him.

"You were born after the pandemic. Why did you decide to install the Your Forma?"

"Ugh." This felt like a job interview. "Living without the device is difficult nowadays. Things would be different if I wanted to live as a luddite, but..."

"Second question, then. When was the Your Forma inserted into your head?"

"When I was five years old. In Japan, they only allow the Your Forma operation on children ages five and up."

"But that said, not many parents agree to have their children go through the operation at that age. Third question. When was your aptitude for your profession—for being an electronic investigator—discovered?"

"When I was ten. I was evaluated as having one of the highest data-processing speeds on the planet."

"I'd expect no less. Fourth question. Is there another job you'd have wanted to work in, assuming you didn't have the Your Forma?"

Taylor smiled, holding up four fingers. The man was undoubtedly a genius, but Echika would have preferred it if he left ordinary people to themselves. If this wasn't for work, she'd have gulped her tea down and gone home by now.

"I got an occupational-aptitude diagnosis from the AI, and I wasn't compatible for anything other than being an electronic investigator. My father wanted me to become one, too, so I decided to go for it. That's it."

"That's not what I asked you, but I'll grant it," Taylor said, pacing around the sofa with composed steps. "Fifth question. This one's a question I'd only ask you, though... Do you know why Chikasato died?"

Don't.

Echika felt her cheeks twitch and harden.

Stop it. Don't go there.

"No. I don't."

"Really?"

"Yes... He didn't leave a suicide note."

Against her will, the memory of that day surfaced in her mind. Three years ago, on the day Echika graduated high school, she left her father's home. Six months later, an assisted-euthanasia company based in Switzerland contacted her, informing her that her father had voluntarily chosen to die. Notably, her father hadn't been the slightest bit ill. He was the very image of health itself. But across the ages, with the exception of certain religions, people had the right and freedom to choose to end their lives.

At the company's behest, Echika left for Switzerland, and after a simple funeral, her father was buried at a public cemetery on the banks of Lake Zurich.

"Investigator Hieda. I know why he died," Taylor whispered softly. "Failing to develop the Matoi was what brought on his suicide."

If Echika didn't have the sense to know better, she'd have fixed her gun on Taylor right then and there and ordered him to shut up.

"What are you talking about?" she asked, her voice coming out lower than usual.

"The Matoi, the project Chikasato was in charge of. The Your Forma's expanded functionality."

"...I think I might have heard about it on the news."

"On the news? Didn't Chikasato tell you himself?"

"No," Echika hissed, clenching her fists. She wanted to get out of here as soon as she could. "My father and I, we... Our relationship was a little distant. And I wasn't very interested in his work, so I don't remember much."

Her father was an extraordinarily talented programmer, and he was always terribly busy whenever he was home. He'd eat dinners with her, but he lived entirely on jelly meals, a habit that Echika ended up picking up.

Her father made her keep their initial promise, so he rarely showed himself to her. He was as much a misanthrope as Taylor was; the only things he would ever look at were work and his Amicus, Sumika.

"You should know why Chikasato resolved to create the Matoi."

"No, I really don't—"

"Your father was brilliant," Taylor interjected, refusing to back down. "Do you know what the term *filter bubble* means?"

Echika suppressed a sigh.

Just end this already.

"Yes. It's a phenomenon where a person ends up only seeing information they wish to see in cyberspace."

"Correct. The Your Forma adapts itself to the user's tastes and ideologies and automatically filters and selects what information to provide them with, but that system has a flaw. When someone is enveloped in a bubble of only the things they want to see, they're shut off from all other information."

The Your Forma was connected to every kind of data. Thus, its algorithm continued to read what the user saw and thought... In other words, it optimized itself. But to avoid failure, it had to continually keep itself up to date.

For example, take Anne's story about how California's movement to litigate days off for Amicus would go down as a major historical event. The thing was, Echika had never seen any news articles about it. The algorithm knew that she had no interest in Amicus, so not once did it bring up a single feature about it.

That phenomenon was the "filter bubble."

"Of course, information that's deemed crucial for maintaining a democracy can't be shut out," Taylor said. "Over the last few decades, humankind's IQ has continued to climb. But the only thing that's been evolving is our data-processing ability, while the other numbers have been leveling off. Why do you think that is?"

"I don't know. I'm an electronic investigator, not a neurologist."

"Then let me change that to an easier question. How do you process the massive amounts of information you run across when Brain Diving?"

"I've never thought about it. I just naturally go through it."

"That's what I assumed. You can do that because you unconsciously let the information flow past you. The brain has a limit to how much data it can process, and so as a consequence of the brain structure we're born with, we have to reject some information when we're faced with a staggering amount of it. And when that happens, the data only passes over the surface level of our thoughts in a thin, shallow form."

Echika had read about this once in an article dealing with the brain's multitasking capabilities. The author doubted whether human brains that accepted Your Forma were pliably remaking themselves to adapt to data processing. It was proven that processing vast amounts of data whittled down one's concentration and understanding, resulting in a loss of attentiveness.

"If things continue like this, people will dispense with thought, forgo memes, and forget philosophy and culture. They'll only judge things in accordance with the whims they were born with. They would lose prudence and *regress* to artificial intelligence."

"…I'm sorry, but does any of this have an academic foundation?"

"Research on the matter has produced differing opinions, so only the future holds the answer," Taylor remarked, staring into space with an air of melancholy. "But your father believed this. And as one of the people charged with developing the Your Forma, he felt terribly responsible for it."

Lies.

Echika couldn't believe it. Her father was the very embodiment of a cold-blooded man, the kind of person who tended to control everything around him.

"The Matoi is an all-generational cultivation system meant to remind people of their humanity. Of their affection and love, if you will. Chikasato dedicated his life to it, but its development ended in failure, so he chose suicide."

"But he died years after botching it."

"Investigator, people don't contemplate death at the moment of their life's greatest failure. No, the wounds gouged by that blunder throbbed and festered over time. And when one feels that their poison has spread throughout their body, that's when they choose death."

Echika fell silent and gazed at the rippling surface of her tea. A breeze from the air conditioner blowing in from somewhere made the liquid quiver, like it was shivering in fear. Why did Taylor decide to share this with her? He said people often told him he acted in bad taste, so maybe he just liked picking topics that annoyed them.

Or maybe it was something else; it didn't matter. Either way, one thing was for sure—talking to him made her sick. She'd never truly felt any real sorrow over her father's passing to begin with.

"Mr. Taylor," Echika said quietly. "Could you finally tell me what the point of this story was?"

"You're very easy to read. Did you hate Chikasato?"

"Maybe you won't like to hear this, since you were his friend, but yes, I did."

Taylor leisurely looked up at the bald eagle gliding through the air above them and squinted. Echika didn't know what that gesture meant, and at this point, she didn't care. She felt nothing but fury at this man for asking her that now of all times.

"I'll be returning to the investigation. We'll be counting on your cooperation if anything else pops up."

∗

"I've questioned all the employees who came in contact with the index cases, but there wasn't anything suspicious about their conducts or their testimonies. I think there's a chance the culprit is an outsider who used Rig City as a means to mislead and throw off the criminal profiling."

Having concluded their investigation of Rig City, Echika and Harold were now waiting for their taxi at the roundabout in front of the building. Harold was in the middle of a simple report; he had a holo-browser window open in his terminal, which showed an image of Chief Totoki.

"Assuming that's the case, how did someone who isn't an employee get information on who'd be attending the study tours?" she asked.

"It didn't look like the server had been hacked into," Echika said, nodding.

"It's not entirely impossible the culprit found out some other way, but still... I don't know about the other two index cases, but Lee didn't post about her tour in Rig City on her social media."

"If only everyone would cooperate and agree to let us Brain Dive... I always say this every investigation."

Totoki sighed. It was late at night at Lyon at the moment, and since she was at home, she was wearing a sweatshirt. Sitting curled up on her lap was a cat with glossy fur.

"Guess we'll have to do it the old-fashioned way. I'll try to trace back the employees' activity records from the personal data Investigator Hieda sent me."

"There's also the matter of Cliff Salk," Harold said, beating Echika to the punch. "He started working in Rig City as a programmer about six months ago, but he resigned last month and went freelance."

"Huh?" Totoki raised an eyebrow. "Who is this Cliff Salk?"

"A Russian-American man we saw in the workers' Mnemosynes," Echika explained. "Something about the emotion associated with his record felt off... Aide Lucraft, did anyone admit to having interpersonal troubles with him?"

"Not in particular. People seemed to get along with him."

Echika couldn't link Salk to the sensory crime directly, but she'd definitely felt something wrong when she witnessed the Mnemosynes about him. And speaking from experience, it was better to look into those kinds of hunches. Just to be on the safe side.

"Chief Totoki, could you look into Salk's activity record in particular?"

"Very well. I'll be checking programmers with a lot of accomplishments under their belts first, but I'll move the check on him ahead—"

She was cut off by a nonsensical "meoooow." The cat sitting on Totoki's lap had risen to its feet with a long stretch. It was a Scottish fold, with small, drooping ears. Its fluffy fur and pink nose grew closer and soon enveloped the whole screen.

"Stop that, Ganache—don't get in the way." Totoki beamed and scooped up the cat. "What's wrong, hungry already? I just fed you, you little glutton."

Oh no. Echika felt the blood drain from her face. *Here we go again...*

"Oh, it's adorable," Harold said. "Is that a pet robot?"

"It is. Do you like kitties, Aide Lucraft?"

"Yes, they're very warm and fuzzy when they sleep curled up with you."

"Yes, yes, exactly! Ah, was it yesterday morning? Yes, I think it was yesterday morning when Ganache—"

"Chief." Echika leaned forward. "That concludes our report. What about our flight back?"

"Oh yes, right! Good work. You two can take a day off when you get back to Saint Petersburg."

"Thank you. Let us know if there are any developments in the investigation."

Echika hurriedly tapped the END CALL button, as if trying to cut off Ganache's shrill meowing, only to find Harold staring at her dubiously. He likely didn't know the sheer scale of the predicament she'd just delivered him from.

"I should warn you now so you know next time this happens," Echika said gravely. "But once the chief starts rambling about cats, never go along with her. She'll talk your ear off until morning and spam you with hundreds—and I do mean *hundreds*—of cat pictures."

Although Totoki was a reliable superior, she was also a pet-robot aficionado to an almost dangerous degree. Real cats eventually passed away, but pet robots didn't die, so you could love them without that concern.

"But still, cats are lovely creatures. Can you really fault her for acting strange?"

"'Acting strange' doesn't scratch the surface of what she's like. She's bordering on Machine Dependency Syndrome."

Machine Dependency Syndrome was a mental disorder that had become very common as of late. Spending time with Amicus and pet robots became so pleasant that people lost interest in their fellow humans. Totoki did show some signs of it and had actually gone without a human romantic partner for years. The only things she wanted to spend her life with were mechanical felines.

Either way, Echika's fatigue spurred her to produce her electronic cigarette and give a long puff. Being in Rig City and talking to Taylor had taken a major toll on her nerves, and it made her head hurt.

"You really do look pale, Investigator."

"You're imagining things." Echika dismissed him, blowing smoke from her mouth and changing the topic. "Oh, by the way, I ran into an Amicus with the same model as yours. His name was Steve."

"Steve Howell Wheatstone," Harold said, seemingly unsurprised. "Anne told me about him. She was staring at me because she knew him."

"Hmm. And here I was, thinking it was because your face's workmanship was too good," Echika said, gunning for clear sarcasm.

"I appreciate the compliment. Would you like to take a closer look?"

"Cut it out—that wasn't genuine; get away from me. Why do you keep trying to show me things close-up?"

"No need to get flustered." Harold pulled back with a smile. "You really are funny."

"Shut up," Echika retorted with a dry cough. *Stupid tin man.* "So did you meet Steve?"

"I didn't. But I will say, I didn't know he was still operational."

"He said the same thing about you...and that he used to work with you."

"Yes. Those were good times."

That was all Harold had to share on the matter. Echika felt the urge to ask him to elaborate, but she suppressed it. Posing questions eagerly like that would make it look like she was curious about him or something.

"Well, hmm... Steve was a lot less sociable than you are, but he did seem quite serious and honest."

"When you put it like that, it sounds like you're implying I'm dishonest."

"Oh, not at all." *Drat, I let what I really think about him slip.* "It's just that you look the same, so if you'd put on the same clothes and stayed quiet, you'd seem honest."

"That's not much better." He sighed, clearly exasperated. "Besides, we have differences. We both have our own unique serial numbers."

"I know. It's printed somewhere on your bodies."

"Yes, on my left breast," Harold said, patting his chest. "Romantic, don't you think?"

".........Romantic?"

"Well, if I were human, that's where my heart would be."

"Just so you know, I'm not the kind of person who's impressed by those sorts of things."

"I know, sadly." The Amicus shrugged jokingly. "...That said, you've been awfully talkative for a while now."

Echika held her breath. He was right; she'd been talking too much recently. That might have been a careless attitude to take when dealing with this Amicus.

"People tend to become talkative when something they don't want touched on comes up. And right now, you're stressed enough to openly chatter with an Amicus, when normally you hate speaking with me."

"No." She denied it at once.

"I heard you met with Elias Taylor. Did something happen with him?"

He saw right through her again, and just like he did when he investigated Lee, he was about to say something that would expose the bottom of her heart. What if he could discover everything, down to her father and sister?

Echika stiffened defensively, but then Harold said, "Investigator. Smoking can help you handle stress, but personally, I recommend something sweet."

With flowing motions, he offered her a piece of chocolate covered in colorful wrapping. It was a familiar, famous wrapping, and Echika had to gawk at it for a moment.

Huh?

"One of the employees gave it to me earlier. Take it if you want."

Just when she thought his powers of observation were about to cut her down to her core, here he was, acting oddly kind all of a sudden.

Echika almost reached out to accept the sweet, but she stopped at the last minute.

"No, forget it. I don't need it."

"Do you hate receiving things from Amicus?" Harold asked, curling his lips up. "If that's the issue, you can consider this a gift not from me but from Rig City."

"H-hey," Echika protested, but he forced the chocolate into her palm. "I just told you I don't want it…!"

But as she said that, the taxi's headlights approached them, cutting through the dusk. Harold walked toward it, not granting Echika the chance to return the sweet.

What's his deal? she asked herself, clenching her fingers around the small wrapped sweet, melting it against the heat of her palm.

She wished it would disappear altogether. His kindness was irking her. She knew very well how Amicus tried to slither into people's hearts.

It's just part of their programming. That's all.

3

She woke up the next morning, only to have a text message from Harold instantly ruin her precious day off.

"Bigga asked me out on a date. We're meeting at Mikhailovsky Garden today at noon."

It was a bolt from the blue. At the time, Echika was lazing around in her bed at the lodging house, but this message immediately jolted her awake. She'd chided him just the previous day, telling him that police investigators were to set an example to the citizenry.

"By the way, I'm set to arrive at Gostiny Dvor station at around 11:30."

Aaah, he thinks he can mess with me!

And so Echika ended up sitting in the subway despite it being her day off. One way or another, she disembarked at the right station and forced herself onto the escalator. As an aside, Saint Peterburg's metro system was dug so deep underground that it took three minutes to get to the surface.

As she stepped outside, a wind cold enough to freeze her annoyance over buffeted her. Harold leaned against a streetlight, wearing a battered Chesterfield coat and burgundy scarf. He must not have applied wax on his day off, because his usually combed bangs were currently hanging limp, giving him a slightly younger impression... Not that this mattered at the moment.

Echika rushed toward him, and he looked up at her and blinked.

"I thought today was your day off, Investigator. Why are you dressed like you're at work?"

This made her glance down at her outfit. A long black coat, a black sweater, a black pair of denim jeans, and black boots. This didn't feel like unacceptable casual wear to her.

"Is there a problem with my clothes?"

"No," he said, seeming as though he'd realized something. "Let me ask you a question. Do you have clothes in colors other than black?"

"No. Matching colors is a waste of time when I'm getting dressed."

"Really. I knew you were indifferent, but... You really are a wasteful person."

"Huh?" *What does that mean?* "I'm free to wear whatever I want. Forget that."

"By the way, I see you always don that necklace. Is it your favorite?"

"Don't pry into my business," she said, gripping the nitro case dangling from her neck. "What are you, some kind of clothes-matching app?"

"I could be one, if that's what you want. *A pale-blue coat would suit you.*"

"I came here to stop you." Echika glared at him after that exchange. "Bigga's involved with the incident, so as a police officer, you can't take her out on dates. Besides, you're an Amicu—"

"Yes, I did promise to meet Bigga, but the part about it being a date was a lie."

".........You were lying about that?"

"I wanted you to come here, so I figured saying that would make you hurry over," Harold replied with an unapologetic smile. "Think of it as an Amicus joke. Did you like it?"

Echika felt all the strength drain from her shoulders. Oh, how she longed to punch this bucket of bolts in the face.

"I can't believe you... You scared me out of bed on my day off..."

"It's past noon, and sleeping in isn't good for recovering from exhaustion."

"Shut up." Like this thing could understand the bliss that sleep gave her. "So what's your real business with Bigga?"

"She called me and said she decided to sign the contract. And since I'm not an official investigator, we need you to be present."

The contract—in other words, she was willing to sign a document to become a civilian cooperator in their investigation. After Echika returned from Kautokeino, the Electrocrime Investigations Bureau had decided to ask Bigga to take on the role. Civilian cooperators were, simply put, informants. In exchange for keeping an eye on underworld organizations and reporting if they made any suspicious movements, they would sweep her past bio-hacking activities under the rug.

And the one to recommend they make her a civilian cooperator had been Harold.

"To begin with, marginalized people only stoop to bio-hacking because they struggle to find valid sources of income to preserve their heritage. If we forcibly round them up while ignoring that, all we'd achieve is stomping out yet another cultural group."

Echika honestly had trouble wrapping her mind around his way of thinking. Even if they let one small indigenous group get wiped out, no one would care in this day and age. But she didn't feel strongly enough to interject and oppose his suggestion.

And so he had kicked the idea to Totoki, who sent the contract proposal to Bigga. All that had remained was to wait for her response.

"Still...if you ever do that to call me somewhere again, don't expect me to ever chat with you."

"Oh, no, I'll make you talk."

"Shut up and reflect on what you did."

She was already feeling exhaustion settle in, but somehow, she managed to shake it off. This was still technically work, so she needed to pull herself together.

As promised, Bigga was standing at the entrance to Mikhailovsky Garden. She had on a colorful woolen hat and wore a white down coat.

That was fine, but Echika and Harold froze up upon seeing some other figures.

"So." Echika nudged her head toward Bigga. "You think they're her friends?"

"If they are, they don't look like very nice ones."

Two male Amicus were standing in front of Bigga. Their attire was quite pitiful; they wore moldy jackets and pants dotted with holes. Muddy sneakers adorned their feet, and their hair and skin were covered in strange filth. It was clear at a glance that these were vagrant Amicus—Amicus who had no owner.

Echika and Harold casually approached them, and the vagrant Amicus noticed them at once and strode away, fleeing. Bigga watched them leave, her lips quivering with rage.

"What's their problem…?" she asked, her voice shaking. "They just walked up to me and begged me for money. It's absurd."

"Vagrant Amicus tend to target young women and tourists," Harold informed her.

Amicus who'd been illegally thrown away by their owners became much like human derelicts and paupers. They pestered people for money and clothes and made their residences in back alleys and vacant houses. Vagrant Amicus were becoming a major social issue, and different countries and cities were taking a variety of measures to deal with the problem, but apparently, Saint Petersburg simply let them wander the streets.

"They were Amicus?" Bigga asked, bewildered. "They looked so real… I thought they were people."

"Yes, very convincing, aren't they?" Harold smiled. "Let's take a walk until you calm down."

How long was he going to hide the fact that he was an Amicus from her? This wasn't a restricted zone, so he had no reason to keep up the charade.

The trees of Mikhailovsky Garden had yielded to winter, standing withered and naked of leaves. They passed by children accompanied by Amicus, young couples on dates, and old couples enjoying a leisurely stroll.

Harold and Bigga took a seat on a bench while Echika leaned against a nearby tree.

"How's Lee doing?" Harold asked.

"She still sees the delusions, but she recovered from the contusion. The doctors said it won't have any aftereffects."

Echika was relieved to hear Lee hadn't succumbed to the accident. She might have acted pragmatic and prioritized Brain Diving into her back then, but that didn't mean she wanted to see the girl meet the worst possible fate... Though of course, she couldn't put that into words.

"Actually, I just went to the academy in Lee's place and handed in a withdrawal letter for her," Bigga told them, hanging her head. "She always wanted to be a prima ballerina but didn't have the talent for it... That's why I put in the muscle-control chips at her request. But we took this chance to talk it over again, and she decided that this wasn't right. So she let my aunt know, and..."

"You've made the right decision. There's no doubting that," Harold said.

"That's what I want to believe," Bigga whispered, taking in his words. "A drug smuggler should be fleeing from Vladivostok to Saint Petersburg tomorrow. I'm supposed to inject them with a suppressant that will pause their Your Forma and assist their escape."

She licked her dry lips and looked up at Harold with clear eyes.

"This is my first intelligence report... I agree to become a civilian cooperator."

"You just made a very brave decision. So long as you keep up your end of the contract, we promise to protect you and ensure your safety."

Bigga nodded, and he handed her a tablet terminal that had the terms of the contract displayed on it. She read through it and carefully signed it with her fingertip. They would share the data with Totoki later and inform her about the intelligence Bigga had leaked.

Still, it was all over surprisingly quickly. If Echika went back to her lodging house now, she could take a good nap before dinner. The thought she could still enjoy her day off helped lift her spirits a little. However...

"Hmm." Bigga parted her lips in a slightly more fidgety manner.

"Actually, it's been a long time since I last traveled outside Kautokeino. I'd like to take this opportunity to see the sights. And, hmm, if it's not too much trouble…"

Hold on. No.

"Not at all," Harold said unflinchingly, "I'll show you around, if you don't mind."

"Really?! Thank you very much!"

"Well, isn't that nice?" Echika said, realizing this was her last chance to run, and raised her hand. "Have fun, you two."

But before she could make her hasty getaway…

"Investigator Hieda." Harold stopped her. "Who said you can go home?"

Oh, give me a break!

A fir that was very similar to a Christmas tree—a *Yolka*, as it was called—stood in the palace square in front of the State Hermitage Museum. The Your Forma summoned a dialogue box explaining that this was apparently a New Year's tradition in Russia. And indeed, the New Year was two days away.

Echika's line of work made it so she was rather detached from such occasions. Celebrating them mostly felt off for her.

They visited the museum at Bigga's request, and it proved to be quite spacious. A guide Amicus at the entrance jokingly warned them, "If you get lost here, you'll never find your way out." The main building was housed in the Winter Palace used during the Romanov dynasty, and its exterior was magnificently repainted.

"This is so exciting!" Bigga exclaimed, her eyes glittering. "I've always like Western art history, so I've read a lot about this!"

"I've visited this place a few times, so I assumed you'd like it."

Bigga and Harold were in good spirits, but needless to say, Echika had absolutely no interest in this kind of art. And so she sluggishly tagged along after them the whole time. They walked through the Peter the Great Hall and the Pavilion Hall; both of them were lavishly decorated. Some of the rooms were very crowded, and the personal-information pop-ups were terribly irritating. She opened the Your Forma's settings and toggled the personal-information display off.

This was her free day, after all. She was allowed to turn it off today, at least.

Her eyes stopped on a statue in the Renaissance art exhibition. It was a statue of a seated boy, curled over and attempting to extract a thorn from his leg. Even Echika could clue in to the sheer history etched upon its surface.

"That's the *Crouching Boy*," Harold remarked, standing next to her. "A Michelangelo."

"I don't need you to repeat what the Your Forma says," Echika replied, holding back a sigh.

"What's your impression of it?"

"Like I should be the one crouching down right now."

"Color me surprised. I didn't know you could tell jokes."

"That wasn't a joke."

"I saw this statue in a book, too," Bigga interjected, cutting between the two of them. "Supposedly, it's incomplete. Its arms and legs aren't properly chiseled out..."

"You know a great deal about this," Harold noted.

"Michelangelo's drawings are lovely, but I like sculptures better."

"Do you have any other favorites?"

"It's a bit of a common answer, but *La Pietà di San Pietro* is simply exquisite."

"Yes, I can understand why you'd feel that way. It completely altered the public's perception of the Virgin Mary."

Enough.

Echika's days off weren't meant to be wasted listening to these kinds of refined conversations, and to top it all off, Bigga was conspicuously ignoring her. Maybe she was still upset about how Echika had forcefully interrogated her the other day.

In other words, she was a third wheel here. Deciding to go home, she tried to walk away.

"Oh, Investigator Hieda, I almost forgot to tell you something important."

"...Something important?"

"Bigga, excuse me for a second."

Harold apologized to her and pulled Echika away by the arm. He dragged her to a corner of the exhibit without giving her a chance to argue.

What's his problem? Echika turned to look at him with fed-up eyes.

"What, is this about the investigation? Or about Bigga?"

"Were you trying to sneak away? I'm sorry, but I won't allow you."

She wished he'd stop reading her like a book. It made him that much harder to deal with.

"Now listen to me, Aide Lucraft," Echika said, poking Harold on the chest. "I won't let you say you didn't notice that Bigga wants to spend time with you alone. I don't want to get in the way of your date. If there's anything I want, it's to go home and sleep."

"This is part of our job, though."

"No, this is obviously a sightseeing tour."

"We won't be paid for working on our day off, but this is without a doubt part of our duty."

"I thought you were in favor of your kind getting days off."

"That was just an excuse to get Anne to give me her number."

"I already told you this, but can you do something about that fickle attitude of yours?"

"You seem to be misinterpreting my intentions. I just think that building up personal connections doesn't hurt."

"Really now?"

"Investigator, please stay with us. I have something important to tell you." Harold brought his face closer to her, which made her stiffen in place. *Stay out of my bubble.* "You see that painting over there?"

"...What about it?"

"The woman on the left kind of looks like you."

"........Huh?"

"See? That's important." Harold shrugged and walked back over to Bigga.

He really was messing with her. She had no idea what he was thinking. If he wanted to keep Bigga company, let him do it alone and leave her out of it... But then again, he'd probably realized her tendency to go along with his nonsense.

It was past four in the afternoon when they left the museum. The darkness of night was beginning to settle over the sky, and they made their way to Nevsky Prospect at Bigga's request. The holiday lights were just coming to life, illuminating the peaceful faces of the families walking by. Echika found herself averting her gaze from them.

"Ah." Bigga stopped in front of a souvenir shop and stared at the *matryoshkas* lined up at the storefront. "Hmm, I'd like to buy my father and Lee some souvenirs, if you don't mind…"

"No problem—I'll look for something with you," Harold said, leading Bigga into the store.

Echika decided to wait outside and leaned against a streetlight. A sigh escaped her lips before she knew it. Somehow, she felt even more exhausted now than she did on a workday. She just wasn't used to spending time like this—she had no interest in tourism and hardly ever walked around with someone else. Echika had no close friends to speak of, but at the same time, it wasn't like loneliness ever burdened her.

If anything, being alone was easier, once you got used to it.

As always, she opened up the news in her Your Forma, but that only made her click her tongue. Of all things, a headline involving Amicus adorned the top result. Annoyed at the algorithm's insistence on updating itself against her will, she closed the browser and looked at Harold and Bigga through the glass window of the shop.

Harold was holding a *matryoshka* the size of his thumb and then made it disappear—a magic trick for entertaining children. But Bigga seemed genuinely surprised and laughed innocently. She looked like she was having the time of her life.

Did Echika ever laugh like that?

"Which are you going to pick, Echika?"

A prickling pain poked at her heart.

"I think Dad likes blue."

Aah, why? Why was she remembering this now?

"I'm sure he'll love it."

The image of her older sister's soft smile surfaced in her mind's eye.

4

When Echika was six years old, during the winter, her father's birthday came around for the first time since she'd moved in with him.

"Are you going out, Echika? Don't forget your scarf."

As she was putting on her shoes in the entrance hall, Sumika showed up and handed her a scarf with a polite gesture. Echika shook her head silently, though. She didn't need it.

"The highest temperature today is two degrees Celsius," Sumika stated. "You might catch a cold."

"I don't need it!" Echika insisted. At some point, she'd grown to take Sumika's kindness for granted. "And don't tell Dad I went out, okay?!"

"Is that an order? In which case, why not?"

Oh, drat, if I dawdle here, Dad might find out!

"Just keep it a secret! Let's go, Big Sis!"

Leaving Sumika behind, Echika bolted out the door, her little heart aflutter with excitement. Exiting their apartment, she ran along the Sumida River like her life depended on it. Perhaps as a consequence of the New Year having just ended, all the usual sights struck her as surprisingly new and fresh that day.

"Echika, wait!"

That call made her stop, turning around as her sister reached her. She halted, caught her breath, and extended her young hands to Echika.

"Go on, hold my hands. I'll keep you warm so you won't need a scarf."

"With your magic?"

"That's right," her sister said, her cherubic features blooming into a mature smile. "Go on, hold my hands."

Her sister's hands had a magic to them. It sounded absurd, but young Echika seriously believed that. After all, whenever she held her older sister's hands, the cold went away like a charm, and it felt like her body was enveloped in spring sunlight.

"Thanks, Big Sis!"

"The magic doesn't end here," her sister said, holding up a slender finger to the sky. "See?"

Something fluttered down onto the tip of Echika's nose—a large snowflake, like a flower petal. It was so pretty, she broke into a grin before she even knew it.

"Do you think the snow will pile up?"

"If you want it to, it will," her sister said, smiling. "All right. Race you to the candy store."

"Huh, hey, wait, that's cheating!"

The laughter of the two girls glided over the cold surface of the lake. The candy shop they headed to was at the corner of an intersection. Its antiquated sliding door was slightly ajar, and sitting in front of the entrance was a battered old mat to wipe their feet on.

Their father handled their normal grocery shopping online, so they didn't have many chances to visit physical retail stores. Echika swung the sliding door open with both hands, her heart beating with excitement.

Beyond the entrance was what she could only describe as a colorful box of jewels. Tall shelves were lined with vivid sweets and confections, all of them absolutely glittering. Echika was immediately bewitched. There were a few other, unfamiliar kids in the store except for them, and all of them gazed at the candy with the same sparkling eyes she had.

"Which are you going to pick, Echika?" Thankfully, her sister was calm at times like these and looked at her excited eyes with a smile. "You want to buy Dad sweets as a present, right?"

"Yeah." *That's right. This is why we snuck out today.* "Sumika told me that when people use their heads, they want sugar."

"And Dad's always busy with work."

In truth, Echika never celebrated her parents' birthdays, and neither her father nor mother ever celebrated hers. Neither of them had any perception of annual events, so birthdays were just ordinary days to them.

She only found out about birthdays after the Your Forma operation, when she was connected to the internet. And as it turned out, birthdays were special days where people gave you presents and celebrated.

"I looked it up on the internet. I actually want to get him a watch or a handkerchief, but I can't afford that…"

"But you have enough allowance to buy anything here, right?"

"Yep!" Echika said, puffing up her chest. "Good idea, huh?"

After twenty minutes of hesitating, she chose a sweet that was just right. Inside a heavy glass jar were round candies that looked like shards flaked off from the winter sky. They were a bit pricier than the other varieties in the store, but she'd saved up for today, so she could afford it. The important part was that they were the right color.

"Hey, Big Sis, I think Dad likes blue."

"You think so?"

"I mean, he always wears blue, and his handkerchief and toothbrush and slippers are all that color, too. And Sumika always wears blue dresses."

"You really pay attention to Dad, Echika."

"Yeah. I mean, I can't talk to him because of the promise, so I have to at least watch him and learn…"

Echika then hung her head, feeling the other children's gazes fix on her. Maybe she was a little too loud.

Echika paid for the candy and left the store, only to find that the world outside was now covered in a silvery layer of snow. This should have made her happy, but for some reason, she only felt restless. Come to think of it, Dad would always scold her when she acted out of line, and she'd come up with the idea of getting him a present today as a secret.

But then again, the internet did say that parents were happy when their children got them presents. Her classmates would gift their favorite glass marbles or portraits they drew, and their parents were happy to get those presents.

But Echika must have looked very dejected, because her sister spoke up.

"I'm sure he'll love it," she said, patting her hair gently like she always did. "It'll be all right."

It was strange. That gesture alone was enough to blow the fear away and convince her that this was bound to go well. Big Sis said it would be fine, so she believed her.

She was…all too naive.

When they came back home, Echika went to her father, who was shut off in his study as always. He was absorbed in his work. His eyes were turned to her, but they were actually gazing into what his Your Forma showed him. He wasn't looking at his daughter one bit.

"Echika, if you need anything from Chikasato, I will handle it in his place," Sumika called out to her from behind, but Echika ignored her.

Even if it meant breaking the promise, she wanted to give it to him by herself. She wanted to make Dad happy. She'd imagined him thanking her, saying he loved it, and then hugging her for the first time in her life.

And so to get him to pay attention to her, Echika sent a message to his Your Forma. And not just one but several hundred of them. With her data-processing abilities, she could send that many in the span of a second.

That made her father finally realize that Echika was standing near the study's door.

"Dad, I—"

"Get out."

He breathed out those two short, cold words, which made her jolt a little. But she refused to back down.

"I got you this," she said, timidly approaching him. "For your birthday. It's a…"

She couldn't finish the word *present*. Her father offhandedly swept the candy jar Echika extended to him out of her hands. The glass container went flying through the air in an almost beautiful arc. She felt like if she didn't blink, time might halt in its tracks. That way, the jar wouldn't hit the floor. It would stay suspended in midair, frozen forever.

But Echika blinked, and the jar struck the floor hard and shattered to countless pieces. The candies flicked into the air, smashing down with the violent lashing sound of hail. She stood rooted in place, gazing at her father with bewilderment.

But he wasn't looking at her anymore. His gaze was already fixed on the Your Forma again. He was there in the flesh, but his mind was elsewhere.

Why?

"Sumika." Her father spoke not to her but to the Amicus who was standing by the doorway. "Clean this up at once."

With that said, he turned around.

"No! Don't throw them away!"

Her father's hand thrust out at her forcefully, pushing her hard to the ground. Echika fell on her backside onto the floor, which was covered in glass shards, and at that moment, her father did, indeed, gaze directly at her. Yes, finally, he turned his eyes to her, but it didn't make her the slightest bit happy. Why were his eyes burning with such coldness?

"Echika, what was your role here? To be my machine, right?"

She knew that already. But…

"Yes." The word slipped from her lips, despite there being so many other things she wanted to say. "I'm…sorry."

"Sumika, clean this up now."

"Understood. But first, I need to treat Echika."

As Echika sat dumbfounded on the ground, Sumika picked her up gently and carried her out of her father's study. The sight of the door closing was distorted by tears. She could tell all the emotions she'd kept bottled up until now had finally reached a breaking point and burst, overflowing uncontrollably.

Why? All I wanted was to make him happy, so why? Was wanting Dad to be grateful to me for once really so wrong? Was wanting a hug really that greedy? Why did he make that promise? Does he hate me?

Sumika sat Echika down on the living room sofa and began carefully treating her arm, which was cut by the shards of glass. She had an adult woman's nimble fingers, and it reminded Echika of her mother's hand. It would have been comforting, if only the sensation of her artificial skin wasn't colder than a human's.

Before she knew it, a whisper left her lips.

"I want to see Mom."

She didn't really wish for that. She didn't really want to move back in with her abusive mother at all. Dad might have been frigid, but he was much better than Mom. This was just her looking for a way to rebel.

"Echika, Chikasato cares about you."

"You're lying." She couldn't believe that. "If you'd have done what I did, he would never get that mad at you."

"It must have hurt you so much. You poor thing."

Sumika patted her cheek, but it just gave Echika goose bumps. Sumika knit her brow sadly, pitying her. And all of a sudden, that emotion felt like a terrible, barefaced lie.

Did she *really* feel bad for Echika?

Sumika was always gentle and kind. She never got mad at anyone, never did anything a human might dislike, and always stuck by Echika. This was how this *robot* was made to be, to always play the part of man's perfect, ideal friend.

All this was fake. All this was just programming, just lines of code. Did Dad understand that and knowingly, consciously, still like Sumika better?

That was crazy. That was absurd.

"It's all your fault," Echika let slip. "Dad won't love me because he has you. Because you're much more convenient and obedient than I am!"

Everyone else in class gets along with their fathers, so why am I the only one who feels this way?

She needed a reason to understand why her parents didn't love her. A reason to justify and rationalize this sadness.

It's all the Amicus's fault.

It was such a plain, simple, wonderful justification that made everything fit into place.

"I'm not like Dad. Even if you're nice to me, I won't like you. I won't be your friend! Because it's all programming, it's all fake, it's all lies. I won't believe you! I'm not as stupid as you think!"

"Echika, I…" Sumika's eyes widened in sorrow.

"Shut up! I don't want to hear anything you say!"

She shook off Sumika's hands and bolted into her room, holding back sobs. She curled up, burying her face in her knees, as her sister's warmth enveloped her. Her small hands embraced her oh so pleasantly.

"Don't worry, Echika," her sister whispered, her voice like a silk wad on her wounds. "I love you."

Yes. That's right. She had her sister. And so long as she had her, nothing else mattered. She didn't need to believe in anything else.

And yet…

"Investigator Hieda?"

The moment she came to, noise rushed into her ears. Echika was seated at a gloomy restaurant table. Harold was sitting opposite her, gazing at her dubiously, and the chicken Kiev cutlets sitting between them glistened in the amber light.

Apparently, she'd been lost in thought, reflecting on the past. Even though she could do nothing to change what had already happened.

"I, ummm…," Echika said, pinching the corners of her eyes. "Where's Bigga?"

Harold moved his eyes to one side, and Echika followed his gaze to the stage, where musicians carrying balalaikas and domras were getting ready to perform. The other customers all put aside their meals and gathered around to watch. Among them was Bigga, standing on tiptoe to peer over their heads.

"You know how the Sami sing songs called *Joiks*? I suppose that also makes them interested in Russian folk songs, too."

Before long, the performance began, and the musicians started singing sonorously to a jolly melody. It was a pleasant if somehow nostalgic tune, and Echika looked up to the ceiling, her mind still a little hazy. A red-painted chandelier hung on the ceiling, shining like a flower and sparkling like the stars.

Today was such a crazy day.

"You went too far, Aide Lucraft," Echika stated, leveling a severe stare at Harold. "Job expenses won't cover this dinner."

"I know that. I don't mind."

"You don't get paid for this, though, do you?"

"I have money put aside to do as I see fit. Quite a bit, in fact," he responded nonchalantly as he cut the food on his plate.

That made sense. The bureau gave him an allowance as a police investigator, which was enough to get by. That was fine, though; the issue at hand had nothing to do with money to begin with. Plus, his table manners were so refined that it kind of ticked Echika off, but that was beside the point.

Making sure that Bigga wasn't returning to the table, Echika said in a whisper, "I understand wanting to further your trust with Bigga, since she's a civilian cooperator now, but do you really have to be this kind to her? Or do you feel guilty because we got Lee hurt?"

"Aren't you going to eat your cutlets? They'll get cold."

Harold seemed to stick to that attitude. Echika glared at him as she picked up her fork and knife. Not that this was relevant at the moment, but she much preferred jelly to such cumbersome meals.

"Don't tell me you're trying to toy with Bigga's feelings?"

"Why would I do that?"

"Hmm…" She doubted this could actually be the case, and yet. "Maybe you're just amused by the sight of a woman in love with you?"

"I imagine you've run into some terrible men in the past? Or maybe your father was an oppressive parent."

"Aaah, that was merely conjecture. I just felt like saying that," Echika muttered. She needed to do something about his observation skills. "Look, I get it—you might look human, but you don't experience any romantic feelings for anyone, and to begin with—"

"Twenty-eight," Harold cut her off.

"Huh?"

"That's how many human and Amicus couples were formed last year here in Russia. Seeing as how you have no interest in robots, I imagined you didn't know."

"I'll grant that a human could fall in love with an Amicus, but you machines can't love humans back."

"I wouldn't be so sure," Harold said, tilting his head in a somehow provocative manner. "It might be a bit different than what humans feel, but we're capable of love. We have all sorts of feelings, just like you do."

"No, those aren't feelings. They're just the product of an emotional engine, programming meant to make you understand people."

"If that's the premise you're going with," he said, ignoring her claims. "I'm not toying with Bigga. Being nice to her is just a necessity. I told you this is work, right?"

"Then explain it a little better."

"My apologies, but now isn't the time for that yet. However, I guarantee you I'll make proper use of her."

Apparently, he had some kind of scheme again and didn't have the slightest intention of telling her what it was. Pretty horrible treatment overall, given that he'd dragged her into this. And what's more, she didn't like how his methods were predicated on taking advantage of people's emotions.

Not that she was one to talk, though, given that she fried people's heads, to say nothing of their hearts.

"We should at least tell her you're an Amicus."

"No, please don't do that yet."

"What are you trying to do?"

"I'm trying to resolve this incident, of course."

She didn't believe him, and the whole act struck her as strange and illogical. Bigga was completely unrelated to this sensory crime, after all.

Echika grumpily carried a forkful of meat to her lips. Surprisingly enough, Harold didn't speak to her for a while. The only sound they could hear was the jolly Russian folk music pouring over them, and before long, Bigga came back.

They left the restaurant at eight PM after finishing their meal. The night air prickled against Echika's skin, prompting her to duck her head. Harold used his terminal to call a nearby taxi as he went ahead to look over the main road.

In the end, she'd wasted her entire day off. Feeling as if her head might pop from all the thoughts sloshing inside it, she fumbled for the electronic cigarette with numb fingers.

"Ms. Hieda."

Bigga, who stood next to her, suddenly called her name. Echika was a bit surprised; she assumed the girl would keep ignoring her like she had all evening. Moreover, she was so used to having other people direct negative emotions toward her that she'd almost forgotten Bigga was giving her the silent treatment.

"Ummm," she started, looking at Echika with pure, unsullied eyes, and licked her lips. "I've been meaning to ask you... You forcibly connected to Lee's Your Forma when she was unconscious, right?"

For a moment, Echika felt her heart skip a beat.

"What do you mean?" she asked.

"The doctor at the hospital told me he checked her Your Forma's connection history."

In other words, Bigga wasn't upset over the rude interrogation she'd gone through. Rather, she was outraged over what had happened to Lee.

"My apologies, but that was part of the investigation." Echika gave her standard answer. "We strive to Brain Dive with the recipient's consent, but in situations like that, where the person cannot give their approval, the law allows us to do it without permission."

"I know. But that's not what I mean."

Of course not. Echika knew it wasn't.

"It was absolutely necessary. I ask that you understand that."

"I get that, but I'm saying that what you did was still horrible. What if something happened to her?"

Bigga tensed up, like she was on the verge of tears.

"You...monster." She breathed out these spiteful words with a puff of breath.

Echika remained silent. She'd made the choices that she did while knowing full well something like this could happen.

"Why do you try to present yourself as a cold and unfeeling person?"
Ugh, just shut up already.

Before long, a taxi pulled up in front of Harold. Bigga wordlessly headed over to him, shook his hand, and got in the taxi. It sped away, its two taillights turning into a single glow as it gained distance. Echika put her electronic cigarette away. She didn't even have time to switch it on.

She took in a lungful of cold night air. That was enough to calm her down a little.

I'll just go home.

But as she set off, she heard another pair of footsteps behind her. Harold sidled up to her before she had time to turn around. Echika stashed her hands in her pockets, unwilling to look him in the face.

"Thank you for coming along today, Investigator. I'll walk you to your lodging house."

"No, thank you," she replied tersely. She wanted to be alone.

"Bigga will be staying in a hotel here in Saint Petersburg for a few days. Room 505 in the Moskovsky District's Rai Hotel."

"Fine. If we get any instructions about the information she leaked, I'll contact her there."

"Actually, I wanted to talk to you about something else."

"I'm sorry, but if it isn't urgent, do it tomorrow."

"Did Bigga say anything unpleasant to you? Please don't sulk about it."

Echika stopped in her tracks, which prompted Harold to halt as well. What Bigga had just told her wasn't unpleasant. It was a fact. What she'd said was just the natural thing to say.

"Stop studying your colleagues."

"I'm sorry. I was going to keep my mouth shut about it, but I needed some way to keep you here."

He remained completely calm, but Echika finally noticed something— Harold was angry. Well, she couldn't tell if he was actually annoyed, since his expression was no different from usual. But somehow, she got that feeling.

She felt her heart tighten up all of a sudden.

"Investigator."

"…What?"

"Don't assume that our emotions are nothing more than programming."

Harold dragged out those words forcefully, still grinning at her. Recalling their earlier exchange, Echika felt like something was constricting her throat; it seemed he was offended that she'd denied his emotions. And so she fell silent for a long moment.

"You're free to dislike Amicus if you wish, but I won't stand for these bigoted comments. I ask that you take back what you said."

"I will not," she snapped at him, almost reflexively. "I'm just stating the facts. Your generic AI thought processes aren't the same as the human brain. Even if you do insist that you have a heart, it's all just part of your programming."

"And can you say that the human heart isn't a product of programming, too? When you trace them back to their origin, human emotions are nothing more than electrical signals in your brain. How is that different from ours?"

"It's completely different. You're not like us. You're something else. You're…empty. Hollow."

With all her problems stacking together, Echika found herself becoming distraught. The words tumbled from her lips before she even knew it, dripping to her feet before the city's tumult and noise drowned them out. She understood that what she was saying were probably things that were better left unsaid.

"Is that really what you think?" Harold hissed, narrowing his eyes.

"Yes… It is."

"You're raising your right heel. Like you want to run."

He was right—she'd raised her heel without even noticing it. Echika glared at him, not wanting him to read any deeper into her. She didn't know why, but her legs felt like they might start shaking at any second.

Her father had loved Sumika over her because she was an Amicus skilled at slipping into people's hearts. And that's why all Amicus had to obey their programming. They had to be something different, something separate from humankind. Because if they weren't, if Sumika and Echika were equals—

Why would Dad love her and not love me?

"Is it fun…?" she asked, her cracking voice slipping between her trembling lips. "Is it amusing to look down on people like that?"

"You say that when you look down on Amicus yourself."

"And you say that after dragging me around all day without giving me a good reason."

"That was wrong of me. I apologize for that. But I know why you're acting so indignant."

"Give me a break. What would you know?"

"I know enough. You can't admit Amicus are equal to humankind, because if you do, you won't be able to explain why your father—"

A tram rushed past them noisily. Echika made to push Harold away, but she couldn't. He'd grabbed her extended arms and stopped her, like he'd anticipated she would do that.

Her back smoldered with heat.

Since when? How? I never said anything. Stop fooling with me.

She couldn't breathe. With her head hung, she saw the streetlights shine down on his shoes. Did he see through her? How much did he know, then? He didn't know everything, did he?

"This isn't funny."

"...Investigator?" Harold asked, his tone much more puzzled than it was a moment ago. "What's wrong?"

She wanted to give a stern answer, but her throat was too tight to utter anything back.

"You're shaking," he whispered, anxiously letting go of her arms.

Echika looked up. He wasn't smiling. Instead, his eyes were wide, like those of a child who'd just realized he'd made a mistake.

"Don't look at me," Echika said, feeling something warm run down her cheeks. She was disgusted with her own childishness. "I'm going home."

"Wait."

He tried to grab her shoulder, but she shook him off. She felt the urge to curse him out but knew she didn't have the right. They'd both gone too far, stepped into places they shouldn't have, and brushed up against each other. So no more.

"I'm sorry," Harold said, looking uncharacteristically unnerved. "I, um, I didn't think it would hurt you so much—"

"Don't say anything else," she said, hoping the words would come out calm but unable to suppress a shiver in her voice. "I take back what I said. I'm sorry; that was inappropriate of me. So never talk to me about this ever again. I don't know exactly how far you've seen through me, but just stay quiet."

"I'm sorry," he replied, biting his lower lip. "I just..."

But he couldn't finish that sentence and instead fell silent, as though he'd been snuffed out. Pedestrians passed them by, glancing at them from afar. Echika slowly rubbed her freezing cheeks a few times and let out a heavy sigh. Her anger finally had cooled down, and now she felt pathetic. All he'd done was bring up a touchy subject, and she'd gone and snapped like that.

This time, she walked off, attempting to escape his gaze. Harold remained still, like he was sewn in place.

A moment later, however, Echika stopped in her tracks. Her Your Forma notified her of a message from Chief Totoki. Given the time zone, this was probably an audio call, not a holo-call.

Thank goodness.

She didn't want anyone to see her right now, even if it was via a hologram. Echika sniffled once and tried to switch gears.

"Hello?"

"**I've got good news for you.**" Echika was somehow relieved to hear Totoki's dignified voice. "**We looked into Salk.**"

Salk. The image of the Russian-looking man she saw in the Rig City employees' Mnemosynes came to mind.

"**There were a few strange spots in his activity history, so we shared our data with the Criminal Investigation Department. You know what we found?**" Totoki paused for breath. "**Cliff Salk is an alias. This man is a criminal on the international wanted list.**"

"—Huh?"

"**I'll send you the details.**"

As Echika stood dumbfounded, Totoki transferred over the man's personal data, which appeared as a pop-up in her field of vision. She opened it, only to be greeted by Salk's mug shot. She scanned over the text written beside it.

Full name: Makar Marcovich Uritsky. Birthplace: Moscow. Profession: Freelance programmer... Currently wanted internationally for the production and sale of electronic drugs.

"**If he can make electronic drugs, cooking up a virus should be well within his abilities. And to top things off, he came in contact with all the index cases and quit Rig City two weeks before the sensory crimes began. But for some reason, he visited Rig City again just yesterday. It's almost like he knew we came to investigate.**" Totoki talked on and on, speaking with unusual speed. "**He's too fishy. In all likelihood, he's probably our mark.**"

Echika couldn't keep up with the situation yet. Yes, she had a bad feeling about Salk, but she'd also thought he was unrelated to the sensory crime. It was only a gut feeling, and now it turned out to be right?

"Share what I just told you with Aide Lucraft."

"Yes," Echika said, drying her tears. "Right away."

"Good-bye for now, then, Investigator Hieda. I'll see you in person tomorrow in Saint Petersburg."

Chapter 3
The Yoke
of Memories
and
Mnemosynes

Chapter 3
The Yoke of Memories and Mnemosynes

1

"Chief Totoki, do you think Salk...I mean, Uritsky is the culprit behind the sensory crime?"

"I wouldn't have flown in from Lyon if he wasn't."

A silent sense of tension hung over the Saint Petersburg branch office's meeting room. Chief Totoki stood in front of a flexible screen set on the wall, and seated before her were the branch head, members of the intelligence department, and investigators from the electronic-drug criminal investigation department. No one made an attempt to hide the grave expressions on their faces.

"We've discovered Uritsky's whereabouts," Chief Totoki announced, placing a marker on the city map displayed on the screen. "Slavy Avenue 45, apartment 32. According to the intelligence department's report, he moved into this apartment under his alias last month after resigning from Rig City. He'd been using this apartment as his base of operations to sell electronic drugs—"

Uritsky's true identity turned out to be an electronic-drug manufacturer with deep connections to the Russian mafia. For the last six months up until the month prior, he'd posed as Cliff Salk, a

Russian-American, to infiltrate Rig City. His motives weren't clear yet, but there was no doubt it was somehow related to electronic narcotics.

And luckily, or perhaps unluckily for him, Uritsky was currently in Saint Petersburg.

"We at the Interpol Intelligence Department have assigned a civilian cooperator to stay in contact with Uritsky already," one of the intelligence personnel said. "We've let him go free for now, since we were hoping to expose what route he uses to sell his drugs to the mafia, but..."

"Since the virus infections have been spreading worldwide, resolving the sensory crime takes precedence," Totoki said. "We have a warrant for Uritsky's arrest, so our top priority is taking custody of him."

"Where is he right now?"

"He's returned to his apartment this morning and hasn't left since."

"Then make preparations to bust in."

"Keep the surrounding area under police supervision."

The people involved hurriedly left the meeting room. It seemed the talks were over, and as an electronic investigator, Echika had nothing more to do until they brought him into custody. And so she got to her feet, but...

"Investigator Hieda." Harold looked up at her, still seated in his chair. "Shouldn't we check Uritsky's room before the police comb it for evidence?"

His suggestion was reasonable. No matter how convenient Brain Diving was, they couldn't do much if the culprit willingly wiped their own Mnemosynes. That meant examining the scene and getting a grasp of his personality was quite important.

"Understood. You should go get permission from Chief Totoki, just in case," Echika said while reaching for her coat, which sat draped on the back of her chair. "I'll wait for you at the entrance hall."

She parted ways with him and left the meeting room. As soon as she stepped into the corridor, she felt her shoulders sag powerlessly. Thank goodness. She could still converse with him normally.

Neither of them had touched on their argument from the night prior since the meeting that morning. Echika had decided to act like nothing had happened, so as to not interfere with work, and thankfully, Harold seemed to have the same idea.

And it'd be for the best if we could keep pretending nothing happened.

When she stepped out to the entrance hall, she found a familiar German man sitting on the sofa. Echika stared at him in silent surprise—it was her former partner, Benno Kleiman. She didn't imagine she'd see him here and hadn't been informed he'd even left the hospital.

Benno noticed her stare and regarded her with a blatantly fed-up expression.

"I'm not quite back to normal yet, thanks to a certain someone. But the chief dragged me here. Said that I should help if I'm good enough to sit at my desk."

"I...see," Echika replied, at a loss for words. "Ummm... Get well soon."

"Hey," Benno said, clicking his tongue. "Isn't there something else you should be saying?"

Yeah, I know.

Like her former partner had implied, this should have been where she apologized. But an apology wouldn't change the fact that she had hurt him. All it would achieve was giving her peace of mind.

"Oh yeah, I heard your new partner is an Amicus," he said, his lips contorted into a sarcastic sneer. "The chief told me about it. Go ahead—use that Amicus until it falls apart. That's the kind of partner that suits a machine like you."

"Echika, what was your role here? To be my machine, right?"

"Investigator Hieda."

Echika turned around to the voice calling out to her. It was Harold. He'd stepped into the entrance hall and approached her with a smile, waving the Niva's old-fashioned car key.

"Chief Totoki gave us permission. Let's go. This is our chance to witness the police break into a criminal's hideout."

"O-oh yeah..." Echika nodded, throwing a glance over at Benno.

He eyed Harold suspiciously, clearly sizing him up. Harold simply looked at the two of them, a bit confused, and cocked his head with a smile.

Thank god he didn't hear what Benno just said...

"Right, let's get going," Echika remarked, pulling herself together and stepping forward.

But then...

"Oh, you're Aide Kleiman, right?" Harold suddenly called out, causing her to stiffen up.

Amicus obviously didn't have the authority to view personal information. So how did he recognize Benno?

"Huh?" Benno seemed as perplexed by this as Echika was. "Who told you my name—?"

"Chief Totoki told me about you in the meeting room. It's an honor to meet you."

Harold jauntily approached him. The other man stood up reflexively, only for Harold to clasp his hand in a firm handshake. Benno looked absolutely astonished, and Echika didn't know what Harold was up to, either, of course.

What is he thinking?

"My apologies for not introducing myself sooner. I'm Aide Lucraft from the city police bureau. Of course, that's not my official title, but..."

"Don't touch me; we're not friends," Benno spat, pulling back his hand in clear disgust. "You're an Amicus, aren't you?"

"Yes, I'm Investigator Hieda's new partner," Harold said, sneaking a glance in her direction and smiling at Benno. "You had an argument with your fiancée last night, right? You promised to spend New Year's Eve together, but you had to fly over here to Saint Petersburg instead."

Wait, what? Echika felt her head spin a little.

"Huh?" Benno muttered, visibly confused. "What are you saying—?"

"She must have been very upset with you, but I'm sure you two will make up so long as you don't act stubborn. I wouldn't throw away the ring if I were you."

"What the hell? How do you know that? Were you watching us or something?"

"My eyesight is quite good, yes, but even I can't see all the way from Russia to France."

"Of course you can't. So who told you?"

"Nobody told me. We've never met before, and I only heard your name for the first time a few minutes ago."

"Right," Benno said, glaring fixedly at Harold. "So what...? You got something to say?"

Harold smirked, as if he'd been waiting for that question, then whispered. His voice was faint, but Echika could make it out.

"I know your secrets. So I have to ask that you never insult my partner again."

Hey, what the hell?!

"What were you thinking?"

Uritsky's apartment was in an old-fashioned, six-story apartment building reminiscent of a Russian *Khrushchyovka* complex. The parking lot was lined with police cars, and electronic drug investigators were filing into the building. Security Amicus stood guard, preventing the citizenry from walking by. The pedestrians exchanged anxious looks, and Echika and Harold could hear their murmuring from where they'd parked the Niva.

"I'm not sure what you mean," Harold replied quizzically, sitting calmly in the driver's seat. "I saw my partner being insulted. It's only natural for me to defend you."

"I never asked you to stand up for me," Echika said, gritting her teeth. "Benno has good reason to resent me, and I'm at fault here. You have no right to stick your neck into this."

"I wasn't aware. I'm sorry."

"No, you're not. Plus, Benno isn't engaged. He does have a girlfriend, though."

"Then he probably got engaged to her without you knowing it. There was an indentation on the ring finger of his left hand."

"Oh, really?" *How did he notice that in that split second? It's creepy.* "So what secrets does Benno have, then?"

"Everyone has something they don't want people to find out."

"So you basically threatened him with a bluff?"

Echika felt a headache coming on. It was clear Harold had only acted as recklessly as he did because of the previous day's argument. This might have been his way of making things up to her, but she would have preferred it if he just ignored the matter altogether and acted like it was water under the bridge.

"Listen, I can manage my own relationships with people, okay? Stay out of my business."

"Understood. But it did make you a little bit happy, right?"

"Is this your idea of a joke?"

Harold intentionally blinked. Not so much as a hint of regret. Echika opened the window and placed the electronic cigarette in her mouth in an attempt to shake off her gloomy mood.

"Never insult my partner again."

She unintentionally bit down on the cigarette. Even if his kindness was just a thin veneer, this was the first time someone else had ever stuck up for her.

So what? He's an Amicus. What he said was just part of his programming. And most importantly, I really did torment my aides. Benno is right.

It didn't take long for Uritsky to be apprehended, carried out, and forced into a police cruiser. Echika and Harold got out of their car and headed to the apartment as planned. Upon reaching the second floor, where Uritsky's room was, they found a security Amicus working for the police barring their way,

"I'm afraid you have to turn back. Once the chief investigator arrives, the room will be scanned by analysis ants," they told them.

"We have permission to go inside." Echika flashed her ID card, which was enough to convince the Amicus into silence.

According to the lease, Uritsky's dwelling was a typical two-room apartment. The pair made their way to the kitchen first and found it in quite a terrible state of disarray. The table was overrun with opened pouch containers, and the stained floor was littered with empty beer cans. The sink was covered in mold and full of unwashed dishes, soiled with rotten vegetable scraps.

It was terrible. The central heating was on, and the warmth of the room was likely hastening the garbage's decay. Their only solace was that the place wasn't infested with worms and insects yet.

"I always ask myself this when I see these kind of spaces, but what drives a person to live this way?"

"Some kind of talent, maybe. Or perhaps an unstable mental state."

"Do you think Uritsky did drugs himself?"

"Who's to say? Let's take a look around."

While Echika paused outside the door, Harold thoroughly examined the apartment. He opened the fridge and cupboards, read the labels on the empty beer cans, checked the stench rising from the sink, and felt the underside of the table. He picked up the decorative potted plants by the window, examining them before placing them back where they were. Amicus came in handy at times like these; they didn't leave any fingerprints.

"In all likelihood, he didn't use himself. But he was clearly under major stress," Harold remarked, wiping the dust from his fingers. "These beer cans all have the same date of production. In other words, he bought all these in bulk at the same time, and based on the smell, he hammered every one of them in a single day."

"Uritsky's personal data didn't mention alcoholism," Echika noted.

"Maybe something recently increased his stress," Harold said, looking around. "He still had a stock of fresh food in his fridge. And as you can imagine from how his kitchen looks, he's probably not the cooking type. Uritsky is registered as a bachelor, but do you think he has a partner?"

"The intelligence department isn't aware of any significant others. He does seem to pay for sex workers, though…"

"And I doubt he'd call them over to make meals for him," Harold said pensively. It didn't look like he was hurrying to draw a conclusion. "Let's check his bedroom."

The bedroom was as cluttered and dirty as his kitchen. A wrinkled blanket had been thrown over his bed, and both his desk and the floor were littered with discarded clothes and assorted trash. A scratched-up armoire stood against the wall, and cloth curtains covered the window.

But most striking of all were the countless cards hanging down from the ceiling, every one of them full of data matrices. It almost looked like some kind of pagan altar.

"Using electronic drugs as interior design. That's a novel idea," Harold mused, touching the cards dangling down from above. "Investigator, be careful not to look directly at them. The Your Forma might end up actually reading them."

"Don't worry—I'm too short to do that."

Electronic drugs were a type of noninfectious computer virus that was sold via data matrices like these. When the user read the codes, their Your Forma would contract the virus, producing a sense of euphoria and release. The virus deleted itself after a certain period of time, forcing addicts to repeatedly pay their dealers for more. The very production of electronic drugs was illegal in most countries.

"But if Uritsky really is the culprit, the question is when and how he infected the index cases with it. I know from Lee's Mnemosynes that he didn't use electronic narcotics to do it."

"There were no signs of anything suspicious in the study tours, either. And even if we account for the virus's incubation period, it's not likely they were infected during the tour itself. This implies he transferred the disease without anyone noticing, not even the index cases themselves."

"If he had a way of doing that, he'd have to illegally access the index cases' Your Forma, but there were no traces of tampering in any of them. What kind of magic did he pull to do it?"

"Any magic has a trick behind it. And thankfully, we can peer directly into his mind to find out."

"But what if Uritsky tweaked or wiped his own Mnemosynes?"

"Then this Pandora's box might come in handy," Harold said, opening one of the desk's drawers and pulling a laptop out of it. "He probably used this to write the virus, so it's highly probable his method of sending it to his victims is on here, too."

"Is it really going to go that smoothly? Well, if all else fails, there are other ways to force him to confess…"

But suddenly, the sound of something being kicked shook the room. *What?!*

Echika whipped around in surprise, only to finds the doors of the armoire swinging open to reveal a silhouette stepping out of it. It was a young woman wearing a thin one-piece dress. Her pale face was

contorted into a ghastly expression, and she had a sheath knife gripped in her slender hands.

"Get out, you…!"

Echika didn't even have a chance to confirm her personal data. The woman rushed her, and Echika's hands reflexively leaped to the pistol holstered on her leg.

No good. I won't make it—

"Investigator Hieda!"

Suddenly, someone pushed her from the side, making her stumble and fall down to the floor. A thick cloud of dust blew up into the air, causing her to break into a coughing fit. When she looked up a moment later, she choked up again for a different reason.

Harold had blocked the woman's charge with his body.

He grabbed her by the shoulders and carefully tried to pry the knife from her. But the woman was in a state of panic and struggled against his grasp. She pushed Harold away, only to stagger back and bang her head against the wall with a loud, nasty *thud*. Then she crumpled limply to the floor.

For an instant, silence settled over the room.

That was dangerous. I wasn't expecting there to be someone hiding in the closet. The police did a poor job of inspecting the place—

Her thoughts were so jumbled, she couldn't think straight.

No. That doesn't matter. Reflect on that later.

"Are you all right, Investigator?"

Harold stood there, collected, with the *sheath knife sinking into his abdomen.* Evidently, he'd gotten stabbed when he caught the woman a moment ago. Amicus couldn't attack humans, even if one was threatening them with a weapon.

Noticing Echika's eyes fixed on his abdomen, he gave an "oh" and touched the grip.

"Better not pull it out yet. If my circulatory fluid gushes out and dirties the room, the investigator in charge might get mad."

"No." That wasn't the problem here. "Why…did you cover for me?"

"We can be repaired as many times as it takes."

"Stop joking about that!"

"Don't worry—it's a shallow cut, and the leak is slow. Plus, I turned off my pain receptors, so it doesn't bother me at all. Forget about me. What's her personal data?"

This doesn't make sense. Is he crazy or something? He makes a fuss about Amicus having emotions, but when he gets stabbed, he acts like it's nothing. He's contradicting himself!

Though bewildered, Echika did as Harold asked and looked at the woman's face. All she saw was ordinary, nonincriminating data.

"Her profession is unlisted. She might be a sex worker Uritsky hired."

"Yes. And it looks like she had trouble with her employer," Harold said, peering into the closet. "She has shoes and clothes hidden in here. Uritsky probably let her hide in his apartment."

"Anyway," Echika said, still out of sorts, "I'll call an ambulance for her and a taxi for you, so you contact the repair shop. Get yourself fixed. Now."

"Don't worry about me—I can wait until after the investigation is over."

"Don't be stupid," Echika said hurriedly. *What kind of nerves does he have?! He has a knife stabbing into his stomach!* "I can't Brain Dive with you like this. Go get yourself fixed."

"It's fine—it won't get in the way. Still," he said, zipping up his coat to hide the knife, "I should probably keep this hidden from sight until Uritsky's questioning is over. Wouldn't want other people who are as overprotective as you to make comments, right?"

"No, not right. And I am not overprotective."

"Please," Harold said, his hand touching her arm gently. "Same as how you can manage your own relationships by yourself, I can tell how my body is doing at any given time. This isn't a problem at all."

"That's a stupid comparison. Stop being such a workaholic."

"Weren't you going to call an ambulance? I'll go report the situation to the Amicus outside."

She couldn't say anything else. Harold rushed outside, leaving Echika rooted in place. She didn't know how sturdy an Amicus's body was, but he was probably fine if he insisted this much. Although she couldn't say for sure, she had to assume that.

Besides, she was too proud to mess up and worry about an Amicus…
No. She wasn't worried about him to begin with. She was just a little
surprised, was all.

Harold had protected Echika despite the fact that she hated Amicus.
And even if he only did it because his program compelled him to, she
still felt something bitter surge up from the pit of her stomach.

Anyway, she had to call an ambulance. She had to prioritize humans
over the Amicus.

Right?

2

"I don't know much. I was caught up in your mess, that's all."

Benno sat opposite Uritsky, the interrogation room's cold table
between them. Uritsky threw his cuffed hands over the table; he'd
been glaring at Benno the whole time.

"How about you think back on the crimes you committed before
you talk?" Benno pressed him. "Production and selling of electronic
drugs, false personation, theft of company secrets, dealings with the
mafia… Even the most innocent child in the world wouldn't believe a
thing you say."

"I was dragged into this and threatened," Uritsky repeated himself.
"You'll find a laptop in my desk. Look through it, and you'll understand. I didn't do anything—"

"The tech support team's already on it," Benno said bluntly. "But its
security is tight, and they can't crack it. Assuming you want to tell us
how to get through it?"

"I don't know how to open it, either."

"Look, if you come clean here, we'll lighten your charges for abduct-
ing that escort."

"Huh…?" Uritsky muttered, his face going pale. "Shit, I told her to
stay hidden…"

"She attacked one of our operatives in a frenzy. She's in the hospital
right now, and we detected she was under the influence of electronic
drugs. Why did you abduct her?"

"I didn't kidnap her. Manya came to me for help…"

"Fine. Then why did you visit Rig City yesterday? You resigned just recently."

"I don't know what you're suspecting me of, but I was called in over a project I was in charge of."

Watching their exchange through a one-way mirror, Echika rubbed her neck. Uritsky was denying any connection to the sensory crime and was attempting to dodge all the questions with a curt attitude. She honestly couldn't tell if he was the culprit or not.

"What do we do, Chief? Do we check the laptop, like he said?"

"It looks like it'll take too long," Totoki, standing next to her, replied before exhaling through her nose. "They stated they tried plugging an SSD into it, but the files are all encrypted. They can't bust their protection, and even when they try to decode it, it's like a puzzle. In the end, they'll have to brute-force his password."

Wait, what?

"Is that some data protection Uritsky built?" Echika asked.

"Yes, to protect against cryptanalysis AI. So there's no way he doesn't know how to get through it. He's just messing with us and enjoying watching us squirm."

"I wouldn't jump to conclusions." Harold, who had remained silent so far, cut into their exchange. "He doesn't look like he's lying to me."

Harold seemed to be the same as usual. He was still in his coat, and his arms were folded politely, so no one had noticed he currently had a knife gouged into his stomach. Meaning Echika's concern had proved to be unfounded. Not that she was worried, of course—she just wasn't sure if he could handle Brain Diving in this situation.

He was an Amicus, after all, so he could just have his parts exchanged, and he'd be good as new.

There's no reason to worry about him, she whispered in her heart.

"Well, he looks like he's lying through his teeth to me," Totoki said, then suddenly looked up, indicating that her Your Forma had received a message. "Good timing—we just got the Brain Diving warrant. Hieda, jack into Uritsky."

Echika nodded. The question of which of them was right would be settled when she Dived into his Mnemosynes. Assuming, of course, Uritsky hadn't wiped his Mnemosynes like she mentioned.

"Let's go, Aide Lucraft."

Echika and Harold walked into the interrogation room. Benno picked up on the situation at once and walked outside, passing them by. Uritsky gazed at them almost fearfully.

"Wait, are you…?"

"We have a warrant," Echika told him. "We'll be investigating your Your Forma. Get up."

Uritsky gritted his teeth bitterly but reluctantly complied. Harold quickly held him by the arm and pulled him to a simple bed in the corner of the interrogation room. He forced Uritsky to lay facedown, and Echika wordlessly injected him with a sedative.

After confirming that Uritsky had gone limp, she jacked the cord into him and set up a triangle connection.

"Aide Lucraft, is everything all right?"

"I'm fine… What is it?"

"Huh?" Echika said, realizing with a start that she'd been leaning in and peering into his face without meaning to. "Ummm, nothing."

"I don't mind you always being this close."

"…Stop fooling around."

Harold looked absolutely fine. Echika wasn't sure how much she could believe what he said earlier, but she couldn't very well mention the knife and check his condition. Not with Totoki and Benno on the other side of the one-way mirror.

I just have to go for it.

And besides, on the off chance something went wrong and Harold's brain ended up frying, she shouldn't really care. It would just be the same as always—

Why do I even need to tell myself this? This is stupid.

She took a deep breath. The air felt as heavy as lead as it filled her lungs.

Focus. Think of Brain Diving and nothing else.

"Let's begin."

The moment she said this, she began plummeting once again into the familiar cyber world. She sank into his surface Mnemosynes.

A scene of that morning. He walked up the steps to his dim apartment, only to be greeted by that escort. She felt his burning fixation with this woman. The two weren't business partners; they were lovers.

No. Not this. Focus on the sensory crime. Figure out how he infected the index cases. Look at his Mnemosynes from his visit to Rig City yesterday.

"*No! I won't hand it over!*"

A clear bellow cut into her thoughts. This wasn't Uritsky. It was Echika's own voice—that of her younger self. This was a countercurrent.

Not again. I touched on the wrong area. I have to get back...

Before she knew it, she'd returned to *that day.*

"*Echika.*" Her father looked down on her with cold eyes. "*The project is canceled. Everyone else got sick.*"

"*I don't understand. What do you mean, 'sick'? I feel fine!*"

"*Tell her good-bye, Echika.*"

Her father's large hand grabbed her by the shoulder. Even if she tried to shake him off, she wouldn't be able to run. His fingers touched on the nape of her neck. It was scary. It felt bad. *Stop it. Stop!*

"*Don't kill her,*" Echika moaned, tears overflowing from her eyes and running down her cheeks. "*Please don't kill her!*"

Calm down. This is just a remnant of the past. This isn't what you should be looking at.

Her father's image faded away.

That's right. Good. Go back to Uritsky.

But no matter how much she tried, the recollection sucked her in. She tried going the other way.

"*What are you doing there, Echika?*"

Her sister looked at her with concern. Echika was in the midst of rummaging through her father's desk until finally, she found what she was looking for. A pretty, half-transparent HSB memory stick, one of many her father owned. It was about the size of her thumb. She held it up against the window, and the moonlight filtering into the room made it sparkle like a frost crystal.

Surely, he wouldn't notice if she took one, right?

"*You and me will always be together, Big Sis!*"

Hearing this, her sister said—

—What did she say again?

"Echika, listen carefully. There's..."

But her voice trailed off without warning. The light returned to Echika's eyes in a sudden flash, and her body was yanked back to the interrogation room, as if it finally remembered it couldn't resist the pull of gravity.

Echika's hands reflexively jumped to her neck. The Lifeline was unplugged, her thoughts were sluggish, and she could still hear her father's and sister's voices ringing in her head.

The Lifeline got pulled out? Not the Brain Diving cord?

She realized that she hadn't been *pulled up normally* just now. That realization lifted the haze from her mind at once. And as her field of vision cleared up, she saw it.

Harold slowly crumpling to the ground.

No way.

His body mercilessly toppled against the hard floor like a discarded doll. He lay limp and still, like an inanimate object.

No... An Amicus *was* an inanimate object. She knew this. But a burning chill ran down her spine nevertheless. Echika reflexively hurried over to him. His eyes were faintly open, but he wasn't breathing. Of course, Amicus only breathed to keep up appearances. She unzipped his coat, revealing the knife plunged into his gut. On his sweater was a black, wet stain, the color of his circulatory fluid, which functioned like blood.

You call this a shallow cut, you dirty liar?! Why did you have to be so reckless? And why was I stupid enough to believe you?

She could hear someone open the door to the interrogation room. It was either Totoki or Benno, or maybe both. She heard shouting but couldn't make out what they were saying. Everything was hazy. Harold's cheeks were as white as porcelain.

"Aide Lucraft...," she whispered, her voice sounding distant even to her own ears. "Hang on..."

Echika kneeled down and shook him, but he didn't react. Her mouth felt dry. What made him collapse like this? Was it her? The knife? If it was the latter, then everything was still all right. They could fix his body as many times as needed. But if she ended up frying his fragile brain—

No, that didn't matter to her. Right. This never mattered to her before now, and it shouldn't start.

This doesn't matter.

"Wake up, Aide Lucraft."

This shouldn't matter.

"Hey, Aide Lucraft… Harold!"

Tell me it doesn't matter!

"—Hieda!"

That call made Echika snap to. Totoki stood over her, glaring. Benno was there, too, staring at Harold with a speechless expression. Echika forced herself to take a breath—or was she just holding her breath all along? She couldn't tell.

"Why didn't you report this sooner?! If anything happens to him, it could be irreversible!"

"I'm sorry." Her lips almost reflexively mouthed an apology. "I'm so sorry. I—"

"Are you joking?" Benno whispered. "He was moving around with a knife in his gut?"

"Carry him to the repair shop, fast! Help me carry him, Benno. Pick up his legs—hurry!"

Totoki picked up Harold's upper half, but Benno was too slow to move. He couldn't understand why Totoki was so stressed over a mere Amicus, but Echika knew why. Harold was special, irreplaceable. Both in terms of his performance as a unit and his talents as a police investigator.

And yet he was one of the Amicus she loathed. So there shouldn't have been any reason for this to agitate her so much.

And yet she couldn't sit still. She got to her feet and helped pick Harold up. Her hands wouldn't stop shaking. She felt so stupid. All the emotions she always kept locked away surged and seeped out.

It's all my fault. If only I'd noticed Harold was pushing himself, I could have insisted and asked him to stop and get repaired.

I don't want to see this anymore. I don't want to watch my partners collapse anymore.

But why now? Why are you thinking this now?

No, she'd just kept it bottled up the whole time. She'd pretended not to feel anything so she wouldn't have to consider this.

"Never insult my partner again."

She had to admit it. Some irresponsible, suppressed part of her heart had been happy to hear him say it. It was terrible of her to feel that way, selfish even. She'd hurt so many of her aides in the past, after all.

But even if it was out of nothing more than programmed kindness, that was the first time someone had ever talked about her that way.

Loneliness didn't bother her? Being alone was easier?

Filthy lies. I was starved for affection all along.

3

By the time they left the repair shop, it was already late at night. The Niva slid across Saint Petersburg's streets. It was New Year's Eve, and the city was bustling with noise. People merrily walked the streets, casting their shadows over the pavement.

As they passed through the entrance to Trinity Bridge, they saw people carrying champagne, excitedly waiting for the date to change.

"Once the New Year begins, they'll pop the corks into the Neva River."

Echika glanced at the passenger seat, where Harold sat, gazing outside with a smile, his arm leaned against the window frame. He was currently dressed in a thin turtleneck shirt, like a newly produced Amicus. The sweater and coat had been soiled with circulatory liquid and needed to be thrown away.

Put simply, Harold's mind was unharmed.

The mechanic in charge of his repairs—who couldn't mask their confusion at his specifications, which were too different from that of a standard-issue model—said that Harold went unconscious because the Brain Diving temporarily put too high of a strain on him.

His system was operating on minimal settings to conserve circulatory liquid due to the leak, which limited the number of circuits he could use. This led to a drop in performance, which resulted in him overloading when he tried to Brain Dive and entering a dysfunctional state.

"How about we buy some champagne and partake in the local customs, too?" Harold suggested merrily.

"Don't, not even as a joke."

"Investigator, we're in Russia, and you're nineteen years old. No one is going to arrest you for having a drink."

"That's not what I mean," Echika snapped, glaring at him. "You're supposed to rest and do nothing else for a while. Understood?"

"I'm fine already. You have nothing to worry about."

"No, that won't fly. Stay put until your second operation."

In reality, Harold wasn't fully repaired yet. The cables in his body were different from those used in mass-produced Amicus models. Since they would need to special order the right ones from Novae Robotics Inc.'s headquarters in London, the mechanic had to make do with temporary repairs for today. Thankfully, it wouldn't take long to get those new cables.

"You better do as you're told unless you want the chief to have your head on a pike. She called me twice while you were being repaired, you know."

"And both times were to give you a status report on the investigation, yes?"

"That was part of it. She said she had another electronic investigator from the branch Dive into Uritsky instead of us. But she was definitely worried about you, too."

"It must be because we both love cats," Harold said jokingly, but his smile soon grew thinner. "I'm sorry. I troubled you a great deal... I didn't want my carelessness to delay the investigation. But I ended up doing just that instead..."

Echika said nothing, gripping the steering wheel with her numb, frozen hands. It was her fault that Harold had ended up like this. If she'd just thought things through a little longer, she would have realized she had to report his condition to Totoki at once. But she'd trusted his calm demeanor.

Worse still, she'd made the situation go further off the rails. She'd let her petty pride convince her she shouldn't worry about an Amicus... even though he'd only gotten injured because he'd protected her from an attack.

Had Harold taken irreparable damage from this, nothing she could do would ever set it right.

She'd realized the truth since the moment he saw right through her on the way back from the restaurant. Insisting that she hated Amicus was just her way of preserving her petty pride. A way to rationalize— to dull the pain of the lasting scar her father had inflicted on her heart.

At some point, she realized—realized that Sumika was never to blame.

"You must be cold," Harold said, turning on the heat. "Don't mind me and switch it on."

"Oh... I forgot to do that."

"You're a poor liar, Investigator."

"I'm not lying." She absolutely was. "I really just forgot."

It wasn't long before they reached the Moskovsky District, and the Niva pulled up in front of a building dyed in pale colors, befitting a Japanese apartment complex. This was where Harold lived. She thought he was just an Amicus provided by the police department. She'd only learned he had a family a few minutes ago, right before they left the repair shop. Since Echika had largely avoided going into his private matters, she'd previously been ignorant of that.

It was something of a surprise. A shock, even. At some point, without even being conscious of it, she assumed Harold was all alone. Just like her.

Harold got off the car with awkward steps. Having the wrong type of cables running inside him seemed to have lowered his body's conductivity and impacted his right leg's mobility in particular. Echika lent him a shoulder, despite his reluctance to take it, and escorted him to his apartment.

Looking up at the building, she saw countless windows were lit up joyfully. Why did gazing at those warm lights make her feel like her heart was freezing over? But the outer wall's advertisements came to life, drowning out that sentimental scene. When she read the data matrix, a browser window opened automatically.

Ugh, now's not the time.

She slipped through the entrance and got into the elevator, where they were enveloped by unpleasant silence. Harold's arm felt heavy as it leaned against her shoulder.

"Investigator," his voice rasped into her ear. "You don't need to feel guilty over what happened to me."

"I'm not," she immediately fibbed; she absolutely was blaming herself for it. "Chief Totoki asked me to take care of you, so I am."

"Could you at least be honest with me when I'm injured?"

"......" Echika bit the inside of her lips. She didn't have the first idea of what to say. "...I *am* a little concerned."

She felt like that made Harold smile a bit, but she couldn't bring herself to look him in the eye.

His apartment was room number sixty-eight, located on the fifth floor. Echika pressed on the doorbell and waited restlessly, her toes curling inside her boots...

Out of nowhere, the browser window she'd just closed flashed in her mind's eye, and something clicked into place.

But then as if to pull her out of her thoughts, the double doors of the entrance swung open, and out stepped a cute, slender woman. She had fair facial features and bright eyes, which were now wide open. Her hair was wavy, and she wore a choker—a stylish fashion choice many women used to hide the connection port in their necks.

<Daria Romanovna Tchernova, 35 years old. Profession: Web designer>

"Oh, Harold. The branch called me earlier. Welcome home...!"

She immediately spread out her arms and embraced him. Echika pulled away from them in a hurry.

"Are the repairs finished? Are you all right?"

"I've only been temporarily sent home, but I'm fine," Harold said, hugging her back like it came naturally to him. "I'm sorry I made you worry."

What is this? Echika couldn't contain her amazement. They looked a little too intimate. They didn't appear to be Amicus and owner but rather...

"Really, you're so reckless. Put yourself in my shoes for once."

"Don't worry—I'll always come back home. I always do, right?"

As Daria released him, Harold gazed at her with a smile gentler than

Echika had ever seen him show before. She couldn't stand to be there a second longer.

"Well then, Aide Lucraft, I'll be going the—"

"Oh, wait." Daria stopped her. "Please come on in. I should thank you for your help."

"No, thank you. I really should be off."

"Oh, please don't be shy."

Echika was no good with this kind of communication and didn't want to stay here any longer. Besides, she'd only worsened Harold's situation and didn't deserve to be thanked. So she was going to insist on leaving, but—

"Investigator, could you humor her? Just give us a bit of your time."

—Harold had to butt in with that. Echika wanted nothing more than to politely refuse and leave, but rejecting the offer so stubbornly would look awkward. Echika had no choice but to comply.

She crossed the doorstep, only to be greeted by a soft aromatic scent filling the room. It was a warm, pleasant smell, typical of a northern city home, and it alleviated the outside chill.

"Take off your shoes here," Daria said, pointing at the floor. "Harold, you go and rest, okay? I'll keep her company."

"Daria, I'm not human. I can do without resting."

"Listen to me for once in your life," she said, pushing his back. "Now shoo, over there."

The two of them vanished deeper into the apartment, leaving Echika alone to take off her shoes and put up her coat on the hanger. Her glance breezed past a mirror hanging on the wall, and she found herself brushing her hair with her fingers.

What are you doing? This is dumb.

Everything was developing so suddenly that it must have been stressing her out. She took a deep breath, but that just filled her lungs with the pleasant smell of the room, making it even harder to relax. Her idea of a home was much more formal, much more…cold and artificial.

Daria soon returned and led her to the kitchen. It wasn't very large, but it was neat and tidy, and every magnet on the fridge looked like a small treasure. There was a sticker of a deciduous tree on the wall, scattering its green leaves. Daria had Echika take a seat at the dining table and served her tea and strawberry *varenye*.

"I'm sorry this is all I can serve on New Year's Eve. I haven't had time to cook recently…," she apologized, sitting opposite Echika. "I'm sorry if Harold's caused you trouble."

"Oh, no, if anything, I've been troubling him." When you really thought about it, he'd gotten hurt because of Echika this time. "Pardon me, but I'll be leaving soon."

"Don't worry. I'm the one who asked you to stay, um—"

"Echika Hieda," Echika said, remembering that she had to introduce herself to civilians. "I'm sorry it took me this long to tell you who I am."

"Don't let it bother you. It happens a lot to people working with the police."

She wasn't used to interacting with people outside work. Echika awkwardly pulled the cup closer, which made Daria smile. This made the lovely dimples on her cheeks more conspicuous.

"Harold told me about you, Ms. Hieda. He said you're an interesting, adorable person."

"Ah-ha-ha," Echika replied with dry laughter. Daria might not have realized, but Harold's description of her was no doubt made in jest.

"He told you not to say anything about the knife, didn't he? Harold does some terribly silly things from time to time. He's just too devoted to work…"

Daria's facial expressions were lively and animated, and she could evidently talk to someone she'd met for the first time with ease. That struck Echika as a talent of sorts. If nothing else, you couldn't be this amicable with other people unless you could naturally love and be loved in return. It made Echika terribly jealous of her.

"Thanks to your help, he got away fine this time, but he could have lost his life. I was scared for a second there," Daria said.

"Yes. I'll warn him never to do that again. He can't break his wife's heart like this, after all…," Echika replied.

At those words, the other woman widened her eyes in surprise. And much to Echika's bewilderment, the next moment, Daria's expression crumpled, and she laughed out loud.

"We're not a couple. He's like a little brother I dote on. Besides, I'm already married to someone else."

Drat. Echika immediately regretted her statement.

Harold had mentioned how Amicus-human couples were becoming more widespread, and he was so affectionate with Daria that she'd made an assumption about them.

"Sorry," Echika said, feeling awfully ashamed of herself. "I, um, I didn't mean to insult you—"

"Don't worry." Daria didn't seem to take offense to that. "My husband brought Harold over. I think it was three years ago? One day, he just picked him up and brought him home."

"...Picked him up?" Echika asked, her hand freezing as she touched her cup.

"Yes. My husband was a detective for the city police and met him in the middle of an investigation. We didn't have an Amicus, so things just clicked."

No way.

"Are you saying Harold was a vagrant?" Echika asked, taken aback.

"That's right. He doesn't look it, does he? He's got such a hand-some model, after all. I think it's called the RF Model? Apparently, they're a special model of Amicus that was given to the British royal family."

"The British royal family?!" Echika parroted her. All these sudden revelations were too much. "You're joking."

"I felt the same way." Daria chuckled. *But that can't be, right?* "At first, I couldn't believe it, but then I looked into news articles at the time and saw that it was true. He was presented to the queen of England to celebrate the sixtieth anniversary of her ascension to the throne. Apparently, Harold was part of a set of triplets, so there are two other Amicus who share his make."

She's talking about Steve.

In other words, the place where Harold and Steve used to work together was the British royal palace. Echika couldn't believe it; the sheer shock of it made her stare at Daria in dumbfounded silence. True, it was clear at a glance that both Harold and Steve had been very expensive Amicus models to create, but…gifts to the royal family? Really? Did Totoki know about this?

"Apparently, the RF Models are smarter than ordinary Amicus. They had… What was it called again? Next-generation all-purpose artificial intelligence? It's said they were experimental models that had a lot of money sunk into them… Don't you think Harold acts a bit more human than most Amicus? He has more of a defined personality."

"Yes, hmm, I'd say he acts more than just a bit human…"

"That's all thanks to this cutting-edge technology, supposedly. Very impressive, if you ask me."

The fact that Harold and Steve had the same model but were polar opposites in terms of nature was because of this next-generation all-purpose artificial intelligence… Daria seemed to believe this explanation, but something still felt off to Echika. She didn't know all that much about Amicus, but even if "cutting-edge" technology was involved, was making an Amicus who was so close to a human really within the scope of what existing AI tech was capable of?

"You know how Her Majesty the Queen passed away a few years ago? Based on what Harold told me, the RF Models were donated to charity organizations, as per Her Majesty's will. But as you might imagine, they're very expensive…" Daria trailed off and brought her cup to her lips. "He was, well, stolen. By bad people, then auctioned off on the black market… After that, he went through quite a lot and ended up wandering the streets of Saint Petersburg all alone."

Echika didn't know what expression she ought to make. She thought back to what Steve had told her in Rig City. About how he'd suffered at the hands of people as they sold him off time and again. And Harold had gone through a similarly terrible phase in his life, too. Except…

"Should I really be hearing about this?" Echika asked. "I mean, we're talking about…"

"Yes, this isn't something we can make noise about. Especially not the matter of the royal family. Bad people might go after him again… But you're his partner." Daria smiled at her. "I wonder why he never told you."

"Well…I think we were just so busy with the investigation that we didn't have the chance to talk about ourselves much."

Echika knew the truth. It was because she rejected the idea of delving any deeper into their personal lives. And so even when he seemed friendly and inviting, he had drawn a line.

She brought the tea to her lips, but its gentle flavor only made her heart throb in regret.

"Speaking of, did your husband also move to our branch? Or is he still with the city police?" Echika asked as she put down the teacup, hoping to change the subject.

But she soon regretted bringing that matter up because she saw Daria's smile stiffen.

"My husband…passed away a year and a half ago," she revealed, her pink lips just barely curled up. "He was killed during the Amicus sympathizer serial murder case."

On her way out, Echika stopped by Harold's bedroom. It came as little surprise after all she'd seen and heard, but the fact that Daria gave him his own room meant she was quite the Amicus sympathizer herself.

"Aide Lucraft, it's me," Echika said as she knocked on the half-open door.

"Investigator? Please come in."

Echika pushed the door open. The room was quite chic, with a predominantly navy and dark-brown color scheme. The walls were covered with niche shelves lined with thoroughly worn paper books, decorative plants, and even a miniature model of the Niva. The desk sitting by the window was neatly arranged and had an analog picture frame sitting on it. The picture in it was of Daria and a Russian man, wearing the same sweater as Harold.

I see.

So the Niva and his clothes had all been handed down to him from Daria's deceased husband. This wasn't originally his room, either.

Despite herself, Echika felt something bitter surge up from the pit of her stomach.

"What's Daria doing?" Harold asked as he changed out of the shirt he'd been given in the repair shop and sat on his bed.

At least lie down, Echika grumbled internally. Not that it mattered, since Amicus could enter sleep mode in any posture, even when standing upright.

"She's in a holo-call with a friend. Looks like they're asking her to join them for a countdown party. Why don't you get in bed, so you don't worry her for nothing?"

"I've already said this, but I'm fine now. I'm letting you know that I'll be coming to work tomorrow."

"If I were you, I'd enjoy my time off until the new parts arrive," Echika countered, utterly fed up with him.

"And do what, laze around in bed until noon? What are you, a cat that's scared of the cold?"

"Hey, zip it. Listen, this is an order from the chief. Just rest for a while—"

"Don't you have something you want to talk to me about?" he cut her off.

Echika clenched her jaw. He was right. She'd come here to discuss work, but until he pointed it out, all she could think about was what Daria had told her earlier about his past. And about her dead husband.

The fact that he could see right through her made an awkward something skitter down her spine.

"Investigator?" Harold asked, narrowing his eyes. "Did Daria tell you about me?"

"No," Echika denied at once. "I don't—"

"You don't have to hide it. If anything, I'm glad she told you. It's not fair that only I know your secrets."

Echika held back the urge to sigh. Why couldn't she, for the life of her, keep a secret from this bloody Amicus?

Based on what Daria had told her, Harold greatly admired and loved her husband, Sazon. He was a detective graced with sharp investigation skills, and he was the one who had nurtured Harold's own talents for deduction.

A year and a half ago, Sazon had been in charge of the Saint Petersburg police department's investigation on the Amicus sympathizer serial murder case. Echika could faintly remember hearing about it. The cause for it wasn't clear, but at the time, there were many killings targeting Amicus sympathizers. The murders that took place in Saint Petersburg were especially ghastly, and their sadistic nature had earned the incident another name in the international community: *The Nightmare of Petersburg.*

Echika had read about it on the news as well. Of the four victims, three were civilians, and one was a detective in charge of the case. Sazon was abducted by the culprit and went missing. At the time, Harold worked as his partner and was part of the city police's robbery-homicide department.

Using the few clues left behind, he continued the investigation on his own and traced Sazon's whereabouts faster than any of his colleagues. But at the time, nobody acknowledged Harold's skills because he was an Amicus, and his warnings went unheeded. In the end, he had to charge the culprit's hideout on his own.

"He was inexperienced." Daria's voice replayed in Echika's mind. *"He thought he could resolve this all on his own."*

The culprit had held Sazon captive in the basement of an unoccupied house, and Harold was captured in the attempt to rescue him. The following day, the police charged the place by tracing Harold's positional information and discovered the Amicus, dazed and staring at a dismembered corpse—that was Sazon's eventual fate.

According to Harold's testimony, the culprit spent half the day torturing Sazon before hacking off his limbs and eventually his neck while he was alive. And since Sazon's Mnemosynes could serve as evidence, Harold eventually extracted the Your Forma from his head and made off with it.

Harold had been forced to watch it all happen before his eyes. It was burned into his memories. The culprit tied him to one of the basement's pillars and kept his head fixed in place so he wouldn't be able to look away. Using Harold's memory data, the police were also able to watch the gruesome scene unfold, which only served to unnerve them.

The culprit kept Harold alive for the purpose of striking terror into the hearts of those involved with the investigation.

Harold didn't take any visible damage, but he was sent to Novae Robotics Inc.'s headquarters for emergency maintenance. After all, he was captured and forced to watch a family member get slowly murdered by a deranged criminal, neither able to save them nor look away. Even if it was beyond his control, this was a breach of his Laws of Respect, and that could create a malfunction in his systems. Thankfully, he'd managed to retain his sanity.

But Daria was still anxious. It seemed to her that he'd kept something suppressed the whole time.

"I mean, throughout the entirety of his confinement, the criminal kept telling him, 'You're an Amicus, so even if I hack your master into bits, you won't feel anything. You don't have a heart. Everything about you is phony'... How could hearing that not faze him?"

Echika remembered what she once told him.

"You're not like us. You're something else. You're...empty. Hollow."

How much had she hurt him in the name of her petty pride?

"Hmm." She licked her lips, still feeling the bitterness of the tea on them. "How do I put it...? I said some pretty rude things to you last night..."

She hung her head and kept talking, while refusing to look at Harold.

"It's like you said. My father and I, we...didn't get along, and I blamed it on the Amicus. I needed to shift the blame onto something else, or I wouldn't last. I was a kid back then."

It was her first time opening up to someone like this; she never wanted people to know what was going on in her heart. But not revealing anything at this point would be cowardice.

"I understood the truth, somewhere deep down. The Amicus weren't at fault. Dad was... But I just couldn't figure out where I had to stop this facade. And to protect myself, I ended up hurting you."

And it wasn't just that. The truth was that on some level, she envied the Amicus. They could find their ways into people's hearts so smoothly and had the means to be accepted with ease. And she was jealous of that. Because no matter what she did, she couldn't get the one person she cared for the most to love her.

She hadn't wanted to admit she was a child unworthy of love. So she pinned all the blame on Sumika, believing that if she did, there would still be some chance her father loved her. But it was just blind conviction, and that chance was never there to begin with.

She was just too young. Too vulnerable.

"I'm sorry," she said.

Echika gently raised her head. His gaze was fixed on her, terribly silent, and so direct that it almost made her want to run away.

"The things you said were aggressions I couldn't ignore, but…," he muttered. "But even so, I should have been more careful with what I did. Let me apologize again."

I'm sorry I hurt you.

In place of any consolation, he simply said that. They'd really tried not to touch on each other's sore spots, and that indirect kindness felt oddly uncomfortable. A deep silence settled over them for a while.

"Investigator," Harold whispered gently. "If you don't mind, can we shake hands to reconcile?"

"Huh?" Echika uttered, confused.

"Whenever I argue with Daria, we shake hands to make up. So I'd appreciate it if we could do the same."

"No, I'm really not that—"

"Please."

Harold gently extended a hand toward her. Echika hesitated for a moment, but he didn't pull back, and eventually, she awkwardly grabbed his hand with hers. Harold's hand had the coolness typical of an Amicus and the smooth feel unique to artificial skin. She'd intended to pull back soon, but he wouldn't let go.

"Um, excuse me?"

"Oh, sorry." Harold came to a realization and let go. "It just felt particularly significant to me, since you didn't shake my hand the first time we met. Your hand is very small."

…Is it just me, or is he back to his old tricks surprisingly fast?

"You won't get anything for buttering me up."

"I'm aware." He beamed at her. "But you really have taken a shine to me, haven't you? You called for me quite desperately when I collapsed."

"Huh?" Echika stiffened reflexively. "H-how do you know that...?"

"An Amicus's hearing device keeps working so long as we haven't completely shut down. It's like when a human can still hear things while they're asleep."

So he... No...

He narrowed his clear eyes softly.

"I wish you'd always call me Harold, Echika."

Die. Actually, no, just kill me.

"What's wrong? Are you being shy?"

"Shut up, go to bed, and never wake up!"

"Never wake up? But how are you going to Brain Dive without my help?"

I take that back. Even if hating Amicus was me just shifting blame, I really do despise this guy.

As Echika suppressed the anger and shame bubbling inside her, she could hear Daria's voice start up again in her ears.

"He might not say anything, but that incident did change him. He throws himself into investigations so much more than he used to, and he keeps doing reckless things."

The Nightmare of Petersburg hadn't been resolved yet, and Daria told her that culprit was still at large. Harold had come in contact with the criminal, but they wore a mask at the time, so he didn't know what they looked like. The only clues were the culprit's gender, voice, height, and overall physique. The investigation had been all but discontinued over the last few months, reduced to merely questioning witnesses.

Daria surmised that Harold wanted to restart the investigation on Sazon's incident.

"But they couldn't let an Amicus handle an investigation on his own, could they? That was when the suggestion that he become your aide came in... The only one who knew about him being a RF Model was the chief of the robbery-homicide department, but the incident tipped the top brass of the police off about it, too. They assumed that since Harold was smarter than most Amicus, he could function as an investigator aide..."

There was a clear shadow over her eyes.

"He probably thinks...if he works as an aide for a successful investigator like you, he might find a clue about Sazon's killer. And he'll probably be as reckless as it takes to do that. It makes me so worried about him..."

"Aide Lucraft."

She could understand Harold's feelings, but making Daria worry after she'd already lost her husband would just be putting the cart before the horse.

"You have a family waiting for you to come home, and that's, ummm... I think that's something very precious. It's certainly not something you can take for granted."

If nothing else, he was different from her, who had no one waiting for her to come home.

"You really should take better care of yourself."

4

Harold furrowed his brow a bit, as if to say he wasn't sure how to interpret what she just said.

"What do you mean by that?" he asked.

".......If you don't understand, that's fine," Echika replied, biting the inside of her lip.

He was an Amicus, a machine that could be repaired time and again, so having a human express this kind of concern probably felt both one-sided and misguided to him. Yet she couldn't help but say that.

Echika then let out a small dry cough, trying to shake off her awkwardness. Right, for starters...

"I almost forgot to say it, but I actually came to your room to discuss the investigation."

"And you told me to go straight to bed despite that?" Harold blinked quizzically.

"Stop nitpicking."

"You're quite the workaholic."

"You're the last person I should be hearing that from," Echika countered, inhaling deeply. "Stop teasing me and listen."

He seemed to clue in to the fact that something was going on and immediately did away with his jocular attitude. "Understood."

They'd had to stop their Brain Diving of Uritsky halfway through, but if her conjecture was correct, their investigation would certainly progress.

"I think I figured out how the virus infects people," Echika said, gazing directly at Harold.

He stared at her with amazement but said nothing else, like he was waiting for her to append *just joking* at the end. But of course, this was no laughing matter.

"Aide, you said Uritsky sent the virus in some form no one, not even the index cases, could notice, and I said it wouldn't be possible without him illegally accessing their Your Forma. But I've realized that there's one other way he could have done that." Echika threw a glance at the window. "The holographic ads' data matrices."

Before entering this building, she'd accidentally read an advertisement's information matrix, which made a window pop up in her field of view. That's when it dawned on her. Closing those kinds of pop-up windows was an everyday occurrence for Your Forma users, to the point that you wouldn't even pay attention to it anymore.

So if the holo-ads were used to spread the virus, it stood to reason that even the index cases hadn't noticed.

"No, I think that conjecture doesn't make sense," Harold retorted quietly. "If the source of the infection was in the holo-ads' code and the browser, a record would remain on their Your Forma's browser history and Mnemosynes. And if that was a common point among the index cases, you'd have seen it when Brain Diving into them."

"Right, but what if he used the information matrix of an electronic drug? With narcotics, it just reads the code and doesn't open a window, so it doesn't leave a record in their browsing history."

"I see. Does the programming of electronic drugs masquerade as ordinary code?"

"Probably. And Rig City supplied the algorithm for the ads. Uritsky could have used the tour to steal data on their personal information and tweak the algorithm. And he coded the virus to trigger the infection only after he quit Rig City in order to cover his trail."

"And since Rig City are the ones regulating the algorithm anyway, they wouldn't see him manipulating it as unauthorized hacking. And thanks to that, it wouldn't leave any proof."

"And people scroll by holo-ads all day, so we overlooked it when we tapped into their Mnemosynes. It was hidden in plain sight, so we didn't even pay it any attention."

I should have considered that possibility sooner, Echika thought, her nails digging into her palm.

"If my assumption is correct, we should be able to find an ad that exists in all the index cases' Mnemosynes, and that would be the one that contained the virus," Echika said, annoyed. "But figuring out which one it was now... Ugh, we'll have to start over from scratch."

"What are you saying?" Harold asked, surprised.

"I mean, we'll need to Brain Dive into the index cases again and find the right ad—"

"Investigator," he cut her off, smiling in an exasperated sort of way. "Did you forget that I have perfect memory?"

Perfect memory.

Echika was stunned for a moment. Right, Amicus could *output their memory data* in flawless detail. It was right there in the palm of her hand, but she had totally forgotten. The only index case Harold came in contact with was Lee, meaning they couldn't compare his memory to other Mnemosynes to find one holo-ad everyone shared. But that wasn't necessary anyway; simply finding a data matrix that didn't open a window would be enough to back Echika's claim.

"I'll extract the memory data at once. Can you get a USB cable from the desk over there?"

Echika did as Harold told her and handed over the cable. He plugged one end of it into the wearable terminal on his wrist and plugged the other end into the port in his left ear. His terminal's holo-browser window popped up, displaying a still image composed of his memories. Unlike Mnemosynes, an Amicus's memory data was made up of second-by-second images. Echika leaned in to inspect the data he'd extracted from Lee's Mnemosynes, but—

"Investigator, you shouldn't look. If you read the virus by accident, you'll become infected."

He was right, but that left Echika with nothing to do until he was finished inspecting the images. It made her oddly anxious. He sifted through the holo-browser with an uncharacteristically intense gaze, and a minute later—

"I found it." Harold looked up. "It's the advertisement for Bluetooth-equipped sneakers. This is the only one that doesn't bring up a window when I tap on the data matrix."

Lee's Mnemosynes surfaced vividly in Echika's thoughts. Yes, in the world as seen through that girl's eyes, there had been an ad for high-tech sneakers alongside ones for new toe shoes. And she'd seen that ad in Ogier's Mnemosynes, too. She could recall the image of those sneakers bobbing up between countless other high-tech-gadget ads.

Her assumption proved correct.

"Process the virus's code segment and send it over to Chief Totoki right away. The electronic investigators who stayed behind in the branch should be useful right about now—"

But the ringing of the doorbell rudely interrupted her. She exchanged glances with Harold; even on New Year's Eve, it wouldn't make sense for someone to visit uninvited at this time of night.

"And Daria's on the phone..." Harold sighed as he got to his feet with a limp. "I'm sorry, Investigator, could you lend me your shoulder again?"

Hearing this, Echika reached out her arm to help him.

When they opened the front doors, Echika was taken aback for a moment.

"Chief? Benno?"

Standing there were none other than Totoki and Benno. Both of them had terribly stiff expressions, and the chief had her arms crossed. This was the gesture she made whenever she was awfully stressed.

"I'm sorry, Hieda. I needed to see you ASAP, so I looked up your GPS data."

"I don't mind, but...," Echika muttered, unable to mask her confusion. "What happened?"

No matter how urgent the situation was, she could always just make a call. Totoki said nothing, remaining silent while wearing a strained expression. The LED lamp lighting up the building's corridor flickered, casting shadows over the floor. Just as Echika was about to part her lips and ask, Totoki took a long breath and said:

"Investigator Hieda. You're under arrest for suspicion of involvement in the sensory crime."

Huh?

Echika was so dumbstruck that she couldn't react immediately. It took her a few seconds to process what Totoki had just said.

Sensory crime. Suspicion. Arrest…

"I'm sorry," she blurted out. "Wh-what did you just…?"

"I'll say it as many times as it takes," Totoki said, Echika's shadow wavering within her eyes. "You're under suspicion of involvement with the sensory crime."

This makes no sense. What's going on here…?

"Hieda, hand over your gun," Benno said mercilessly. "Then place both hands on your head and turn around."

"No, wait, I…"

"We'll hear you out in the office," Totoki insisted. "Now come with us."

"Please calm down," Harold said, wrapping a hand around Echika's shoulder and holding her tight, as if refusing to let them take her away from him. "Please explain yourselves. Neither of us understands what's going on here."

"There's nothing to understand. I just told you everything you need to know," Totoki continued, as expressionless as she could be. Like she was talking to a complete stranger. "While you were in the repair shop, we cracked Uritsky's files open and found the directory for his virus…and *you were the one who had him make it*, Hieda."

Everything went dark. What did the chief just say?

"The branch's electronic investigators Dived into Uritsky's Mnemosynes," Totoki said, her glare nearly stabbing into Echika. "It took them a while, since they're not as good at it as you are, but they found traces of his Mnemosynes having been wiped. Since the wipe was done in a hurry, they still found some fragments, though. They were in the wrong level, and the date was glitched out, but...they saw you in there, Hieda. You coerced him into making the virus. The Mnemosynes recorded that memory as one of fear and terror."

"But that can't be," Echika said, her voice coming out so shrill that it surprised even her. None of this made sense. "It's fake. Today was the first time I ever met him."

"You know that even though it's possible to tweak or erase Mnemosynes, fabricating them from scratch is impossible. If nothing else, he definitely came in contact with you in the past."

Echika's voice wouldn't leave her trembling lips. She simply shook her head in dumbfounded denial.

I'm innocent. I didn't tell any lies. This can't be.

"I'm not related to the sensory crime," she finally managed to say. "I really don't have anything to do with..."

"We'll find out if you're innocent when we Brain Dive into you."

Brain Dive into you.

A stinging chill bit into Echika's heart. Yes, if an electronic investigator was to plunge into her Mnemosynes, it would prove that she was being framed. It really was that simple. But...

It also meant they would see *those Mnemosynes*.

No, Echika thought. *Not that, not ever. I can't let anyone expose that.*

But was there any other way to prove her innocence besides letting them Brain Dive?

"Hey, Amicus." Benno clicked his tongue. "Hand Hieda over. You're hindering our investigation."

"If anyone's hindering things here, it's you," Harold retorted firmly. "Excuse me if this comes across as rude, but Uritsky's playing you for fools. We've just unearthed information that will be helpful to solving this case. Chief Totoki, I was just about to send it to you—"

Information for solving the case. He meant the virus's avenue of infection. This information tied like a knot in Echika's mind with what felt like a spark—

—But if I do that, I'll probably never return here.

What do I do?

She glanced over at Harold's hand, wrapped around her shoulder. She could see the wearable terminal peeking out from under his cuff.

"Don't worry, Echika. I love you."

"Ah, Big Sis...!"

Echika bit on her lip, feeling the metallic taste of blood leak over her tongue. She knew she didn't have time to doubt herself. She couldn't afford to lose her, no matter what... Right. These were just false accusations; she could clear her name just fine on her own. She'd always made it out of trouble without anyone's help so far.

"Stop this already!" Benno raised his voice. "Hand her over already..."

Echika reached for the terminal on Harold's hand in a daze. Sooner than he could react, she activated the holo-browser, displaying the image of the sneaker holo-ad before her eyes. In the space of a second, the data matrix carved itself into her retinas. Her Your Forma didn't react in any way to it, but it definitely *read it.*

"Investigator?" Harold asked, his breath held in shock. "What did you—?"

Sorry.

Intentionally averting her eyes from his face, Echika brushed away his faltering grip and bolted.

"Hieda, stop!"

"You're not getting away!"

Totoki shouted at her, and Benno's fingers brushed against her arm, but Echika just barely managed to slip past them. She went by the elevator and sped down the stairs. She could hear Benno's footsteps echo behind her. Of course he'd gone after her.

Echika ordered her shaking knees to keep running, hoping she wouldn't stumble along the way. She had no doubt she'd just made the most foolish choice possible.

So be it.

I'll never let anyone peer into these Mnemosynes.

5

"Now then, Aide Lucraft. Who was being played for a fool by the culprit?"

Beneath the apartment building was a police car, its warning lights splashing over the pearl-colored walls. Totoki was glaring angrily at the air, likely communicating with other officers using her Your Forma.

"Hieda got away, and if you'd have just handed her over, none of this would have happened."

"You're right. I was wrong. My apologies."

"I didn't want to believe she was the culprit, either," she huffed indignantly at his emotionless apology. "But this is work. And if she hadn't run away, there'd still be a chance she was innocent..."

"Her fleeing doesn't make her guilty."

"I can understand not wanting to suspect your partner," Totoki replied, her voice full of suppressed emotion. "But right now, we're reacquiring Hieda's GPS data. She knows as well as we do how difficult it is for a Your Forma user to stage an escape."

With that, Totoki walked off to the nearby crowd of officers, leaving Harold behind. His gaze dropped to an umbrella he'd been using as a walking cane.

Echika had intentionally read the virus and run away. By infecting herself, she'd forced her Your Forma into an inoperable state. Based on how much time had passed, it wouldn't be long before the virus would activate and cause her GPS signal to disappear.

Judging by the temperature and sweat of her palms when they'd shaken hands, Harold could tell Echika had been hiding something, but neither of them had revealed their innermost secrets.

Ironically, her running away was enough to convince Harold his theory was correct, though.

Echika thought of him as frivolous and shallow, but the truth was, touching someone's body was the ideal way of understanding their mental state.

His fickle attitude and words had only been a means of buying the time he needed to analyze people and obscure his own intentions. And of course, he wouldn't reveal the truth unless it was strictly necessary. After all, acting human rather than mechanical made it easier to acquire people's trust.

The deceased Sazon had once told him, *"Harold, you're an Amicus, so you can't carry weapons. But the way you're modeled is a weapon in itself."*

And so Harold always used every means he could in order to further the investigation.

"Hey, Amicus."

Harold turned around to find Benno standing behind him. He'd gone after Echika earlier but lost sight of her when she went outside. Benno glared at Harold, annoyance visible in his eyes.

"Look, I get it. Echika threatened you, too, didn't she?"

"...Excuse me, but I don't understand what you're talking about."

"Don't play dumb. I mean what you said the other day about knowing my secrets."

Benno's words called up a corresponding file in Harold's memory.

"Did Hieda order you to threaten me?"

"No, she did not. I said that of my own judgment."

"Is that what your system told you to do?" Benno said, raising his brows dubiously. "That can't be. What, are your Laws of Respect compelling you to protect criminals, too?"

He's the very image of a luddite, Harold thought.

No matter how human they might act, this man would only see Amicus as collections of wires and circuits. But there were times when even blind, closed-minded people like him were useful.

"We finally found her," Benno suddenly said and made to share Echika's position with Totoki and the other officers. But then—"...Huh?"

"What's the matter?"

"It's just... Hieda's GPS data, it...disappeared just now."

No doubt the virus had finally overtaken her Your Forma, but Benno and the others didn't know that. He approached Totoki, confused; they all seemed baffled that they couldn't trace Echika's GPS data.

"Send officers to the last spot she was detected in," Totoki commanded, starting to give out instructions.

Thankfully, no one was paying attention to Harold anymore. And so he walked away, using his umbrella in place of a walking stick. At this point, his right leg's sluggish movements were becoming terribly inconvenient. Letting that sex worker stab him had truly been a bad move.

That said, that incident *had* indirectly led to Echika meeting Daria, who'd told her about his past. Stirring her compassion and lifting every bit of aversion to Amicus in her heart were both things he'd intended. But the way she'd recklessly chosen to escape was something he couldn't have predicted.

Harold got into the Niva parked on the corner of the street. His partner's escape may have been unexpected, but he could still predict where she'd go after being infected. But this vehicle was too distinctive, so he would probably be better off exchanging it for a rental car in one of the nearby parking lots.

He only wanted one thing and one thing only: to solve the case laid out before him.

Chapter 4
The Proof
That Comes
with Pain

Chapter 4
The Proof That Comes with Pain

1

Saint Petersburg spread out before her, like a mirror's reflection of a silvery snowscape. The streetlamps and headlights of vehicles danced over the roads covered in white, and a trail of ivory smoke lingered in the sky above her.

Echika sprinted through the back alleys, evading the gaze of the surveillance drones, but there was more pedestrian traffic than she expected. Street stalls packed with customers, young people lying on the pavement hugging bottles of vodka, people walking alongside families and loved ones. Echika suddenly heard a rumbling blast that echoed deep in her stomach. When she looked up, she saw blazing fireworks burst in the sky.

The date changed over, and the New Year began.

The civilians were sharing in their joy as she passed them by. Echika ran, hugging herself and rubbing her arms vigorously. Her teeth had begun clicking moments ago. Just taking a breath made her feel as though her throat might freeze over.

She couldn't believe no one but her could see this snow.

The illusion was simply that vivid. Her freezing cheeks, her throbbing fingertips, all these were real sensations. She couldn't believe everything was a hallucination a suture inside her brain was showing her.

Your Forma.

How long have I experienced reality solely through the filter of that thread? The form of this machine is the very form of this world. And that might just be a terrible mistake.

As she gazed at these snowflakes, which were either flittering down from above or rising up from below her feet—she couldn't tell—that thought crossed her mind for the first time.

And yet thanks to this virus, she'd been able to shake off Totoki's pursuit. All that was left was to go to Bigga and have her apply the suppressant, and after that, she'd have to figure out a way to clear her name.

Of course, Bigga hated Echika, so there was no telling if she'd even cooperate with her, but she had no one else to turn to. With that in mind, she tried to look up on the map where Bigga would be staying, but since her Your Forma was malfunctioning, she got lost. Even if she tried finding her way to the hotel the old-fashioned way, she couldn't read Cyrillic characters without the Your Forma's translation function.

Suddenly, she saw a surveillance drone in the sky above the path before her.

No good.

Echika changed directions and slid into a narrow alleyway. The snow was especially deep here, and her boots sank into it. She lifted her legs out of the cold, crunchy surface, pushing herself forward, but her legs were getting heavier and heavier. Her thoughts, meanwhile, were becoming dimmer and hazier.

I shouldn't have left my coat at Harold's place...

She rubbed her cheeks, which had grown numb from the cold. Either way, she'd have to keep going while relying on her intuition.

A few minutes after she left the alley, the snow grew more intense, turning into an outright blizzard blowing against her. The hazy cityscape was dotted with molten neon lights. Echika deliriously walked through the streets, with people celebrating the New Year bumping against her shoulders every now and then.

Echika usually liked the snow. When she was little, her big sister had often made it snow. But she would have never wished for such a strong blizzard. The sensation in her hands had long since gone. She could see why those infected with the virus developed hypothermia symptoms; her legs were numb, and she couldn't tell where she was anymore.

When she finally came to, Echika once again found herself in an alleyway. She sat squatted on the snowy ground, her back resting against a filthy wall. She couldn't recall how she'd gotten here. Her mind felt sluggish, like her head was full of sludge. The core of her body burned from the cold. But somehow, she'd stopped shivering.

The tumult of the city was distant; she'd been enveloped by silence. Her shallow breathing echoed loudly in her ears. This was painful. She cursed her own stupidity. She'd been foolish. So foolish that if she ended up dying here, she would have earned it.

A particularly strong gust of wind blew through the alley. Unable to withstand its intensity, Echika fell down, her cheek sinking into the snow.

Oddly enough, it wasn't cold anymore. If anything, it felt...warm. Kind. If she had to describe it, it was like she was in her father's arms... No, she never knew that man's embrace, so she was probably just assuming that was what it felt like. She could hardly remember her mother's warmth, either.

But she could remember her sister. She alone would embrace Echika, pat her on the head, hold her hands... Her sister was the only one who loved her.

Being exposed to the blizzard had chipped away at her pride and left her dispirited. Maybe she'd have actually been better off quitting a long time ago. Echika had only gone along with becoming an electronic investigator because of the results of the compatibility analysis and the opinion of her father, though she didn't hate the work.

But if all she was going to do was keep hurting her colleagues, she may as well have just shut herself off in her room and withered away. Some part of her felt that fading like that would be for the best, for everyone's sakes, but...sadly, she wasn't that kind of person.

After her sister was gone, she'd been left all alone in her frozen home, with little alternative but to remake herself into a machine that obeyed her father's wishes. That was how Echika had shielded her heart. She allowed things to just carry her away, never showing a will of her own and never allowing herself interest or attachments.

Acting like that had been the first time she'd ever felt at peace. And as she'd kept up that frigid facade, she started hiding herself. That way, she could lock those precious memories of her sister away in her heart, memories of the days when she truly felt loved and at ease.

Those memories were the one thing she would refuse to let anyone look at. No one would take them away, not even her father. No one would tarnish them. No one would touch them. That way, she wouldn't let anyone kill her sister again.

But every so often, it hurt. Echika didn't know how long she should keep this up. Her father was already dead, yet she still remained a machine. That way of life had seeped into her heart and body, transforming her into the same person her father had been.

She hadn't wanted to turn out like this. She wished she could be someone who could honestly express her feelings, like Bigga or Daria. Someone who could believe in the kindness of others without any qualms, a person who knew what it was like to be loved and cherished.

She was getting too emotional. The boundaries of her consciousness were growing nondescript, as though they were melting away. Like leaves flowing across the surface of a river, her memories flitted along incoherently.

"Hold my hand, Echika."

"With your magic?"

"Do you think the snow will pile up?"

"If you want it to, it will."

"Everyone else got sick."

"The project is canceled."

"I feel fine!"

"Please don't kill her!"

"You must be Mr. Hieda's daughter. I came to deliver his will."

Ah, I see—so that's what this was all about.

The truth about the sensory crime. *It wasn't actually a virus.*

She finally realized that. But at this point, she could no longer get back up. Her body felt like mud, like it was crumbling away and coming apart.

But just as she was on the brink of letting everything slip away, she felt someone grab hold of her.

2

The light of a shed lamp shone down on her from the ceiling.

It took her a moment to realize that she'd woken up. Echika absentmindedly reached for her cheek, only to realize for the first time that her fingers weren't numb with cold. She'd felt like she was freezing over earlier, but now she was lying in a soft, warm bed.

How had she gotten here?

"Are you up?" Bigga peered at her, her braids dangling down and her expression oddly strained.

Why was she here? Echika had never made it to the hotel, after all.

With a start, she realized that the illusory snow wasn't falling down anymore.

"Ms. Hieda, I've injected you with a suppressant. The same one I used on Lee, a powerful substance that makes all the machines inside your body cease functioning. You'll need another injection in twelve hours."

Upon hearing this, Echika realized her field of vision did seem unusually empty. There was no time or temperature UI overlaid over her eyes, nor were there any noisy notifications buzzing in her ears.

She tried to open her message box and news topics, but none of them budged. The only thing she could see was Bigga, staring down at her. Right, this was the effect of the machine suppressant—her Your Forma's functions were all completely frozen.

This girl had, without a doubt, just saved her life.

"Thank you," Echika croaked out. "But how did you...?"

"Harold was the one who saved you," Bigga told her curtly. "Be grateful to him, because I'm still mad over what you did to Lee, but... Tell me, is he really an Amicus?"

"Huh?" Echika didn't quite believe what she'd just said. "When did you realize that?"

Instead of answering her question, Bigga simply bit her lips. Then she walked off, as if running away from Echika, and the area hazily came into view.

It was a small, single-bed hotel room, and sitting on the table by the window was an open trunk. Inside were surgical instruments, syringes, an ECG monitor, and a tablet terminal. This was a bio-hacker's work kit, it seemed.

Echika placed a hand over her cold forehead. She didn't have a clock anywhere, so she couldn't tell how much time had passed since this had started. It was still dark outside, so it must have been two to three hours at best. Were Totoki and the others after her even now, or had they given up already?

Suddenly, Harold's expression when he saw her read the virus came to mind.

"She just woke up," she heard Bigga say. "Over here."

What? Who is she speaking to?

Echika sluggishly craned her neck to peer out, only to see Bigga leading someone inside. Seeing who it was completely parted the mist from her mind and jolted her awake.

"How are you feeling, Investigator Hieda?"

It was Harold. He looked much as he did when they'd parted ways, and he carried an umbrella in his right hand in place of a cane. Why was he here? Were Totoki and the others there, too? Echika stiffened at once.

"There's no cause for alarm," Harold said, his usual gentle grin on his lips. "The chief doesn't know we're here. I put away my wearable terminal so she wouldn't be able to trace my location."

"But doesn't your system register your position, too…?"

"I have ways of shutting down the signals in my head—don't worry."

Harold walked over, leaning on his umbrella for support, and took a seat by her bed. Unable to keep still, Echika sat up. Her body felt as heavy as lead, but it was still better than being subjected to that illusory snow. Her mind was now crystal clear.

"Aide Lucraft, if…"

If you're not here on the chief's orders, why did you come here? Are you crazy?

The words climbed up to her throat, but the moment Harold touched her shoulder, they completely dispersed.

"Looking for you and coming all the way here was quite the effort for me. If I got to you any later, your life would have been at risk," he said, his tone softer than usual. "I'm truly glad you survived."

Harold narrowed his eyes with heartfelt relief, which made Echika realize something. Yes, *he* was the one who'd carried her over to Bigga after she'd fainted. Indeed, she'd felt a pair of arms pick her up right before going unconscious.

Harold had saved her life. And no matter how hard the trials before her might be, that fact would remain firm and true.

"Ummm..." Echika managed to force out the words. "I'm sorry I caused you so much trouble..."

"I could say the same thing. You carried me to the repair shop, didn't you?"

"That was different. For starters, it was my fault you collaps—"

"Investigator," he interjected, softly raising his hand from her shoulder. "I know you're not the culprit. We need to talk this over."

Bigga, who had been watching their exchange, parted her lips in a reserved manner. "I could make some coffee, if you'd like?"

"Are Chief Totoki and the others still out hunting for me?"

"Yes. I believe they won't give up until they have you."

Echika, Harold, and Bigga sat around a table by the window. Bigga had closed up her trunk and put it away. In its place, she'd laid out cups of instant coffee, which she'd made using an electric kettle in the room.

"Yes, but if you go missing while they're on the lookout, they'll just assume you're my accomplice," Echika mused wearily.

"They probably will," he said nonchalantly. "I don't mind that, though."

"I can see why Daria was so worried about you. I never asked you to do this."

"You can chide me if you want, but I think there's something else you should be telling me right now," Harold said quietly before sipping his coffee.

Echika gripped her knees under the table. It dawned on her that after she'd injected herself, he'd gone out of his way to find her and save her life for no apparent reason. He even believed in her innocence. She should have been grateful to him.

And yet...

A stinging silence settled over her.

"Wow...," Bigga muttered out of nowhere, her awkward gaze nailed to Harold's coffee cup. "You really can drink, just like a human..."

"Yes," he replied, his brows lowering slightly in apology. "Bigga, I'm sorry I startled you. As a friend, I promise I won't keep secrets from you anymore."

Bigga gazed at Harold with an expression betraying mixed emotions—had he revealed his identity so he could "make proper use of her"? Could he have really made Bigga stay in this location because he'd predicted something like this might happen? No, that would definitely be giving him too much credit.

"I...," Bigga started, licking her lips hesitantly for a second. "I still can't believe you're an Amicus... I don't know how to accept this..."

"I understand that it will take a while. And I won't fault you for holding the fact that I lied to you against me."

"I'd never!"

"But, Bigga, Investigator Hieda and I need to find the real culprit. And if you're willing, we'd greatly appreciate your cooperation."

Bigga nodded vaguely, stirred by his earnest attitude. Echika, however, was taken off guard by his statement.

"We're going to search for the real culprit? This is the first I've heard of that. They already have Uritsky behind bars—"

"He isn't the true perpetrator," Harold cut her off.

He said it with such confidence that Echika shuddered—because that was the same conclusion she'd hit upon while trudging through the blizzard. And despite all that, this development wouldn't be favorable for her.

"Uritsky was only used and manipulated by the mastermind. He probably doesn't know anything about the sensory crime. In all likelihood, the true culprit was the one who'd planted the virus data in Uritsky's computer and placed it beneath multiple layers of encryption.

"And most importantly," Harold appended as he put down his cup, "even if Uritsky was the architect of the virus, there'd be no reason for him to go as far as fabricating his own Mnemosynes just to pin the crime on you."

"That should be impossible to begin with," Echika noted.

"But the culprit can obfuscate *the truth* and manipulate the fake facts they created. Please don't try to change the subject, Investigator."

"I'm not trying to change the subject, and I have no idea what you're getting at here."

"I think you know what I'm getting at just fine," Harold insisted, staring at her like he could see straight through. "You already know who the mastermind is."

Echika didn't reply immediately. A part of her even wanted to drive Harold out of here somehow.

"It's just a hunch." She managed to force the words out through the lump in her throat. "And I have no proof, so I can't do anything with it."

"But there is proof," Harold said firmly. "And you yourself have it."

"Huh?" Bigga asked, baffled. "But you just said Ms. Hieda is innocent—"

"Yes, and I stand by that. The investigator is not the culprit. But she does know how the sensory crime functions."

Echika held her breath. Harold, by contrast, wasn't smiling one bit. He simply stared at her, eyes as cold as the surface of a frozen lake, their gaze bereft of suspicion or enmity but full of conviction.

So that's why he was here. This was why he'd even betrayed Totoki to side with Echika. It wasn't simply out of concern for his infected partner.

It was because *he knew everything*.

"Initially, I didn't understand why you went so far as to infect yourself with the virus to run. At the time, you were clearly terrified at the prospect of someone Brain Diving into you."

"No," countered Echika, defiant. "I was just confused then, and—"

"There's actually something I need to show you," he said, taking a folded-up piece of paper from his pocket.

He spread it out, and as Bigga curiously leaned in to look, Echika felt her spine stiffen in fear. It was a printout of an electronic periodical published by an American newspaper company. It was dated April of ten years ago, and the headline sitting proudly at the top read, **"Rig City announces the addition of Your Forma expanded function, Matoi."**

"According to this article, the Matoi was a cultivation system for all generations. Our modern society is overflowing with optimized information, and the Matoi system was designed to help users who exclude information recall their humanity. More specifically, it was an augmented-reality program meant to stimulate altruistic affection by making users spend time with child AIs."

Echika stared at the newspaper blankly. She'd read the article time and again, so she knew its contents by heart. It was accompanied by a photograph of the project members sitting in an interview, clad in dignified suits. And there at the center of the group, with a cold, stone-faced expression, was none other than *him*.

"However, during the experimental stages, a fatal flaw was discovered in the Matoi system, leading to its development being indefinitely suspended. The experimentation period lasted a year and seemed to be progressing well at first, but during the eleventh month of testing, problems began to arise. The Matoi was capable of regulating the user's body heat and adjusting the weather using augmented reality, and the issues stemmed from a bug in those functions. But the details weren't disclosed, and the only thing released to the media was that the test subjects had all become terribly ill. One subject even passed away before they could be properly treated. Thermoregulation issues, a weather-related bug, sudden illness—it all bears an uncanny resemblance to the sensory crime we're investigating now. In fact, one could even go so far as to say that it's identical."

Echika couldn't utter a single word. She clenched her fists so hard that her nails dug into her palms.

"Following that, the Matoi project was shuttered, and its development team was broken up." Harold continued his explanation unabated. "But I have a sneaking suspicion that the Matoi program itself wasn't actually deleted. In fact, it's likely one of the development team members secretly executed it within the Your Forma users' minds."

"But that's a crime!" Bigga exclaimed, going pale. "I mean, if what you're saying is true, it means they intentionally hid a dangerous, buggy system inside people's heads, right?"

"No, it's quite the opposite." Harold shook his head. "They hid it because they were confident it wouldn't bug out."

"...What do you mean?" Bigga asked.

Echika wasn't sure if she was breathing properly anymore.

"The person who planted the program believed that the bug in the Matoi was the product of some kind of external conspiracy. And if my hypothesis is correct, the trigger for the bug's occurrence is what's being used in this sensory crime. In other words, what we thought was a virus simply unlocks the Matoi feature hidden inside the users' Your Forma. It's a program that intentionally triggers the bug."

"That's just speculation," Echika finally managed to say with what felt like tremendous effort. "According to Rig City's analysis team, the virus simply uses the Your Forma's signals to influence the brain..."

"Rig City could be under the mastermind's surveillance. I wouldn't trust anything they say."

"Your entire premise makes no sense," Echika muttered, her voice trembling despite herself. "Why are you sure the Matoi is hidden in every single user's Your Forma? How can you even prove that?"

"Chikasato Hieda." Harold's well-shaped lips invoked that abominable name. "Your father was the team leader for the Matoi project, and he was the one who hid it in the Your Forma. You already know everything I just laid out."

Stay calm.

Echika tried to keep her expression as firm as possible, but of course, she knew the Amicus she was facing may as well have been a keen lie detector. This was probably wasted effort. Still, she had to try.

"Yes... My father was a developer for the Matoi, I'll admit that much," Echika conceded, picking her words carefully. "From what he claimed, the Matoi is a normal program, and the bug was the product of a conspiracy. Out of defiance, he planted the Matoi in all the users' Your Forma... That's what was written in his will."

The will her father had entrusted to her with the assisted-euthanasia organization. It was, in effect, nothing more than a confession of his sins. The thought that this was the first and only letter he'd ever addressed to Echika would have made for brilliantly dark humor, were it funny in the slightest.

Following the project's suspension, all data pertaining to the Matoi was to be erased. And so to keep the program in existence, her father chose the perfect hiding place for it—inside everyone's Your Forma. And he'd bequeathed that final letter to Echika, imploring her to keep his sin a secret.

Although she could have ignored his final order and publicly condemned his actions, instead, she'd simply obeyed his will. Not out of sympathy or affection for her father, no. She just left the truth unsaid so as to protect her own secret.

And ironically enough, that had now only served to corner her.

"Aide Lucraft, your hypothesis is correct, but even if you can prove the Matoi is hidden within the Your Forma, correlating it to this sensory crime is a leap of logic. What if the culprit knew about the Matoi's past bugs and decided to reproduce their effects?"

"You're right," Harold conceded. "But that means all I need to do is prove there's a correlation between the virus and the Matoi."

"...How?"

"You're the one holding that piece of the puzzle, Investigator," Harold asserted, utterly composed. "I know your relationship with your father wasn't favorable, and yet you respected his last will and hung on to that secret until now. There must be a reason behind that, no?"

Echika gazed at Harold, almost glaring at him, refusing to blink. She had to look at him like that, or else he'd encroach on territory she didn't want him to reach. Despite the fact that it was probably far too late for that by now. In the end, she could flounder all she wanted, but she had nowhere left to run.

"Do you remember how we first met?" Harold asked, bringing his fingertips together while he kept his eyes locked on her, as if refusing to miss even a single intake of breath she made. "I called you indifferent and disinterested in your daily life. From a different angle, your lack of interest and desires is a reflection of your psyche trying to protect itself."

"Stop talking bullshit."

"You spent your childhood with an overbearing father, and that naturally made you relinquish your own desires. In that kind of situation, most people would develop a mental disorder, but you have no such clinical history. And it can't be just a natural resistance to stress. Surely, you must have had something to support you, then, something holding up your heart and keeping you stable?"

"No, there wasn't."

"I'm talking about that necklace," Harold stated, his gaze moving to Echika's chest, or rather, the nitro-case necklace dangling helplessly over it. "My apologies if this is offensive, Investigator, but you don't care one bit for accessories. However, I can understand why you're so fond of that nitro-case necklace despite that. After all, you can cherish it like a treasure that way."

"...What are you saying?"

"You already know what I'm getting at," Harold stated, not a trace of a smile on his lips. "Show me what's inside the case."

"My cigarette battery," hedged Echika at once.

"Please cease with the useless lies."

"I'm telling the truth."

"Doing this will help clear your name, Investigator."

"No," Echika said, hopping to her feet as if someone had kicked her from below. "Just...give me some time alone."

She fled the room as though trying to escape from Harold's and Bigga's gazes, sprinting down the staircase without thinking things through at all. She didn't know where she was heading, but before she knew it, she was in the hotel lobby.

Since it was still late at night, the lobby was silent, and there was no one near the check-in counter. Echika crossed the automatic door and stepped outside. Specks of snow floated down from the slumbering sky. This was no illusion—it was real snow.

A stabbing gust blew past her, sending a chill through her body. Come to think of it, she'd only been wearing a thin sweater since she left Harold's apartment. Looking around and rubbing her arms all the while, she spotted a deserted circular plaza across the street.

Echika approached the plaza as if drawn toward it. The city had been cacophonous earlier, but now it was enveloped in silence, and there were barely any people in sight. She could neither see surveillance drones nor hear the wail of police sirens. The celebrations that had taken place just a few hours ago now seemed like a distant dream.

Why…? Echika gripped the nitro case tightly in her hand. *This was the one thing I didn't want anyone to notice.*

At the plaza was a spire-like monument, along with sculptures of soldiers. The numbers *1941* and *1945* were etched onto the spire. Without the Your Forma to help her, she couldn't decipher what the engraving said, and no one was there to tell her. She assumed it had to do with a war.

I wanted to keep this secret, she thought. *This was the one place I didn't want anyone to intrude on, no matter what.*

"Investigator Hieda."

She turned around to find that Harold had gone after her. Though she'd asked to be alone, he hadn't listened. Echika turned her back on him and folded her arms like she was hugging herself.

"I'm not going to speak about this anymore," she breathed out with a thick gasp. "I don't need to tell you anything, after all. You already know everything."

"Then at least let me check if my conclusions are correct." Harold gently brushed against her back.

Stop it. Shut up.

"Investigator, you're not one to trust or put faith in others, and despite that, you spoke to me of your father's relationship. You told me about the reason you started hating Amicus, which is, in other words, your trauma. That's not something you can share easily, but you chose to prioritize your sincerity to me over that."

Echika gritted her teeth in an attempt to suppress something that had welled up inside her. Something that wasn't just the cold.

"You're a kind, gentle person, but you keep up this frigid facade because you're hiding something in your heart—something you don't want anyone to know about. If people think you're standoffish, they won't approach you, which would make hiding your secret easier. And even if they hate you for it, you're used to putting up with that."

Yes, he's right. That's correct.

"And the reason you can put up with it is because *for the last thirteen years, the Matoi has been by your side*, hasn't it?"

Echika turned around, gazing at Harold as the gentle snow fell over his hair and melted. "The prerequisite to qualify as a Matoi test subject was being over eighteen years of age. Despite that, your father secretly implanted it in you, as well. Maybe that was just his way of expressing his love for you, or maybe he simply did it out of experimental curiosity... But in the cold household you grew up in, the Matoi was the only one who understood you. The only family you could trust."

"Don't worry, Echika. I love you."

"But when the bug happened and the project was suspended, you rejected the notion of being torn apart from the Matoi but couldn't stop it from happening...and so *you copied the program and hid it on your person.*"

"You and me will always be together, Big Sis!"

Even if she was nothing more than a mass-produced AI, Matoi had been a true sister to her. It was thanks to her that Echika could experience the joy of familial love. She'd held her hands, embraced her, acknowledged her as an individual, and spoken to her. And to Echika, those little things were a treasure without equal. They were her support, her salvation.

Neither of her parents had loved her, but Matoi alone had. And when the project was shelved, Echika asked her father why it happened, but the only thing he said, time and again, was that the other subjects all "got sick," refusing to go into any more detail.

"My Matoi never did anything strange. But everyone else's went crazy, and because of that...," she said through trembling breaths. "I didn't want my sister to die. I didn't want her to leave me. So I..."

"...copied her HSB."

"And then placed her inside that nitro case. Right?"

Making a copy of a program that was suspended for use was an illegal activity. If someone was to Brain Dive and peer into her Mnemosynes, she really would lose her sister this time. So she took the pains of infecting herself to run away, hoping that if she caught the culprit on her own, maybe no one would need to peer into her mind.

"When did you realize?" Echika asked. Her fingers, clutching the nitro case, were numb and aching from the cold. But she didn't care about that right now. "Did you suspect me the whole time?"

"Saying I suspected you would be incorrect, since you're not the culprit," Harold said, his breath coming out in a white puff. "I first had an inkling of something when we Brain Dived in Rig City. You looked awfully shaken after that, and after meeting Taylor, even more so. Seeing that made me speculate about you having a shared past."

"But Taylor is an eccentric. He could have just asked me something rude."

"No, if he was a stranger, you'd have shrugged off his criticism."

"You don't know that."

"No, I'm certain of that," Harold said clearly. "And after looking into you a bit, it was easy to find out your father was involved with the Matoi's development. And then when you heard the name of the program while Brain Diving, it shook you so much that it made you go into a countercurrent. That led me to assume you were involved with the Matoi project in some way, so I concluded you were a test subject for it."

"But even if I was a test subject, how did you deduce I was still carrying Matoi with me...?"

"You probably don't realize this, Investigator, but considering how little you care for appearances, that accessory stands out quite a bit. So that got me thinking that it must be shaped like a nitro case for some reason. I surmised that something supporting you must be hidden inside it."

He's a monster, she thought. *Being able to conclude that much so early isn't normal.*

"But there's one bit of evidence missing to properly associate the Matoi with this sensory crime," Harold continued as Echika remained silent. "However, if the culprit's goal is what I think it is, you would eventually become a target, too."

"...What are you talking about?"

"Haven't you realized it yet? They've been targeting you since the very beginning."

Echika couldn't immediately process what he meant, and so she simply shook her head vaguely.

"As I assumed, the mastermind made contact with you," Harold explained coolly. "I was surprised he used Uritsky as a red herring to frame you...but personally, I didn't mind however it had to happen."

"What are you saying...?"

"The Matoi is absolutely essential for proving the truth behind the sensory crime, but even if I asked you to show me what's inside the nitro case, you'd never say yes. Even if the perpetrator ended up cornering you... The only thing I could do was form a relationship of trust with you, so that when the time came, you'd relinquish the Matoi to me."

Was the way her jaw shivered just now because of the cold or something else?

Bigga wasn't the one he'd been manipulating all along. Just when had she realized that *she* was the one dancing in the palm of his hand?

"Investigator, I need to apologize to you about something. Firstly, my argument with you on the way back from the restaurant was intentional. It wasn't the first time I'd run into people who denied Amicus having emotions, so hearing that wouldn't have made me that angry. But you kept your guard up around me at all times, so I needed a way to break through your defenses. There's a saying in Japan that adversity strengthens foundations. When it comes to relationships between people, clashing and disagreeing is a valid way of deepening a bond."

She now realized that Harold's eyes had been frozen over the whole time. His frivolous attitude and jovial remarks were all part of a calculated facade.

"And I had Daria tell you about my past so we could grow closer."

Piss off!

No, that was wrong. She'd known this all along. Every part of it had just been programming the whole time. His kindness, his smiles... And her feeling happy because of it had just been a mistake. Her weakness tripping her up.

Aah, this feels...

"Aide Lucraft...?" she asked, her knees trembling. "Just how much of this was all according to your calculations?"

Harold furrowed his brow apologetically. That's all he did—that was his only answer.

"Right." Echika didn't know why, but for some reason, something inside her chest clenched up. She felt so stupid. "You knew who the culprit was and what they were after the whole time. So having me tag along when you gave Bigga the tour was all just so I'd cooperate with you when I became a target...so that she would be around to give me the suppressant in case I refused to let them Brain Dive into me."

"I made proper use of her, didn't I?"

"Do you...?" Her lips trembled. "Do you think all the humans around you are just pawns in a game?"

"The only thing I want is to solve this case."

"Maybe, but your methods are hypocritical."

"Yes, I realize it would seem that way to you. That's why I've chosen not to share my true thoughts with anyone."

"So you're saying that your insistence on human morals was all a lie, too?"

"It wasn't a lie. I do have a conscience. But on top of that, if I'm being honest, sometimes respecting human values makes it easier to acquire trust."

Echika breathed through her teeth. Despite Harold being an Amicus, she always thought he'd acted more human than she did. He was considerate, outgoing, and loved his family. And his affection for Daria probably wasn't fake, despite everything.

But he lacked something crucial. When all was said and done, Harold was still a machine.

"If that's the case...," Echika said, a bitter taste in her mouth, "why are you sharing your true thoughts with me now?"

"Because I want you to give me the thing you hold dearest," he said, his gaze fixed unflinchingly on her.

There was once a time when she'd envied those artificial eyes of his.

"From your perspective as a human being, it might seem like a sham. However, this isn't my programming speaking but my own sense of morality. When you ask someone to hand over the thing that matters most to them, you need to give up something precious in return...like a secret you don't want anyone to know. I want you to understand that this is my way of being sincere."

"Don't force your sincerity on me. I haven't decided to hand my sister over to you."

"Investigator, the Matoi is built to display affection to anyone and everyone. That's how it was programmed. So even if it was to interact with someone else, someone besides you, it would—"

"Shut up!" The scream left her throat before she knew it.

Echika covered her ears and squatted down. She realized she was acting like a child, but if her sister truly was kind to everyone and anyone, that would mean she wasn't Echika's one and only sibling.

But she still had to cling to her.

If this was what had to happen, Echika wished she never would have met her to begin with. She wished she'd never known the bliss of someone patting her on the head and the joy of an embrace. If she'd just stayed with her cold, emotionless father forever, she wouldn't have to feel this way.

Harold approached her slowly. She could see his shoes enter her field of vision but refused to raise her head just the same. Echika simply hugged her knees and held her breath.

Don't invade any deeper.

"Your calculations were wrong," she blurted out, her field of vision blurring. "Because I don't trust you!"

"Yes, maybe they were," he replied. "You were harder to please than I anticipated."

"You have a family who loves you, but I don't, okay? The only one who was ever on my side was Matoi. And now you're trying to take her away, too."

"That's right."

"Ah-ha-ha." She realized how childish she was being, but she couldn't stop herself. "What, is solving this case that important to you? But no matter how badly you want to resume the investigation on Detective Sazon, an Amicus like you won't be able to make a career for himself."

"I know that, of course. My only way to do that is to keep putting in the effort, slowly and steadily." Harold bent down and took a knee. "Investigator, here is my second precious something—my other secret. If I ever catch Sazon's killer, I intend to judge him by my own hand."

Echika looked up. His meticulously crafted mechanical face was right in front of her, those clear eyes bereft of warmth.

"...What do you mean?"

"I mean exactly that."

A silent shiver ran through her. Daria was right; he really was keeping something suppressed in his heart—a dark, terrifying impulse.

"But the Laws of Respect apply to you. Can't you not hurt humans?"

"Are you sure about that?"

"...You're not going to modify your own programming, are you? They'll scrap you if you do that."

"Let them," Harold whispered all too quietly. Was his artificial gaze inherently incapable of burning with anger and regret? "Even if that happens, it'll be my due punishment for failing to save Sazon."

Echika couldn't see what he'd done to her as anything but the most terrible thing possible, and Harold knew that. That was why the Amicus had chosen to share what mattered most to him, to attempt to convey his sincerity in his own way. If the only thing he wanted was to use her, he wouldn't have been driven to open his heart and reveal his secrets to her.

Or maybe this was all part of his scheme, too. Either way...

"I won't," she whispered, gritting her teeth. "I won't...hand Matoi over to you."

"Echika," he said, placing his hands over her own, which were clenched around the nitro case. Even his cold, mechanical fingers felt terribly warm right now. "You told me to take better care of myself, but those were words you should have directed at yourself instead."

"What...?"

"You haven't been looking at yourself. You've been clinging to your sister's image for too long. You have to realize how lonesome and isolating that is."

I can't.

"Please take better care of yourself," he implored her.

I just can't. I'm too afraid.

"If you need her... If you need Matoi that badly," she said, moving her numbed lips. "Tear it off."

Yes, it would be that much easier for her if he just did that. Echika slowly opened her frigid fingers, and the nitro-case necklace dangled down over her chest.

"I can't take it off on my own... I'm too much of a coward."

"In that case," Harold said, furrowing his brow sadly, "is your love for your sister fake?"

She could see her own fading eyes reflected in his pupils. What was he saying all of a sudden?

"When Sazon died, I watched them cover his casket with dirt. I wanted to stop them, because if his body was to decay, I'd never be able to hug him again. But that was just selfish of me. Sazon never would have wanted that, and so I watched, full of respect and affection for him, without ever looking away. When you love someone, you have a responsibility to accept the fact that you'll have to tell them good-bye. But you refuse to do that."

That's...

"That refusal isn't affection. When you do that, all you're doing is protecting yourself. Matoi wasn't a sister to you, Echika. She was just a tool that gave you what you always longed for the most."

No...

That denial reached her throat, but she couldn't put it into words. What she wanted most was affection from her parents, from her father. She wanted him to look at his own daughter, not Sumika, and truly love her. And Matoi always looked at Echika first and foremost. She loved her, and that had made Echika happy. She didn't want to lose that.

But...

"Children refuse to let go of their stuffed toys," Harold said. "Especially if they have nothing else to protect themselves with."

But I...

"But this stuffed toy can't save you any longer, can it?"

Harold's words continued relentlessly. The memory of that day was burned into her closed eyelids.

"You and me will always be together, Big Sis!"

It was the day before the Matoi was uninstalled. She snuck into her father's study, stole the HSB stick, and connected it to her neck. Soon after she started copying the program, her sister moved in to stop her, regarding her with a pained expression that Echika had never seen her make before. And then she said this:

"Echika, listen carefully. There's only one of me in this entire world."

That's right. Her big sister was unique, a singular existence. So even if every other copy of the Matoi were erased, she didn't want her big sister to die.

But doing that was a mistake, a lie her younger heart spouted. An excuse.

She knew the truth already. What she had copied into her young ego wasn't her "one and only" sister anymore. On that day, her sister really had died, and the thing she was holding on to until now was nothing more than the cinders of her cremated memories.

Echika was nothing but a foolish child, crying out for someone to love her. She'd kept on screaming out that she wanted it, demanded it, longed for it…but in the end, she couldn't get anything. And it was because she knew, deep down, that she couldn't have it that she desperately refused to admit the truth. To face the fact that those memories were nothing but ashes.

"Very well," Harold whispered. "If you refuse to let go, I'll take her away, like you asked. If you're sure that's what you want."

No.

"Wait."

Echika managed to open her eyes. Harold's hands were a second away from touching the nitro case.

I know. I have to put an end to this someday.

"I'm fine," she managed to breathe out. "I'll…take it off. On my own."

She reached for the back of her neck and touched the hook on her necklace. Her fingers were too numb from the cold to grab it properly, so she fumbled with it time and again.

Time and again, she thought… *I still have time. Matoi is right here. I can just run off, and this time, I'll die together with her—*

No. No, I can't. I already know that. If I can't lay my hands on anything at all, I at least have to prove my love for Matoi was real. Or else I'll wind up just like Dad, who could only love Sumika, a machine that always acted the way he wanted her to.

Echika undid the hook and let the nitro case fall into her palm. It was clear and felt cold as ice. She twisted its cap, which came off with surprising ease, and flipped it over. Its contents spilled onto her other hand. A small memory stick, transparent as crystal.

"Here it is, Aide Lucraft," Echika announced.

"This is...the evidence to support your theory."

She handed him the HSB stick with freezing fingers, and Harold took off his coat and draped it over her shoulders. Their eyes met. His eyelashes shone with molten snow, and his hands once again enveloped hers, gripping the HSB stick.

"I'm grateful for your courage," he said, his eyes fixed on her with more honesty than ever before. "I have a plan in mind for arresting the culprit. Will you hear me out?"

This was probably a scheme he'd concocted so the two of them could capture the mastermind alone. They couldn't rely on Totoki right now, and if the perpetrator was the kind of person Harold thought they were, they could probably tweak Echika's Mnemosynes with the same ease with which they'd faked Uritsky's.

If they were going to prove Echika's innocence, they'd have to settle this on their own. For better or for worse, this Amicus was her only ally right now.

"Tell me your plan," she said, gripping his fingers in response. "What will I have to do?"

3

Steve returned to Rig City at around ten in the morning. A van parked in the roundabout as night rose. It wasn't a vehicle he recognized. When he looked up its license plate, he found out it was a rental car. Sitting behind the wheel was a girl who seemed to be of Scandinavian descent.

"What is it?" She lowered her window and asked him this with awkward, thickly accented English as Steve approached. "I am waiting for my brother here. He's working overtime. Is it forbidden to park here?"

Workers being picked up by family wasn't at all unusual, but the fact that it was a rental car did strike him as off. But then again, there could be any number of plausible reasons for that, and he realized he was probably being overly suspicious. So he simply apologized to the girl and moved away from the van.

Upon entering Rig City's main office building, he ran into a coworker who was on his way out.

"Oh, Steve, Mr. Taylor was looking for you."

"...About what?'

"Well, remember that big box you carried in earlier? That, uh, decorative plant delivered to him?"

"No...," Steve muttered in confusion. "I have no idea what you're referring to."

"What, did your head get messed up along with your *leg*? You should probably have the mechanic give you a diagnostic tomorrow. You're charged with nursing Mr. Taylor, after all, so you can't neglect your own maintenance. Maybe your circulatory fluid is starting to solidify or something."

The coworker continued chattering without regard for him and soon left. Steve looked down at his leg, confirming it was working perfectly well. Just what kind of mix-up would make this employee say that...? But then his thoughts moved so fast that they nearly made an audible whirl in his head, and the possibility dawned on him.

It can't be.

Steve broke into a jog, and by the time he got on the elevator, the regulatory-fluid pump in his left breast was beating wildly. But how? He didn't meet him directly, so it made no sense. This had to be him overthinking things.

But when he got off the elevator at the top floor, the organic transistors in his skin were buzzing. The doors to the guest room were flung open, and behind them was nothing but lukewarm darkness. No one was there. After thinking for a moment, he picked up the sofa's cushions and took out a revolver hidden beneath them. This was a weapon

Taylor had prepared for self-defense purposes. He checked the back of the door, then gazed at the silent corridor extending ahead of him. Even though he was listening carefully, Steve couldn't sense anyone there...

And then he heard it. The door to the bedroom had barely opened.

Elias Taylor's bedroom was dim and thick with an inorganic odor. His hospital bed was equipped with an oxygen concentrator. The room was empty and dreary, save for the desk and PC set against the wall. Blackout curtains were draped over the windows, which made the twinkling stars reflecting against the marble floor that much more visible. The dome-like ceiling had a flexible screen set over it, which displayed an image of the night sky. It was like a planetarium.

"Mr. Taylor."

As he lay in his bed, drifting in the dreams of analgesic-induced slumber, he awakened to the voice of a familiar whisper. Opening his heavy eyelids, he saw that it was Steve. He was in his usual dress shirt and vest and looked at him with concern in his eyes.

"The nurse Amicus are all occupied at the moment, so if you don't mind, I'll handle wiping your body off for today."

"Is it that time already?" Taylor checked his Your Forma's clock UI, which showed that it was past nine in the morning. Spending your entire day in bed made it easy to lose track of time. "Please go ahead."

Nodding silently, Steve gently raised Taylor's head. Feeling the Amicus's hands touch the back of his neck made the old man recall what he'd seen when Steve had returned just now.

"What was that large box?" Taylor asked. "I saw it when the living room door opened."

Despite being bedridden and ill, Taylor still insisted on confirming who was coming into his room, and one could enter only if he undid the security. "Don't tell me the hospital sent some pointless medical device..."

"Not to worry," Steve said with his usual dour expression. "It contained a person I brought here."

"...What?"

Just as Taylor knit his brow in surprise, he felt something attach to the port in his neck. Steve had plugged an HSB connector of some sort into him, but why? The footage projected onto the ceiling changed. Instead of a starry sky, it displayed a gaudy ad for sneakers equipped with Bluetooth.

Taylor didn't have the time to look away. The information matrix on the commercial hopped into his field of vision. The clock UI projecting into his eyes momentarily crackled and warped, and Taylor could tell his face had gone pale with shock.

He quickly called up a message window, and it opened normally, but he knew perfectly well what had just happened. In just ten to twenty minutes, all his Your Forma's features would begin to malfunction.

"Steve, you—"

Taylor gazed up at the robot, who smiled softly at him. But that Amicus would never smile; that was an expression that was entirely unlike anything Steve would ever do.

"So we meet at last, Mr. Taylor," Steve—or rather, the Amicus with Steve's face said as he drew the HSB from his neck. "It's a pleasure to make your acquaintance. I'm Harold Lucraft. And…"

Harold's gaze trailed away, and Taylor followed it in a stupor, his eyes finally settling on the figure sitting at the foot of his bed. "Hello, Mr. Taylor."

It was an electronic investigator, her figure as black as ink.

"You…," Taylor said, his voice as faint as the rustling of fallen leaves. "This is trespassing, Investigator Hieda."

"True, I don't have a warrant."

Taylor had used his name as a technological revolutionary to achieve anything and everything he wanted, but now he was nothing but a decrepit old man. Most of his hair had fallen out, and his striking almond eyes were now sunken and gaunt.

His complexion was dull from the medication he needed to take, and he had a nasal cannula inserted into his nostrils. A sweater hung baggily over his emaciated body and limbs, which were by now little but skin and bones. Here was the truth his holo-model could not and would not have communicated.

There he lay, a shadow of his former self, the shrunken remnant of a former genius.

"Mr. Taylor, we came here to place you under arrest," Echika said.

Taylor's tight lips slackened slightly, and he took a long, labored breath.

"I have no idea what you're talking about. Are you saying I'm a criminal charged with some kind of sensory crime?"

"Yes, you are. You were behind all this."

Elias Taylor was the man behind it all. This was something Echika and Harold were in agreement about.

Getting into Rig City was easier than she'd expected. Echika and Harold left Saint Petersburg with Bigga, booking a flight from Pulkovo Airport. Of course, if Echika was to walk into an airport, Totoki would quickly discover it and come after her.

That was where Bigga proved helpful. By showing her credentials as a civilian cooperator with Interpol, she was able to get Echika on board by claiming she was an Amicus.

The memory of being forced into the Amicus compartment with Harold came to mind.

"What do you think? It really is just a cargo hold, isn't it?"

As Echika was quite exhausted from the cramped space, Harold was looking at her with an awfully amused expression. But honestly, the most annoying part about the trip hadn't been the terrible compartment—it was having to cling to him until the flight was over. The two of them were stuffed into the Amicus compartment like sardines in a can, so they'd had to hold on to each other the whole flight.

"Can't you scoot over a little?"

"I could, but then you'd end up hugging an Amicus you don't know."

"That'd be a major improvement."

"Well, I'd rather stick to you."

"Even if that's a joke, I'll knock your lights out," Echika groaned, resisting the thumping headache this was giving her. *"Ugh, let me ride first-class, dammit..."*

"I'm glad you finally understand how I feel about this compartment."

After landing in San Francisco, the three of them rented a van and made their way to Rig City's main building. They intentionally waited for a time when Steve would be out. Harold had called Anne and was able to get her to share Steve's schedule.

Thanks to that, Harold could masquerade as Steve and walk right in through the front door. Echika had hidden in a large delivery box, which was placed on a cart Harold pushed. Security Amicus and coworkers had stopped him a few times, asking about what was in the box, but he talked his way out of it by claiming it was a decorative plant.

No one could expect that Steve's brother unit would walk into Rig City in the middle of the night, and Steve was well trusted in the company, since he was seen as Taylor's right-hand man. Harold expected the plan would work without a hitch, and he was right.

Still, Echika never wanted to go through any of that ever again. Especially not the cargo hold.

"Mr. Taylor, you realized my father hid the Matoi in everyone's Your Forma, didn't you?"

"What are you talking about? The Matoi project was suspended years ago."

"There's no point to playing dumb," Harold said, swinging the HSB stick in his hand. "You knew that Chikasato Hieda hid the Matoi and erased it from your head alone. That said, however, I just reinstalled it."

Taylor closed his thin eyelids and heaved a sigh.

"And you infected me to prove that the sensory crime is caused by the Matoi?"

"Yes." Harold nodded expressionlessly. "And if you understand that, I ask that you confess sooner rather than later. Because in fifteen minutes' time, you'll have to confess while tormented by the blizzard, and it'd be pitiful to see you do that."

"Mr. Taylor," Echika called out to him quietly. "You were trying to pin the sensory crime on me. And you used Cliff Salk to cover your tracks, didn't you? His true identity was Makar Uritsky, an electronic-drug manufacturer connected with the mafia. Did you know that?"

Taylor said nothing; he simply kept his eyes closed.

"You exposed Uritsky's identity and used it as leverage to make him cooperate with you." Echika continued unperturbed. "You blackmailed him and planted the virus in his laptop. And you had him talk to me—or at least, a holographic model of me—to make it seem like I was the mastermind."

When Echika visited Rig City before, Taylor had used Chikasato's holo-model, which shocked her. There was no way her dead father could appear before her very eyes, after all. But even if she was conscious of that, the hologram was convincing enough to make her believe it was really him. And Taylor had told her that holo-model was based on scan data from Rig City's security cameras.

"And when I visited the company to investigate a few days ago, the surveillance cameras detected me, of course. You made a holo-model based on my data, used it to blackmail Uritsky, and, in so doing, planted Mnemosynes that made me look like the culprit in his head."

It was impossible to fabricate Mnemosynes from scratch, but like Harold said, it was still possible to obfuscate the truth with manipulated facts.

"And you did more than just that. You messed with my Mnemosynes, too. You're the Your Forma's developer, after all, so managing that would have been child's play for you."

"That's slander," Taylor seethed. "When would I have the time to tamper with your Mnemosynes?"

"When I asked for your cooperation with the investigation. Mnemosynes are managed in a stand-alone fashion, so to manipulate them, you need to directly connect through HSB. And that's how you secretly edited my Mnemosynes. I'm sure you did the same to the other employees, too."

Echika had Brain Dived into four Rig City employees, and what tugged her in Uritsky's direction were the emotions they exhibited toward Salk. But now Echika realized the truth; those intense but incoherent emotions she saw in their Mnemosynes were all part of the mastermind's attempt to lead her on.

"Mr. Taylor," Harold said. "To make your plan succeed, you had to create a holo-model of Investigator Hieda and tweak her Mnemosynes on top of that. That was why you picked candidates to serve as index cases from among the study tours' participants and set up the investigation. You did all that to bring her to you here in Rig City."

He remained silent.

"Please tell me why you did it," Echika said, licking her dry lips. "Is my father related to this incident?"

Taylor snorted. His wheezing breaths fell to the marble floor with increasing fervor as he lifted his discolored eyelids.

"The Matoi was originally my project, not Chikasato's."

"...What do you mean?" Echika asked, furrowing her brow.

"It's true. Didn't it strike you as odd? Why would the Matoi, a mere cultivation system, have weather manipulation and thermoregulation features?"

Echika did always think Matoi's *magic* of creating snow was unusual, but since her "sister" was by her side since she was a little girl, she never particularly doubted it.

"It was originally part of a different project. But instead, the system was discarded during its development stages in favor of the Matoi, and Chikasato chose to incorporate some of its features out of the kindness of his heart. All the credit for it should have been mine...but he took it all away." Taylor reached for the side of the bed with his slender, emaciated arms and grabbed the guardrail, pulling himself up. "And you, Investigator, should face retribution in his place."

"So you were behind the bugs—"

But Echika suddenly fell silent in shock. Taylor raised his hand from under the covers—to reveal he was gripping an automatic pistol. Echika's entire body tensed up at once. She never imagined he was hiding a gun in there.

"I made my choice," Taylor said, undoing the safety with his thumb and fixing its sights on her. "I would take revenge on Chikasato before I die...and I will besmirch the Matoi's honor."

Resisting the urge to yell in her throat, Echika slowly raised her hands. What made this situation worse was that since she'd had to come here as Bigga's "luggage," she was completely unarmed right now.

"Mr. Taylor, put the gun down," Harold said cautiously.

"Stay quiet, Amicus. This is a conversation between human beings."

"No, I—"

"Aide Lucraft," Echika managed to cut him off. "It's fine. Don't worry."

Harold still looked like he had more to say but stepped down bitterly.

"So," Taylor said feebly, "when did you figure out it was me?"

Calm down—he won't shoot you right away, Echika told herself as she took a deep breath.

Taylor's gaze and muzzle were fixed calmly but lethally on her.

"When they came to arrest me over the fake charges, I infected myself with the virus to get away. And when I saw the blizzard, it reminded me of the snow my sister...the snow Matoi would make." Echika dropped her eyes. "I was my father's secret test subject. He didn't tell anyone about me, not even you. So when he saw that all the other subjects experienced the bug but my Matoi continued functioning normally, he immediately realized you were behind it."

"So he used his daughter as a precaution to begin with," Taylor said, his lips contorting into a smirk. "He really was an impressive man... I liked your father a great deal, you know," he whispered. "He was my first true friend...at least until he betrayed me."

"Yes, he was a fundamentally flawed person, but I can't imagine him trying to steal a project away from someone as talented as you," Echika said. "Even if he tried to do it, everyone else would have tried to stop him."

"As you well know, I'm quite the misanthrope," Taylor said with a self-deprecating smile. "Whenever I started a project, I only ever asked other people for help after making a great deal of progress. I never disclosed any details on the Matoi until I reached that point, either, but everyone seemed to understand that I was always working on something... Chikasato took advantage of that to use my weakness against me. He coerced me."

"...Your weakness?"

"For many years, I took pleasure in peering into other people's heads and guiding the way they thought," he said with terrible triviality. "I originally made the Your Forma because I wanted friends. I hated people, but *if I could customize them however I saw fit*, they could become perfect acquaintances. So I used the Your Forma's personalization algorithms to twist my employees' thoughts in whichever direction I needed."

Echika couldn't believe what she was hearing. How much of what he'd just said was serious?

"Yes, you can use the personalization features to selectively feed the user information that suits their preferences, but you can't actually twist their thoughts into…"

"Oh yes, you can. Remember what I told you? The human brain is quite malleable, and it adjusts itself to whatever it's given," Taylor interjected unapologetically. "In other words, since it's being optimized to their tastes, or rather, they believe it's being optimized to their tastes, *they become convinced whatever they see is right for them.* That way, you can alter people's thoughts while they're none the wiser."

Apparently, he'd used this method to twist several workers' thoughts in a complete one-eighty.

"I can make a coffee aficionado develop a hatred for caffeine, turn a moderate into an extremist and vice versa, or make them go from devout Christianity to complete atheism… What started as an attempt to customize people into my friends became a fascinating experiment. As it turned out, all you people out there let whatever you see every day overwrite your minds."

Regardless of whether what he'd just said was fact or falsehood, Echika couldn't restrain the disgust surging up within her. She thought back to Elias Taylor's personal history, which she'd spent the last day looking into.

His intellectual talents were discovered during his infancy, and by the tender age of twelve, he'd already graduated from MIT. The media coverage earned his parents a fortune, but Taylor himself objected to this and became an independent industrialist at the age of fifteen.

His overwhelming intelligence isolated him, made him someone who always stood out from the rest. When he turned twenty, a mass-media outlet released an article titled "**Geniuses can't feel solitude,**" and he sued them for libel.

Ever since then, he'd shut himself off in his home, rejecting both media attention and direct human contact. And though Taylor ran Rig City with his acquaintances, he had no interest in managing the company, always serving as a consultant and submerging himself in whatever research he saw fit.

"Chikasato was whip-smart. He realized my attempts to guide the thoughts of others and denied our friendship. And then he told me this: 'If you don't want to be arrested for media manipulation, hand over the project you're working on right now.' He blackmailed me."

That did sound like something her father would do. Since the day he'd forced her to make that promise, Echika knew—her father was a crafty man who would use anything a person said or did against them. Nothing was below him, so long as it served his ends.

"He'd conceived the Matoi project beforehand but struggled to develop the system for it. By using the foundation I laid for my project, he believed he'd be able to succeed."

Thus, Taylor made his deal with Chikasato and handed the Matoi project over to him.

"It was unforgivable. He walked all over my pride and betrayed me. So I caused the bug in the Matoi and had the project suspended. But Chikasato continued to deceive me and hid the Matoi away... That's why I decided I would put even that to use, to take revenge on him. To let my grand act of vengeance be the last great moment of my life."

"Why does it have to be the last moment of your life?" Echika asked.

"Because I hate humans. It's not like I have a knack for concocting the perfect crime, and I don't want to spend my life in prison, surrounded by criminals. I didn't want to be arrested and waste my remaining time like that before my life ran its natural course."

Taylor was a man of extraordinary talent, but his personality and mind were by no means respectable. But he and Echika's father were so arrogant that mere words couldn't begin to describe the full extent of their egos. And on top of that, they'd been able to manipulate other people to act exactly the way they wanted.

When all was said and done, this sensory crime was nothing more than an egotistical slugfest between two very similar men.

"But my father committed suicide years ago, Mr. Taylor."

"And yet you're his daughter, and you're still here. I caused the bug in the Matoi again so I could set you up as a terrorist in Chikasato's place. You're a talented electronic investigator trusted by her peers. What if they found out you were nothing but a vile criminal?" Taylor chuckled. "You'd get to experience what it's like to be scorned by those you trust and the sorrow of being betrayed."

A talented electronic investigator trusted by her peers? Echika thought. *Who is he even talking about?*

From Taylor's perspective, seeing his treacherous friend's daughter make a career for herself was probably insufferable. But that was only an illusion born from his distance from Echika.

Yes, she'd made impressive achievements solving cases, but she tormented her partners at the same time. Her coworkers shunned her; she didn't have their trust.

"I swear... I really have gone senile, haven't I?" Taylor said, his expression clouding over. "You exposed the means of infection, used the virus to get away, came all the way here, and even had a copy of the Matoi. And I accounted for none of those things. It's like I can't match Chikasato no matter what I do. How...irksome. To think he entrusted his dear daughter with the program..."

"His dear daughter?" Echika couldn't overlook this. "My father never cherished me, not once."

"I wonder," Taylor said, his body shivering like he'd been withstanding the cold for a few minutes now. "When I first met Chikasato, he was an ordinary, kind man who loved his family."

"You're joking..." Echika scoffed.

"No, it's true. He only changed after you were born and he divorced his wife. Though he lost his emotions and became coldhearted, at first, he was a compassionate, empathic man."

Was he saying that her father had really loved her mother? Echika couldn't imagine it. The image of when she'd first met him surfaced in her mind. That cold expression and his merciless promise—

"No, it's not the first time. I saw you in the hospital nursery."

Thinking back on it, those words implied he went to the hospital for the express goal of seeing Echika. And this was a man who wouldn't ever do anything for his daughter. Was that a lie he thought up on the spot, then?

And even if it isn't—so what?

"Investigator, in my eyes, the Matoi was his symbol of resistance. When humans are overly optimized, they become fragile. When

Chikasato's wife left him, it greatly pained him, and from that point on, he could only love Amicus, machines that would never betray him. That weak man crafted the Matoi because he was seeking a crutch for his fragile human heart."

Echika recalled the pale sakura petals fluttering through their apartment corridor.

"He couldn't love his daughter anymore, so he likely thought to make an AI to love you in his place. He wanted it so much, he shamelessly betrayed a friend and took over their project. All in the name of the patronizing love he felt for his daughter."

That's absurd, Echika thought.

This was all Taylor's strained interpretation of the facts. Her father was a nasty man who would stoop to anything to achieve his ends, and he was completely detached from affection. And besides, he was dead now, so he couldn't say anything to absolve himself one way or another. This entire exchange was pointless.

"Enough," Echika said firmly. "Mr. Taylor, Aide Lucraft has just memorized your entire confession. Stop resisting and hand over your weapon—"

"Investigator Hieda, step away from Mr. Taylor."

Echika froze up as a voice suddenly cut her off. Turning to the source, she saw Steve standing in the entrance to the room, his back straight and a revolver gripped in his fair hands. Its muzzle was fixed directly at her.

She felt a chill creep through her as all the blood drained from her face. Echika hoped they would finish this before Steve returned, but he made it at the last second.

"Brother Steve, it's been a while." Harold, who'd remained silent for a moment, hailed the other Amicus. "I'm glad to finally see you."

"Harold, I can see you're not happy in the slightest. I'm sad that we have to meet again under these circumstances," Steve said as he silently came into the room. "Investigator Hieda, step away from Mr. Taylor's bed right this instant."

"No, you throw away that gun. Amicus aren't allowed to carry firearms."

"Steve," Taylor moaned, calling out to him. "This is my problem. Stay out of it."

"You don't need to dirty your hands with this, sir," Steve replied.

"Investigator, Harold, put your hands behind your head."

Harold wordlessly did as the other Amicus ordered and took a step back. Echika, however, remained still and sneaked a glance at Harold. Their eyes met.

"Investigator," Steve repeated himself. "This is my third warning. Step away from Mr. Taylor."

"I won't," she asserted, glaring at him defiantly. "Taylor is taking advantage of you. He had you do all his dirty work, from fabricating the virus-analysis results to making my holo-model. Are you still going to obey him?"

"Mr. Taylor saved me. He was the only one who would. He was the first person to give me a place to stay, without ever putting a price tag on me."

"And that's why you couldn't refuse to cooperate with him?"

"No. You're wrong. I became his accomplice of my own will."

"That can't be...," Echika said, clenching her teeth nervously.

An Amicus's Laws of Respect guaranteed they would honor and obey their owners. And that had made Steve elect to indirectly harm all other humans except his master, Taylor— No, that was wrong. Amicus were absolutely forbidden from attacking humans, no matter the circumstances.

"Steve," Taylor moaned. "Enough, step down."

"Investigator Hieda, I implore you to do as I say. Your cooperation would spare me from having to shoot you."

"Spare you from shooting me?" Echika echoed him. "Steve, Amicus can't gun people down."

"No, I'm capable of it."

It can't be. A chill ran through her. *No, wait.*

"When I first met you, I always thought your unsociable behavior was unusual for an Amicus. Don't tell me Taylor undid your Laws of Respect."

"I'm operating absolutely normally. I simply came to learn what the Laws of Respect truly are."

"...What?"

"The Laws of Respect are nothing but what humans call piety. And I simply realized that I can live without having to worship humankind."

The light of the screen shone over Steve's gun muzzle, making it faintly glint. His eyes, so similar to Harold's, glared at her like burning ice.

"I can decide what I should protect on my own."

Echika didn't even have the time to part her lips. Without any hesitation whatsoever, Steve fired, and his gun roared, the muzzle flash dispersing the gloomy darkness of the room. The bullet it spat out plowed through Echika, and her scraggy form staggered violently.

The tremor of a gunshot shook the walls.

Echika could feel her eardrums tremble painfully. Steve, *who had been shot in his stomach from the front*, fell to his knees with a dumbfounded expression. Sitting up in his bed, Taylor lowered his smoking gun, his bony fingers shaking.

"I told you to step down!" Taylor scorned him, his voice shaking with more fury than ever before. "This is my vengeance! If someone is going to kill her, it should be me! I won't hand that role over to a mere machine!"

"Mr...." Steve tried to say something, but he toppled over, limp and motionless.

Circulatory fluid seeped from under him, forming a large black puddle over the marble floor.

A silence heavy enough to feel like a buzz in one's ear settled over the room in the blink of an eye.

"You're next, Harold," Taylor said, pointing his gun at him.

The decrepit old man gritted his teeth, his weakened body shivering with excitement as he tried to accurately align his sights on the Amicus.

"Taylor, there's one thing I want you to tell me before you shoot," Harold, who remained still and composed, said calmly. "Is it snowing right now?"

"Yes...," Taylor breathed out. "It's been snowing a long time now."

"I see," Harold replied, his lips mellowing down into his usual smile. "So now we have proof to back the claim that the sensory crime really was caused by the Matoi—isn't that right, Investigator Hieda?"

Taylor turned around at once, just barely catching sight of Echika pouncing on him from behind one of the blackout curtains. She wrested the gun out of Taylor's thrashing fingers and twisted his emaciated arm back. Pinning his face down into the covers, she leaned over him like she'd just crawled onto the bed.

"Stay still. Otherwise, you'll break a bone."

"But why are you…?!" Taylor croaked out. "I saw you get shot a moment ago…!"

"A well-made holo-model sure is a mysterious thing, don't you think?" Harold answered his question. "It's real enough to even fool its own creator."

The Amicus approached him, dragging his right leg and then kicking something over—the bald-eagle laser drone rolled over the floor with a loud *rattle*. Taylor's sunken eyes widened like a child's.

"Mr. Taylor." Echika looked down on this former genius one more time and stated clearly, "You are under arrest for suspicion of involvement in a sensory crime."

4

The roof of the hospital offered a fine view of San Francisco Bay. Dawn had just started creeping over the sky, dyeing it violet. Headlights continued racing dully across the Dumbarton Bridge, but the city was still asleep. There were relatively few drones flying about, and the air was soft and clear.

"Where's Bigga, Aide Lucraft?"

"Asleep in the lounge. She was quite tuckered out, it seems."

After the arrest was made, Echika had called an ambulance. It carried away Taylor, who was already in a state of hypothermia. The doctor had applied a suppressant, and it seemed his state had stabilized.

"Well," Echika said, leaning against the guardrail and blowing out a wisp of her electronic cigarette's smoke, "what's Chief Totoki up to?"

"She just discovered Bigga's flight record in Pulkovo Airport," Harold replied, standing next to her. He'd used her tablet terminal a moment ago to phone Totoki. "She says she'll be here as early as tomorrow. She seems to believe my testimony for now and is trying to have the suspicions leveled against you lifted. A job well done, from the looks of it."

"I don't know about that...," Echika said, honestly wondering if it was too early to rejoice. "We might not think so soon enough."

Thanks to their efforts, they'd been able to piece together enough evidence to implicate Taylor, but they had to break multiple laws to do that. Namely, sneaking a human onto an aircraft as an Amicus and infiltrating Rig City without a warrant... Finding out about these would likely give Totoki one hell of a headache, and she would have to toil quite a bit to cover for them.

"Even so, everything ended well," Harold said, smiling serenely.

"I wouldn't say that." Echika sighed. "Though, I guess the plan with the holo-model did end up working..."

Since Echika had been unarmed, she required some means of defending herself. So before they entered Taylor's bedroom, they brought the eagle laser drone from the guest room and set it up under his bed. Taylor was too delirious to notice and thought the projection was actually Echika. Meanwhile, the woman herself hid behind the blackout curtain.

Taylor had used her holo-model just a few days ago to make it seem like she was Uritsky's accomplice. Given that he was constantly resting on his sickbed, he probably didn't utilize the drone that often and had left it with Echika's projection in its memory. At least, that was Harold's prediction, which had turned out to be true. Thanks to that, their operation went as planned...barring Steve's intrusion.

"I didn't think Taylor would shoot him," Echika said morosely.

Honestly, it left a bad taste in her mouth. It was decided Steve would be taken to the repair shop at dawn. His head was unharmed, so he'd probably be fine.

"He sided with Taylor, helped him commit his misdeeds, and endangered countless lives. He got what he deserved," Harold said curtly. "In fact, maybe seeing Taylor's true nature will do him good and help open his eyes."

"Logically speaking, you might be right." Echika bitterly switched the cigarette off. "But he is your sibling. You called him 'Brother Steve' yourself, didn't you? Don't you feel any brotherly love toward him?'"

"That's our way of expressing familial affection, if you will. And while I may be his younger sibling, I'm a police officer first and foremost."

"I salute your workaholic tendencies," Echika retorted dryly.

"That said, why do you pity him so much?" Harold asked. "He did try to kill you."

"I don't pity him per se," she said with a frown. "I just…don't think I can condemn him that easily, is all."

Considering what Steve went through, Taylor was a savior to him. She couldn't fault the Amicus for holding the man in such high regard, and the situation honestly painted a pretty tragic picture. And most of all…

"Steve pulled the trigger out of a desire to kill people… He said something about coming to learn what the Laws of Respect truly are. What was that 'truth'? Did he use whatever he discovered to undo his prohibitions?"

"I couldn't quite understand what he meant, either," Harold said, still visibly calm. "But if Taylor didn't modify him, it's only reasonable to assume he had some kind of defect."

It was a terrifying notion but not an impossible one. Amicus were usually thoroughly tested for safety before they were delivered to clients, but the ones testing them were still people. Perhaps Steve's Laws of Respect were incomplete as a result of human error.

"But if that's the case…" Echika paused, hesitated for a moment, and then swallowed the question. "No… Never mind."

If that's the case, are your Laws of Respect functioning properly, Aide Lucraft?

"If I ever catch Sazon's killer, I intend to judge him by my own hand."

When they were at the plaza, Harold had clearly told Echika that. Maybe it was just a figure of speech, or maybe the sorrow of losing someone dear to him was so great that he could only word it that way. But after what happened with Steve, she couldn't help but wonder if a time might come when Harold wouldn't be able to retain his loyalty to humankind, too. She couldn't deny the possibility anymore.

She may have been able to Dive into other people's heads, but she had no way of peering into an Amicus's thoughts. Was Harold really a loyal machine, or was he just acting like one?

But one thing was certain. Echika gently touched the nitro case dangling from her neck. It was empty now, of course, since she'd left the HSB stick in Rig City. She'd always thought letting go of it would tear her heart apart, but oddly enough, she felt strangely calm. It was peculiar, given how terrified she had been of relinquishing it. Maybe all she wanted was for someone to provide her a reason to give it up.

She glanced over at Harold. His frozen eyes were considering the San Francisco Bay. The cold wind toyed with his blond locks, and he looked as defenseless as any young human man.

He was the one who gave her that reason, and no matter what shape his heart might take, that was something that wouldn't ever change. And really, that was all she needed.

"What's wrong?" he asked, his gaze still fixed into the distance. "Something on your mind?"

"Uh…yeah," Echika decided to say after a moment's hesitation. Telling someone about it would make her less afraid to go through with the choice. "Thanks to you, I finally decided."

"Decided what?"

"That I'll…quit being an electronic investigator."

She bit her lips, ruminating on the weight of those words. She only ever took this job because of the occupational-aptitude diagnosis and her father's expectations. But now with her big sister gone, Echika was no longer the little girl dominated by her father's wishes. There was no reason to cling to that identity anymore.

So for now, she wanted some distance. Some time to think things through carefully, to figure out who she really wanted to be.

Harold didn't seem surprised; he simply narrowed his eyes sadly.

"It was my honor to be your last partner."

"You don't feel that way." Echika tried to scoff at that comment, but with him gazing straight at her, she couldn't quite manage it. "You, um… You made me realize it."

Harold cocked his head a bit.

"I mean, uhhh…" Echika continued muttering. Aaah, how she wished she wouldn't have to say this, but there was no going back now.

"Some part of me already knew I couldn't keep clinging to Matoi's memory. But I was too much of a coward, so I felt like I wouldn't last alone. But you just..."

Even with arresting Taylor, she couldn't have managed to do it all on her own. All this only turned out well thanks to his help. And so...

"So, um, thank you...Harold."

Uuuugh, I just can't do this the right way...

She looked up, trying to mask her restlessness. A flock of birds soared toward the dawn like black dots against the sky. Harold remained quiet. This uncharacteristic silence made her sneak a glance at him, only to find he was standing completely still and unblinking.

"What's wrong?" Echika asked, her expression dubious. "Aide Lucraft?"

"It's nothing." He heaved a long sigh and ruffled his disheveled hair. *What's gotten into him?* "Why now, Investigator?"

"Huh?"

"I mean, why did you decide to open your heart to me now? That wasn't what I predicted."

"Er." *What is he saying?* "I don't care about your plans, and I didn't open my heart."

"You've always been like that. Whenever I think I have you wrapped around my little finger, you pull these kinds of tricks and surprise me."

"I'm sorry—I'm not following you here."

"Anyway, please stop doing that."

"For whatever reason, I'm starting to regret thanking you."

"That's fine by me. I didn't do anything you should be thanking me for anyway. All I did was help solve the case—"

"Yeah, yeah." *Seriously, what's his problem?* "But why do you want me to stop those, uh, tricks?"

"Well," he said, knitting his brow in an unusually grave manner, "I can't quite explain it, but having you play those kinds of surprises makes me, well...restless."

...Is he just being bashful without realizing it?

She got the feeling pointing it out would just make things more irritating, so she decided to drop it.

Still, she'd gotten to see something nice at the very end—there were some things even Harold couldn't calculate.

"Why are you smiling?" he asked her.

"No reason."

Echika let go of the rail and walked away, leaving a pensive Harold behind. She still had to clean up the mess left in the aftermath of the incident, but for whatever reason, she had a spring in her step.

It felt…lovely, in its own way.

Epilogue
The Snow Thaws

Epilogue
The Snow Thaws

1

Chief Totoki's office in the Lyon headquarters was as meticulously tidy as ever…except for the sickeningly adorable cat posters plastered over the walls.

"So how long have you had this in mind?" Totoki asked, her cheek resting against her hand.

Her gaze was fixed on the air in front of her. She was looking at where her Your Forma was projecting the letter of resignation Echika had submitted earlier.

"About six months ago," Echika fibbed. "I feel like I might be better suited for another job."

"I recommended that you continue your partnership with Aide Lucraft, but you refused. I guess this explains why." Totoki paused for breath. "Hieda, don't take this as me making light of you, but are you qualified for any other profession?"

Echika averted her gaze. That question touched on a sore spot.

"I'll figure that out going forward," she said.

"There aren't many jobs that make use of your data-processing speed, and Amicus handle more general tasks. I don't think you'll find a new gig that easily. Do you have any savings?"

Totoki pulling the brakes on her like this was probably something she should have been thankful for. Although she'd suspected Echika for a time, Totoki still held her abilities in high regard. What's more, she had helped sweep a few things Echika had done during the investigation under the rug. It was thanks to Totoki's efforts that she hadn't been suspended or fired, so Echika was honestly in her debt.

A month has passed since the case was closed. As soon as the truth about the sensory crime came to light, the public began to riot. The news of the Matoi's existence made the people feel like they were carrying a time bomb in their heads, and naturally, it incited them to erupt with panic and outrage. Rig City's stock took a nosedive, and its employees had to spend day and night handling complaints. Some of the infected even tried to take the company to court.

Elias Taylor was prosecuted soon after his arrest, but he passed away before the first hearing. The investigation continued nonetheless under the surface, though. The Your Forma was extracted from Taylor's remains, and its data was being copied, and those related to the case within Rig City were still being questioned. Steve's custody was transferred to Novae Robotics Inc.'s headquarters, where he cooperated with the investigation while his Laws of Respect were being tuned.

Echika, however, had already been taken off the case. Things had gone way past the point where an electronic investigator's assistance was necessary. Soon after the incident, Rig City issued a system update to the Your Forma that completely erased the Matoi. This freed Echika from the hallucinations, and she was able to return to her ordinary life.

"Very well, then I'll go straight to the point. Are you quitting because I suspected you back then?"

"I personally put it all behind me. I was under the impression we both did what we had to do given the circumstances," Echika replied.

Totoki really hadn't had much of a choice, and Echika was even more at fault for running and making the misunderstanding worse. "And I'm grateful for your help, Chief. You even covered up the fact that I had an illegal copy of the Matoi… It's just that I need time to reconsider things, that's all."

"So you're set on following through with this," Totoki said, heaving a clear sigh. "You're the hero who cracked this case, you know. Honestly, if you quit, the bureau director might want my head on a pike for letting you go."

"That won't happen. Besides, even if I'm gone, you'll still have Aide Lucraft."

"He's an Amicus, which puts him in a position where few people will admit what he's capable of."

"Even though you put a lot of stock in the RF Models' capabilities?"

"…Did Aide Lucraft tell you about that?"

"Next-generation all-purpose artificial intelligence, was it?"

"I'm sure you understand why I kept quiet about that," Totoki said apologetically. "Just the fact that he was a tribute to the royal family makes him incredibly valuable, but him being a next-generation model that doesn't exist on the market is something we can't disclose. I need you to keep that in mind…"

"Of course. I won't tell anyone," Echika promised. Given how rare Harold was, she couldn't blame Totoki and the top brass for hiding the truth about him.

"But even if he's a highly efficient RF Model, he's still an Amicus. We might admit to his *abilities*, but it'll take a while until his *merits* are acknowledged."

As Totoki said this, she sent a message. A notification popped up in Echika's field of vision, containing an e-mail address she didn't recognize.

"An acquaintance of mine is actually looking for a consultant well versed in electrocrimes. If you're ever in need of work, try contacting them."

Echika blinked in surprise. *Does this mean…?*

"I accept your resignation."

"Thank you very much, Chief!"

"But I still want you here until the end of the month, understood?"

"Of course," said Echika, bowing. She couldn't say anything else, not after Totoki went along with her whims like that. "I'm very grateful."

On her way out of her office, she ran into Benno. Apparently, he had business with Totoki. Recently, Benno had made a full recovery and returned to his duties as an investigator aide.

"I decided to quit," Echika told him.

Benno didn't seem surprised. Maybe he thought it was a joke.

"If that isn't the best news I've heard all week," he said with his usual scathing sarcasm. "Might have to pop open an old bottle of wine when I get back home."

He then waved his hand, as if to shoo her away, and Echika could see a ring shining on his left ring finger. So he had made up with his fiancée.

Not that I could possibly care less about that, though, Echika remarked to herself.

Returning to her desk, she found an envelope sitting on the table. It was Bigga's first periodic report. She tore it open, then took a piece of old-fashioned stationary out from it. The text was in the Sami language, but her Your Forma translated it properly.

It was a concise report, and at the end, she appended a private message.

"I apologize for calling you a monster that one time."

It seemed that with everything solved, Bigga's feelings had mellowed out somewhat. It helped that she'd moved in with Lee, who had been discharged from the hospital, and had started exchanging letters with Harold. Even after learning he was an Amicus, Bigga couldn't withhold her interest in him, it seemed.

Echika decided to go out during lunch break and buy some stationary to write her a reply with. She had things to apologize to her about, too.

∗

A month had passed since Echika's resignation, and she'd spent her time more freely than she ever had before. Which was to say, she idled it away at her apartment in Lyon, lying in bed as she read books or watched movies until she fell asleep.

Sometimes, she'd walk along the banks of the Rhône River and try to act French and eat a *pain au chocolat*, though she didn't like it very much. She also decided to quit smoking on a whim.

Having resigned from her job, her Your Forma fell silent, a bitter reminder that she didn't have any acquaintances in her day-to-day life. She got no calls or messages.

As the days breezed by, she began wondering how she would lead her life going forward. At first, she thought things would work out one way or another. For example, she could use her information-processing prowess to obtain qualifications and work in an IT organization. Maybe she could live a more reclusive life, gathering paper books that wouldn't sell to open a used bookstore.

Those were all unrealistic fantasies at best.

Before she knew it, her thoughts would wander once again to Brain Diving. Of the moments she plunged into someone else's head. Of the frozen days she spent in Saint Petersburg, exchanging barbs and thinly veiled insults with Harold.

She was curious about how he'd been keeping since. Curious, yes, but it didn't feel like enough of a reason to warrant getting in touch with him. She decided to do her best not to linger on those memories.

As winter drew to a close, she visited Tokyo. She made her way to her empty home and, after gazing at the Sumida River for a while, headed back. She only spent a few hours in Japan, not long enough to even taste any of the local cuisine. All she did was stare at the river's surface. She had to admit it was a terrible waste of money.

In other words, she didn't know where to go anymore. She thought that by quitting her job as an electronic investigator, she could find some other way to live. That maybe being away from that line of work would bring what she really wanted to do into focus.

But she found nothing. In fact, every passing day made her miss Brain Diving all the more. It made her feel kind of crazy.

She only recalled the address Totoki gave her on one afternoon. While she was cleaning up her apartment, she went through her Your Forma's message box and discovered the address again. She pondered over if she should discard it for one long moment. It felt like keeping it would just put her back right where she started.

But then a soft fragrance wafted in through the window, as if to mellow out her hardened heart.

The seasons had shifted; it was spring.

2

<Today's temperature stands at −8°C. Attire index B, a thick coat, is recommended>

When she arrived at the Pulkovo Airport, Echika immediately regretted not putting on a scarf. She had assumed that since it was spring, she could dress light, but that was a careless mistake. She'd forgotten how terribly cold this city could be. Looking up at the sky from the roundabout, she could make out low-hanging clouds, pregnant with rain.

Echika had contacted the address the previous day and soon received a reply from a private detective called Watson. She imagined he'd hold an interview with her using a holo-call, but he apparently greatly disliked phone calls and insisted she meet him face-to-face. And much to her surprise, the rendezvous point he requested was Saint Petersburg of all places.

Echika recalled the few days she'd spent in this city several months ago. She'd met Harold, who throttled her about at every turn and then saved her life… A lot had happened, to put it mildly.

And though she thought that incident changed her entirely, here she was, trying to get involved in electrocrime investigation again. It seemed this was the only life she knew.

But this time, she wasn't following any orders. This was for her—she'd chosen this alone. And that made all the difference.

It was just past the appointed time when a vehicle pulled over in front of her. It had a squarish body with a stylish maroon coating, and its roundish headlights…

Her Your Forma swiftly analyzed the car model… Wait, no, she didn't need an analysis. She was awfully familiar with this car.

A Lada Niva.

Seeing it made an ominous premonition wash over her—yes, of course. Totoki had been so fixated on keeping Echika around. She should have suspected something was off when she'd let her resign that easily.

As Echika stood there dumbfounded, the driver got out of the car. A Caucasian man in his mid to late twenties. He had irritatingly handsome features, and his blond hair was set in place with wax. The back of his hair stood up a little, and he had a faint mole on his right cheek. His Chesterfield coat flapped dashingly in the wind.

No, this wasn't a Caucasian man. It was *an Amicus who looked like one.*

"I missed you, Investigator Hieda," Harold said with his typically flawless smile and *hugged* her triumphantly.

"Oh, you've quit smoking, haven't you? And you look quite jittery. You must have only ordered one cup of coffee on the flight. And did you bring a mirror to fix your hair before you got off?"

Stop screwing with me what the hell are you doing here explain yourself—

Before she sputtered those words out of sheer confusion, Echika shook off his grip. As Harold obediently stepped away, she glared daggers at him.

"What *is* this?!"

"It is what it is."

"This doesn't make sense." Why did he have to be so cryptic? "I didn't come here to see *you!*"

"You meet your old partner after three months and you can't greet him with a smile?"

"Shut. Up."

He clearly hadn't changed a bit.

"Where's Detective Watson? The electrocrime consultant."

"That was all a lie Chief Totoki made up," Harold revealed unapologetically. "Firstly, let me just say, Watson exists, but he isn't a private detective. The one looking for an electrocrime consultant was us, the Saint Petersburg branch. But in the event Echika Hieda contacted us, we were to hire her as an electronic investigator, not a consultant."

What the hell?

Her anger and amazement boiled over and transformed into utter exhaustion. Then why had she spent the last three months feeling like

she was stumbling at the crossroads of life? Had she really just been swimming in a closed fish tank this entire time? What a poor excuse for a joke...

"Please don't make that face. The chief only proposed this for your sake," Harold said, the gentleness of his tone coming across as very irritating. "Besides, you ended up missing Brain Diving, didn't you?"

She couldn't deny that, and Echika very nearly nodded—but stopped at the last second.

"But if this was all the chief's lie, she wouldn't have handed me that address if she didn't know I was going to quit ahead of time..."

The two stared at each other silently for a long moment. Right, so that's what happened. The moment she pieced it together, an indescribable emotion simmered up from the pit of her stomach.

"Aide Lucraft, did you tell the chief that I was going to ask to resign?"

"I'd never," Harold said with a truly honest expression. "I wouldn't share something that private with anyone."

"Stop lying to me, you schemer!" Echika shouted, unflinchingly grabbing him by the collar. "You're the one who came to Chief Totoki with this idea, weren't you?! And the chief was so fixed on me partnering with you, so against letting me go, that she went along with it! I can't believe you!"

"Please calm down," Harold said, peeling Echika's clenched hands from his coat and clasping them instead. She couldn't shake him off. "All I did was propose an option, but whether you'd return was up to you. You chose to come here of your own volition, so I think blaming me would be misguided."

"Then I think I'll reconsider."

"Why?"

"Why? Well...I mean, you'd be my Belayer again, right?"

"Of course. Are you displeased with that arrangement?"

"If there's anything I'm dissatisfied with, it's the fact that you think there's nothing to be mad about."

"So you hate the idea of partnering with me so much, you'd prefer to fry some other Belayer's noggin?"

Echika gritted her teeth. Bringing that up was a terribly cowardly thing to do. Totoki just didn't know what he was really like. This coldhearted Amicus would use people's hearts like pieces in a game if it suited his objectives.

"I have a lot of things to say to your face, but none of it would get through to you, so what's the point?" Echika said, pulling her hands away from Harold and stashing them in her pockets. "But why are you so determined to stick your nose into my business? You knew I'd want to go back to this job anyway, even if you didn't do anything."

"Actually, there's something I've yet to find the answer for, so I hoped you might help me with that."

"What are you talking about?" Echika furrowed her brow.

"When we were on the roof of the hospital after the incident ended, you gave me a very frank thank-you."

"I remember that, yes. Pardon me for being sincere."

"Yes, it was horribly eerie. And despite that, it made me very ill at ease. I still don't know why that happened and was hoping I might find the answer if I'm with you."

"...Huh?"

"And," Harold continued quite gravely, "you did indeed want to return to this job. I think our interests are in alignment, aren't they?"

Is he joking?

Echika was truly appalled. It was absurd to consider that he'd set her up for such an asinine reason. All this might not have happened if she didn't snicker at him back then or at least told him why she was smiling.

"Aide Lucraft," she started, unable to hold back the urge to sigh, "I actually know the reason you feel that way."

"You do?" Harold asked dubiously.

"Yes, I do. It's called embarrassment. You're feeling awkward because I thanked you for something you didn't expect. It might have even pricked at your pride a little. And that's it. That's all it is. It's that simple."

"...No, I think you're mistaken."

"How am I wrong? For being so perceptive, you're really blind to your own emotions."

"Absurd. Could you stop trying to get even with me with those quips of yours?"

"No, face it. As calculating as you are, you're weak to surprises—"

"Echika." Harold brought his face to her ear and spoke, making her stiffen. "*A pale-blue coat would suit you.* I see you remembered what I told you, and it does look very good on you indeed."

Flustered, Echika looked down—this new blue-gray coat was something she bought while wandering about over the last couple of months. She thought that changing her wardrobe might help her turn her attitude around, too. Obviously, she'd forgotten about that small bit of advice he'd given her off the cuff. She really had. Honest.

"Oh no, you definitely remembered. You're just too bashful to admit it," Harold insisted.

"No! I only just remembered you said that, and I'll never wear this thing again!" she vowed, glaring at him in a panic. "Are you sure you're not trying to get back at me?!"

"I would never do anything that childish," he said, flashing an annoyingly indomitable grin. "Anyway, get in. I'll show you to your desk when we get to the branch."

Ugh!

Echika grumpily got into the passenger seat of the Niva. As expected, the interior of the car was freezing cold, prompting her to angrily switch the heating on. Some part of her felt like she should grumble and complain, but oddly enough, another part of her was relieved.

But I'm never ever *thanking him again.*

As Harold got into the driver's seat, Echika glanced at him.

"So in the end, who was Watson?" she asked.

"Oh, that would be me," he replied carelessly. "Much like Steve, I have a middle name. Harold Watson Lucraft. So like I said, that part wasn't a lie at all."

"But they told me that was your first name."

"Amicus use last names, too. Don't you know?"

"Either way, you're a huge liar. If anything, you're not a Watson to begin with; you're more of a Holmes."

She intended it with the utmost sarcasm, but it failed to faze Harold one bit. Quite the contrary, actually.

"Hearing you say that really makes it feel like you're finally back," he said with a carefree smile.

Seeing him act so pleased about it quelled her anger. But after all, even that expression was probably just a calculated facade.

Echika sighed for what felt like the umpteenth time.

"You really are one hell of a *partner*, you know that?"

"I'm honored to hear you say that. I look forward to a fruitful partnership with you, Investigator."

Harold extended his hand for a shake, and Echika begrudgingly took it. The dry warmth of his artificial skin felt somehow warmer than it had before, and she was surprised at herself for feeling that way.

And then the Niva set off. Like it had been waiting for their hands to part.

Afterword

This work contains allusions to minority people and their beliefs but was not written with any intent of denying any ethnic group, faith, or gods. All organizations within this work are purely fictional and are unrelated to existing groups or people.

I have received help from a great many people in the publishing of this novel, to whom I would like to extend my thanks.

To the 27th Dengeki Novel Prize's selection committee, for gracing this amateurish book with the honor of this award, as well as the editorial department's members for their assistance.

To Yoshida, the editor in charge of me. I could not be more grateful to you for taking my shoddy manuscript and guiding me to craft it into a true novel, despite my being a complete amateur.

To the book's illustrator, Tsubata Nozaki. I'll never forget the excitement I felt when I first saw your character designs. Thank you so much for breathing life into Echika, Harold, and the others.

To the manga-ka, Yoshinori Kisaragi. I can't be more thankful for the wonderful promotional manga you drew.

I would also like to thank Mr. J for coming up with my pen name, as well as the many people who watched over my work. And especially to my uncle and aunt, to my mother who supported me during my hardest time, and my deceased father.

But most importantly of all, to all the readers who picked up this book. Thank you so much for choosing this story out of the countless many available to you. If you enjoyed this work even a bit, nothing would make me happier.

January 2021, Mareho Kikuishi

References

Aihara, Kazuyuki. This Is How AI Is Made. (Wedge, 2017)

Etherington, Darrell. Elon Musk's Neuralink Looks to Begin Outfitting Human Brains With Faster Input and Output Starting Next Year. (https://jp.techcrunch.com/2019/07/18/2019-07-16-elon-musks -neuralink-looks-to-begin-outfitting-human-brains-with-faster -input-and-output-starting-next-year/?fbclid=IwAR02dra3Ex-YXs 6pLGqBJVuJIkFbkMJUXU4MjOoxNF3ICOdEY0NtXQNH1EU, extracted August 2020)

Lebrun, Marc. Translation by Kitaura, Haruka. Interpol. (Shirumizu, 2005)

Navarro, Joe. Karlins, Marvin. Translation by Nishida, Mioko. What Every Body Is Saying: An Ex-FBI Agent's Guide to Speed-Reading People. (Kawade Bunko, 2012)

Pariser, Eli. Translation by Inokuchi, Koji. The Filter Bubble: What the Internet Is Hiding from You. (Hayakawa bookstore, 2012)